THE NECESSARY LESSON
THE HARCOURT'S: ANOTHER GENERATION

PENNY FAIRBANKS

ALSO BY PENNY FAIRBANKS

Resolved in Love Series:
Behind The Baron's Mask
Healing The Captain's Heart
Finding The Artisan's Future
Embracing The Earl's Dream

The Harcourts Series:
Anna's Decision
Dalton's Challenge
Caroline's Discovery
Patrick's Arrangement
Harriet's Proposal

The Harcourts: Another Generation Series:
A Convenient Escape
The Hidden Heiress
An Unexpected Bloom
The Necessary Lesson
An Impossible Fate

The Necessary Lesson © 2022 by Penny Fairbanks

All rights reserved.

No part of this book may be reproduced in any form or by any electronic or mechanical means, including information storage and retrieval systems, without written permission from the author, except for the use of brief quotations in a book review.

Cover design by German Creative

Family tree by MeganJoyCrafts

This book is a work of fiction. Names, characters, places, and incidents either are products of the author's imagination or used fictitiously. Any resemblance to actual persons, living or dead, events, or locales is entirely coincidental.

First Printing: July 2022

Family Tree Chart

- **Martin Harcourt 'Baron Welsted'** — Born: 4 Jan 1765
- **Bridget Brownly 'Lady Welsted'** — Born: 18 Mar 1768
  - **Anna Harcourt** — Born: 10 Feb 1789
  - **Noah Waynford** — Born: 17 Jul 1784
    - **Elizabeth Waynford** — Born: 30 Mar 1812
    - **Sophia Waynford** — Born: 11 Jun 1814
    - **Robert Waynford** — Born: 19 Sep 1817
  - **Dalton Harcourt** — Born: 20 Apr 1791
  - **Winifred Thirley** — Born: 11 Nov 1791
    - **Hugh Harcourt** — Born: 10 Jan 1814
    - **Helen Harcourt** — Born: 8 Aug 1816
    - **Hannah Harcourt** — Born: 1 Oct 1818
    - **Hayes Harcourt** — Born: 22 Feb 1821
  - **Caroline Harcourt 'Lady Helsden'** — Born: 15 Mar 1794
  - **Sir Arthur Helsden** — Born: 25 Sep 1793
    - **Jasper Helsden** — Born: 4 May 1816
    - **Amelia Helsden** — Born: 19 Sep 1818
    - **Duncan Helsden** — Born: 10 Nov 1820
    - **Sidney Helsden** — Born: 6 Jun 1822
    - **Rebecca Helsden** — Born: 26 Jan 1825
  - **Patrick Harcourt** — Born: 14 Jun 1796
  - **Eloise Beaufort** — Born: 3 Oct 1793
    - **Colette Harcourt** — Born: 18 Apr 1818
    - **Stéphane Harcourt** — Born: 9 Dec 1821
  - **Harriet Harcourt 'Lady Kentwood'** — Born: 22 May 1799
  - **Jonas Drake 'Viscount Kentwood'** — Born: 27 Jan 1796
    - **Felix Drake** — Born: 15 May 1821 (1st twin)
    - **Ezra Drake** — Born: 15 May 1821 (2nd twin)
    - **Margaret Drake** — Born: 20 Sep 1825

CHAPTER 1

September 1836

"Rebecca, what is this?"

Jasper jolted at the sound of his mother's sharp voice directed at the youngest Helsden child. He glanced nervously around the table in the center of Attwood Manor's dining room, surrounded by family. All eyes turned toward his end of the table, where he sat beside Rebecca, their mother on her other side.

The girl sank lower in her seat, shoulders inching up around her ears and thick dark brows scrunching over a narrow nose. "Sweets," Rebecca mumbled under her breath.

All the happy familial chatter in the room instantly vanished. No one so much as let a single whisper of air past their lips. Jasper's grip tightened around the silver fork in his hand. Everyone knew what was coming.

Mama sighed and set her utensils down on the fine china plate, the picture of complete grace and decorum—her youngest daughter's exact opposite. The light from the grand chandelier above glinted against her black hair, the same hair she shared with Jasper and Rebecca. From his vantage point, Jasper noted all the ways Mama and Rebecca looked like mirror images of each other. Papa had even said once that they both carried the same stubborn streak—a fact Mama sorely regretted at times like this.

"Sweets, Rebecca?" Mama groaned, the fine lines around her eyes tightening. Her irritation rose to the surface much faster with each passing day. "You knew we were coming to Attwood tonight to have a nice dinner with our family. And you repay your grandparents' generosity by sneaking in sweets?"

Jasper clenched his teeth together when he felt Rebecca stiffen. She sat up straighter, rising to Mama's criticism. "I do not want mutton and carrots and potatoes," Rebecca shot back. "I want sweets. What is so bad about that? Besides, Grandmama and Grandpapa would have already had all this food prepared whether or not I ate it. What difference does it make?"

"That is not very considerate to our hosts, daughter. Would you want this fine food to go to waste?" Papa added in his quiet, soothing voice from across the table. It had eased many an argument and tantrum for the other Helsden children over the years. But not so for Rebecca.

"No, it certainly is not considerate at all," Mama agreed firmly. "Such behavior will not be tolerated, Rebecca. When will you learn?"

With a disappointed shake of her head, Mama's hand shot out and snatched at the remaining treats nestled in Rebecca's skirts, partially obscured by her napkin. Before Jasper could plead for Mama to stop, a chilling wail tore through the tense air of the dining room.

"Heavens," Jasper mumbled, grimacing as Rebecca's

shriek pierced his ears. He had thought he would be used to this dreadful sound by now, yet it rattled him every time.

"Rebecca! Stop that this instant! You are not a little girl anymore!" Mama cried, all while trying to wrest crumbling tarts and sugar plums from her child's determined fingers.

A chorus of suggestions and mollifying words echoed through the dining room, drowning under Rebecca's screams of defiance, as grandparents, aunts and uncles, and cousins tried and failed to find that magic phrase that would put Rebecca to rights and put this whole uncomfortable ordeal behind them.

None of it worked, of course. Jasper lowered his head in equal parts shame and dismay. Dinner had been going so well. He had even started to hope that they might make it through the whole evening without an incident.

Though he knew none of their beloved family judged them for Rebecca's behavior—and that they all loved her regardless of the tantrums—it had tainted enough of their gatherings and daily lives to make Jasper occasionally wish he could sink through the hardwood floor until Mama and Papa took hold of the situation or until Rebecca went hoarse, whichever came first.

"Come now, Rebecca," Papa offered, hurrying around the large table to kneel beside his wife and daughter. "You are eleven years old now. Is this how an eleven-year-old young lady is meant to act?"

"I can act however I want! Why must everyone care so much about what I do or don't do?" Rebecca retaliated, her face going cherry red. She yanked her hands away, causing Mama to nearly fall out of her chair.

Bits of tart crust and filling and crystals of sugar flew through the air. Surprised, Jasper traced the arc of a large piece of crust through the air with his eyes until it landed in

Uncle Patrick's hair. Lord only knew where the rest ended up settling.

"Look at this mess!" Mama moaned, shaking off Papa's concerned hands from her shoulders.

"Do not fret over that, Caroline," said Grandmama, the regal baroness. Even her usually patient and knowing smile showed signs of strain. "This is nothing a little cleaning cannot mend."

"No, this is not acceptable!"

"Dearest Rebecca, why don't we put all this down on your plate for now? Once we brush off your hands, we can all talk about this calmly and kindly," Jasper suggested, wrapping a comforting arm around his youngest sibling's shoulders.

He shot Mama a pleading look, desperate to help ease his parents' stress. Every once in a while, he seemed to have some sort of power to wrangle the unruly child. It only worked if Mama and Papa stepped back and kept their justified frustrations silent while he grasped at anything to calm Rebecca. A muscle in Mama's jaw twitched, her eyes blazing with exhausted anger. She turned away and forced several deep breaths.

Jasper returned his attention to Rebecca. "See? We are all taking a moment to gather ourselves. Will you try, too? Please, sister?"

Rebecca's dark eyes slowly lifted to peer up at Jasper. Her bottom lip protruded in a pout that had been endearing and amusing several years ago. It had only become increasingly maddening the longer she refused to grow out of it.

"See?" Jasper repeated with a hesitant smile. Had he done it? Had he pulled Rebecca out of her poor temper? Perhaps they could salvage the night yet.

"No, I will not try! Why should I?" Rebecca shrieked, her round cheeks reddening again. She wiggled her shoulder to shake off Jasper's arm, though he noted with minuscule relief that she did put down the sweets onto her still full plate.

"That is enough," Papa said, his exasperated sigh bowing his shoulders as he stood and pulled Rebecca's chair out from the table. Gentle yet firm, the baronet gripped his daughter's upper arm and tugged. Knowing she had finally met defeat, Rebecca begrudgingly obeyed, fierce anger radiating from her small body.

Everyone returned their attention to their own plates as Papa half-dragged half-marched Rebecca from the dining room. A heavy, strangely unwelcome silence fell over them until Mama cleared her throat.

"I pray you will forgive us," she mumbled, lowering her head.

Jasper's heart ached to see his dear mama's usual confidence shaken so severely. Though he could not much relate to that quality, he could certainly understand her embarrassment and frustration. Every child offered their own unique challenges, sometimes positive and sometimes undesirable. Every member of their family knew that from experience, either from raising their own children or growing up alongside many siblings and cousins. Yet none of them had seen a child quite like Rebecca.

"Do not apologize on our account, dear Caroline," Grandpapa offered with a commiserating smile. "We know how hard you have been trying…."

Mama inhaled sharply and squeezed her eyes shut. "Even so, nothing works. I swear I am at my wits' end. I cannot even begin to fathom what we should do next."

Although unconventional, Jasper knew none of the others cared overmuch for proper seating arrangements at an informal family dinner. Everyone chose their seats for themselves save for Lord and Lady Welsted, who maintained their seats at opposite ends of the table. Thus Jasper knew no one would bat an eye when he quietly moved from his own chair to the one Rebecca had just occupied.

He reached a hand under the table and found his mother's hand, curled into a small, trembling fist. With a heavy heart, Jasper wrapped his fingers around Mama's and gave them a gentle squeeze. She sniffled, refusing to let any embarrassing tears spill, and flashed Jasper a grateful smile.

"You know, sister, there is still plenty of time for her to grow out of it on her own," Uncle Dalton, Mama's older brother, offered from the opposite side of the table, his usual shining cheer subdued, though he did manage a thoughtful shrug.

"Indeed," added Uncle Dalton's wife, Aunt Winnie. "Our Hannah has certainly had her moments, especially since she and I are of such different temperaments." The older woman glanced to her daughter a few seats down. Cousin Hannah smiled in encouraging agreement. "Even now, we still have our disputes, but I find they have become fewer and further between and far less severe over time."

Mama only nodded dejectedly, staring down at her now cold mutton. "I still do not understand just how Rebecca came to be this way. None of our other children gave us such trouble. Where did we go wrong?"

"Now, now, Mama. You are forgetting Sidney," Amelia chuckled from her spot across the table. She caught Jasper's eye and arched one brow, the corner of her mouth pulled to the side. Though Jasper's other younger sister did not have as much patience for Rebecca's shenanigans as he did, she possessed a far better talent for injecting small doses of humor into difficult situations.

"Cousin," Colette, Uncle Patrick's and Aunt Eloise's oldest, gasped, elbowing Amelia. Amelia scrunched her nose at her favorite cousin, confident that Mama would not notice such an unladylike expression given the current circumstances.

"What did I do to deserve this attack?" Sidney grumbled, glowering at his older sister, one butter knife raised as if ready to parry another verbal ambush. "And why must we always talk about Rebecca?"

"I saw that, Amelia," Mama chided, ignoring Sidney's minor complaints for the time being. Her voice was far too weary to carry any real weight of consequence in it. "Need I remind you that you will be making your debut next year? Such expressions might not offend your family, but expectations will be vastly different in London amongst the *ton*. Perfection is—"

"She knows, Mama," Jasper whispered, squeezing Mama's hand again.

"Yes, she certainly knows," Duncan, the middle Helsden child, added with a subtle sneer directed at Amelia. "If I have to hear her plod along on the pianoforte for another minute—"

"Plod?" Amelia shot back, leaning over the table and itching to pounce. "I do not plod, Duncan. I am extremely proficient—"

"Amelia, he is only teasing," cousin Colette chuckled. She gripped Amelia's elbow under her puffed sleeve and pulled her back. "Mind your gown or you will dip it in the sauce. I am terribly afraid that it will not suit this lovely blue silk."

"Do not listen to Colette," Uncle Dalton chirped, the humor returning to his eyes. "There is no fashion that cannot be improved by a little spot of sauce."

"My darling Colette, are you sure you wish to spend the entire autumn and winter amongst these mad fools?" Uncle Patrick chimed in from his seat nearest Grandpapa with a mischievous smile.

"Mad fools or not, we are your family, little Patrick," Mama teased, her disheartened mood lifted.

Jasper could not help smiling despite the mild insults flying around the table. His family certainly had a unique way with words. Yet beneath the teasing existed a solid foundation of love and mutual respect that allowed them to poke fun at themselves and each other without damaging any feelings.

Everyone at the table—as well as the aunts, uncles, and cousins not present—knew that the family would be there for them in an instant with words of comfort and encouragement or advice or simply a listening ear should the need arise.

His smile faded slightly as the dining room filled with lighthearted conversation and laughter once more. He only wished Papa and Rebecca could be here to enjoy it.

"I am happy to see things settling back to normal," a kind voice to Jasper's right pulled him out of his melancholy thoughts. He turned to smile at cousin Helen, Uncle Dalton's and Aunt Winnie's second oldest child, an empty seat now separating them. She leaned closer. "Has the new governess been helping at all?" she asked under her breath.

"She handed in her notice last week and left a few days ago," Jasper whispered back. His mouth pressed into a tight line. They had just lost their third governess this year. None of them could survive Rebecca's tantrums long enough to make any real progress.

"Goodness," Helen said, returning her gaze to her plate. "Well, I am sure the next one will be the answer. I certainly pray she will be."

Jasper nodded, forcing a smile. "As do I. Now tell me, how are Miles and little Josiah?"

At the mention of her husband and son, Helen's mind easily discarded any further discussion of Rebecca or the many governesses she had driven away over the years. They could talk about that some other time. For now, Jasper needed to recover from the most recent ordeal. When it came to his married cousins, all new parents themselves, he knew bringing up their spouses and children would always secure him at least half an hour of conversation not revolving around Rebecca's latest antics.

"Miles is such a brilliant father," Helen started with a beaming smile, love shining in her eyes. "I told him he should come to dinner tonight and that I would mind Josiah. He is quite a terrible sleeper, yet so very angelic when he does finally fall asleep. But Miles said I should spend some time out of the cottage with family—family that can converse beyond babbles, at least."

Jasper smiled in return, his burdened heart absorbing his dear cousin's happiness. He had seen Helen's and Miles's friendship unfold over several years until they both finally realized that love had bloomed right where they had met and spent most of their time together—in Attwood Manor's gardens.

Now they were happily married, living in a cottage on the grounds while Miles worked as assistant gardener and Helen learned from her mother-in-law all the necessities of running a household without servants, all while settling into their new role as parents. His cousins Beth and Hugh had also found their happily ever afters full of wedded bliss and children.

It was everything Jasper had dreamed of for himself. Yet with Rebecca in such a state, constantly aggravating their parents, how could he even consider the selfish choice of focusing on courtships, falling in love, and becoming a husband and father? No, all the sweet things Helen told him of now would simply have to wait.

At least Jasper would not have to worry about all that

again until next Season. In the meantime, he prayed that something would shift in Rebecca, something that would soothe her temper and return them to a normal, peaceful family.

After dinner concluded, Mama announced the Helsdens would be returning home early instead of lingering in the drawing room for more conversation with the rest of the family. Her poor husband had suffered enough, missing most of the meal and having to manage Rebecca in some other secluded room.

No one blamed them, though their goodbyes carried a defeated gloom. This was not the first time Jasper's family had had to make an early exit from an event. Nor would it be the last, it seemed.

To everyone's relief, Rebecca had fallen into a sullen silence for the short ride back to Goddard House, the smaller property beside Attwood Manor and the long-standing seat of the baronet, currently Jasper's father and one day Jasper himself. Mama and Amelia shepherded Rebecca upstairs to the bedroom the Helsden girls shared. Cousin Colette, who preferred to stay at Goddard House during extended visits to remain near Amelia, followed after them. Papa retreated to his study with a weary sigh while Duncan and Sidney chattered on their way to their quarters. That left Jasper to slip into the small drawing room alone.

Hands clasped behind his back, Jasper crossed to the far window. The glass failed to reveal anything but the dark of night. A few stars broke through the clouds, drifting lazily across the sky. The weight of the evening's unfortunate turn settled heavy on Jasper's shoulders. He leaned forward and rested his forehead against the cool glass.

"There must be something we can do for Rebecca," he whispered to himself, a quiet, desperate prayer, his breath fogging up the window and fading away just as quickly. "At this rate, we will need nothing short of a miracle."

"Jasper? Are you unwell?"

Surprise jolted through Jasper. He snapped to attention and whirled around to find Colette peering through the doorway, brows furrowed in concern. He certainly had not expected anyone to still be awake enough to walk in on his moment of weakness.

"Yes, yes— I mean no, I am not unwell. I am very well, indeed. Perhaps not very well, actually, but well enough," Jasper sputtered, his cheeks reddening. At least it was only Colette. Some of the other cousins, those less familiar with Rebecca's antics and the situation within the Helsdens' home —might have taken the opportunity to give him a light teasing.

Colette offered an understanding smile and crossed the drawing room, her dark brown hair catching the meager light from the window to reveal red undertones. "I am sorry for tonight."

Jasper's shoulder lifted in what he hoped came across as a nonchalant shrug. "You have nothing to apologize for."

"I know, but still…. What a difficult situation. I am sorry that any of you should have to deal with it."

"Unfortunately, we are all quite used to it by now," Jasper sighed, turning back to the window. "But it does not get any easier. As Uncle Patrick said at dinner, are you sure you wish to remain under this roof until next year?"

The cousins exchanged glum smiles. Knowing Jasper would not mind the slip in decorum, Colette leaned her back against the wall beside the window.

"Certainly. When Rebecca feels compelled to be well-behaved, she is a very lovely girl. Besides, it would be too difficult for me and Amelia to gossip and plot her first Season if I stayed at Attwood with the rest of my family. And

Stéphane and I do nothing but argue these days. Younger brothers become quite frustrating when they approach that age just before adulthood, do they not?" she finished with a bemused shake of her head.

"I certainly hope I was not as frustrating when I was their age," Jasper chuckled. At the age of twenty—and after years of acting as an additional parent for his younger siblings when Mama and Papa had their hands full with Rebecca—Jasper liked to think that he had matured into a patient, levelheaded future baronet. "At least Duncan and Sidney manage to keep their manners most of the time. Even they have sympathy for our dear mother and father and all their struggles with Rebecca."

Colette hummed, narrowing her eyes as a thought struck her. "Say, do you remember this past Season when you told me of one of your London friends? The one who also had a formerly troublesome younger sibling? A brother, I think it was."

Jasper's mouth scrunched to one side as he struggled to remember. So much had happened, as was standard for any Season, yet in the end it had all amounted to nothing, at least as far as Jasper's marital aspirations were concerned. All his minor courtships and outings with friends could not help being overshadowed by the stress that permeated their daily lives.

"Mr. Moore, was it?" Colette added, pinching her chin between forefinger and thumb.

"Ah! Yes, Mr. Moorewell is who you mean. Goodness, I cannot believe I forgot so thoroughly."

"You must write to him, cousin!" Colette cried in triumph, a smile spreading across her features. "Now that you have had another governess leave, this would be the perfect time to call upon a proven expert."

Jasper smiled at his own blurry reflection in the window.

"Yes, Colette, you are quite right. As a matter of fact, Mr. Moorewell provided me with the governess' name and address just before the end of the Season. Rebecca's behavior has been even worse in these past few months since returning to the country that I could hardly think of anything else, and of course we already had a governess until recently. Indeed, the timing is quite perfect. I only hope she will be able to come—and quickly."

His heartbeat picked up speed as the possibility of their prayers being answered, the miracle finally arriving, sank into Jasper's burdened mind. This woman could very well be the answer their family had been seeking.

"Go on then," Colette said, shooing Jasper with both hands and a pleased grin. "You must get that letter in the morning post."

"Of course." Jasper nodded eagerly and pulled Colette in for a brief hug. "Thank you, dearest cousin!" he called over his shoulder as he hurriedly quit the drawing room.

"Does that mean I am your favorite now?" Colette asked, her lighthearted voice trailing down the hall after Jasper.

Though he did not much care for the idea of choosing favorites among family, Colette could very well secure Jasper's top spot if this suggestion did indeed prove fruitful. His own smile widened as he rushed up the stairs, taking the steps two at a time.

A small part of Jasper tried to remind himself not to expand his expectations so soon. After all, the governess might not be available to move from one family to another. The bigger part of Jasper, the one desperate for even just a glimmer of hope, would not be silenced so easily.

After a moment of tearing through the organized contents of the writing desk in his room, Jasper seized a small slip of paper tucked away in the back of a drawer.

There it was, her name and most recent address known to Mr. Moorewell.

Heart buzzing and hope growing, Jasper settled into his chair, pulled out a sheet of paper and a steel nib pen, and began writing.

"Dear Miss Philippa Seymour, I hope this letter finds you well...."

CHAPTER 2

*B*eautiful mature trees, topped in rich oranges, yellows, and browns, lined the drive toward Goddard House—Pippa's new temporary home. She leaned closer to the window to peer up at them, excitement and nerves battling within her chest.

Memories of her most recent charge tempered her interest in the new family, the Helsdens. She had been with her former family for almost a year. The boy had made excellent progress. Though it was not uncommon for Pippa to receive letters from families seeking to employ her while she was still working with one charge, she had to admit the timing had been perfect. Pippa leaned back against the carriage's cushioned seat as the driver pulled the horses into the circular drive before Goddard House. She would have hated to turn down such an urgent plea.

Pippa peered down at the letter resting on her lap that had summoned her to this charming part of Somerset. She picked it up and reread a few lines, her heart moved again by the love she saw in those words.

This letter was different from most. Firstly, it had been

written by her future student's oldest brother rather than a parent or guardian. More importantly, this Mr. Helsden had not simply asked for her to put a stop to the child's madness, as most letters did. He had asked for something no other family had requested before.

"I pray, Miss Seymour, that you will help us as a family to understand what troubles our beloved Rebecca so deeply, so that we might identify the root of the problem and help her live a happier life."

"How sweet," Pippa mumbled to herself as the carriage slowed to a stop, eager to meet both Miss Rebecca and Mr. Helsden.

Tucking the letter away into her reticule, she pressed herself against the window once more to catch a better view of the handsome house—not as large or extravagant as some of the others Pippa had lived in over the years, though it looked very fine and comfortable indeed. She had no doubt that she would materially enjoy her stay here, however long it might be.

"Welcome to Goddard House, Miss Seymour," the elderly butler announced when Pippa stepped into the modest foyer. "Right this way, if you please."

Pippa followed him upstairs while footmen unloaded her luggage, her eyes wandering about the rather exquisite furnishings and artwork. Clearly, someone in the baronet's household boasted excellent and expensive taste. Her expression of wonder and admiration turned to surprise when the butler showed her into the drawing room.

The only occupant appeared to be a young man—a very handsome young man, Pippa noted, when he turned away from the window on the wall to her right. Her wonder returned in full force, heart lodging itself in her throat, as he approached with a soft, grateful smile. The afternoon sunlight of a cool mid-October day glinted off his thick black hair and turned his deep brown eyes a warm honey.

"Miss Seymour, what a pleasure," he said with a graceful bow, his voice just as quiet and lovely as Pippa had anticipated. "I am Mr. Jasper Helsden, the one who wrote you—nay, begged you, I dare say—to bring your expertise to Goddard House."

"The pleasure is all mine," Pippa returned, a touch too breathless. She quickly lowered her head and sank into a curtsey, her gloved fingers clutching the pastel green floral fabric of her full skirts. When she dared to look at Mr. Helsden directly again, she found him wearing a decidedly less enthusiastic smile.

"Allow me to apologize on behalf of my parents, Sir Arthur Helsden and Lady Helsden, as well as my sister, Miss Rebecca. They had planned to be here to welcome you, but, well…we had another incident." The young man looked down at the beautiful azure rug, a sweet shade of pink blooming across his cheeks.

Taking advantage of his embarrassed distraction, Pippa gave her head a small shake, the red ringlets framing her face bouncing frantically. She was here to do a job, a very important job at that—not swoon over a gentleman she had just met.

Besides, she had met her fair share of handsome and charming men over her years of moving from home to home all over the country. None of them—not even the one frowning endearingly at his polished boots—could sway her toward anything more than a passing infatuation.

"Excellent," Pippa chirped, clasping her hands before her and straightening her spine.

Mr. Helsden only partially raised his head, one full brow arched up. "E-Excellent?"

Pippa gave an encouraging nod. "As far as I am

concerned, yes. I am more than happy to begin my work right away, and there is no better introduction than to see the unwanted behavior firsthand."

"Are you positive?" Mr. Helsden asked, his fingers twisting around themselves. Pippa stifled a smile. Something about his nerves made her want to soothe him, too. "You did just arrive after days of travel. Surely you wish to settle in and rest first."

"Not at all," Pippa insisted with a lighthearted chuckle. She dared to take a step closer. "I always feel invigorated and eager to start as soon as I arrive. It will be no trouble at all. Please bring me to Miss Rebecca so I can observe one of these incidents. Sometimes when I first take up my post, my new charge might assume a sort of facade because they are unsure of me. It can take them several days to several weeks to feel comfortable enough to begin testing me and reverting to their old mischiefs and misdeeds."

Both Mr. Helsden's brows rose, his bottom lip jutting out in an impressed pout. "Is that so? I do suppose that makes perfect sense. Follow me, then."

Energized by his admiration, nerves melting away under his kind gaze, Pippa walked beside Mr. Helsden through Goddard House. Every once in a while he offered a brief explanation of a painting or an old family heirloom and pointed out various rooms she might make use of during her stay. Pippa made a note to herself to ask him later if he might take her on a proper tour—just so she could familiarize herself with the place. It had nothing to do with spending more time in his company.

The gentleman fell silent when they ascended another flight of stairs to what Pippa guessed to be the family's private quarters. The long hall stretched out before them, a few doors cracked open for curious eyes and ears. A terrible screeching sound and frustrated shouts echoed all the way to the stairs.

Mr. Helsden stepped forward with another apologetic smile. "Miss Seymour, allow me to introduce some other members of our family. Here we have my younger brothers, Master Duncan and Master Sidney," he said under his breath, gesturing to the door on the left. The two lads slipped out into the hallway to greet Pippa. "And there we have one of my younger sisters, Miss Amelia Helsden, and our cousin, Miss Colette Harcourt." Just like the boys, the two young ladies presented themselves to Pippa with elegant curtseys.

"I am delighted to meet you all," Pippa whispered, matching their hushed demeanors.

"Back into your rooms, all of you. Or go entertain yourselves elsewhere about the house. Or visit Grandmama and Grandpapa," Mr. Helsden suggested. Miss Helsden and Miss Harcourt disappeared back into their bedroom while Master Duncan and Master Sidney scurried away toward the stairs, quietly debating if they should sneak into the kitchens for a snack before racing each other to some place called Attwood.

With a deep inhale, Mr. Helsden marched down the hall toward the racket produced by his youngest sibling. He paused outside the door, hand on the knob, and shot Pippa a glance. Without knowing how, Pippa perfectly understood him. She nodded, signaling that she was ready. Mr. Helsden's Adam's apple bobbed as he turned the knob.

"I do not *want* to change into a new dress!" Miss Rebecca cried from the corner of the room, her round face red, soft black curls trembling with anger. "There is nothing wrong with the dress I am already wearing! Why must I change a thousand times a day?"

"Listen here, Rebecca," said the woman Pippa assumed to be Lady Helsden in as firm a tone as she could manage amidst her own rising exasperation. "There is no need to exaggerate. We are not making you change a thousand times a day. This is only your third dress today! We want you to wear something special to meet your new governess. Is that so horrible?"

Miss Rebecca scrunched her brows together and balled her small hands into fists that clutched the lovely cream skirts of her dress. "Yes, it is! I do not want to change into a new dress, and I do not want to meet my new governess!"

Lady Helsden threw her hands up in defeat and the man beside her—likely Sir Arthur—wrapped his arm around her shoulders. Pippa cleared her throat. All eyes, even Miss Rebecca's flaming ones, snapped to the doorway.

Everyone regarded each other for a surprised, silent moment. Until the girl started wailing again, screaming at her parents that she refused to change and they could not make her.

Mr. Helsden, Lady Helsden, and Sir Arthur all started to speak over Miss Rebecca's impassioned defiance, apologizing to Pippa for the commotion. She only offered a small smile and held up a hand for quiet. The adults obeyed. Miss Rebecca did not. Pippa expected that.

The governess wordlessly stepped into the room, her slippers whispering over the gleaming wood floor. As unladylike as it might be, Pippa sank to her knees before Miss Rebecca, her skirts pooling round her. She had no fear of tarnishing her reputation with such actions. She was no lady, after all. Any skeptical or scandalized parents soon opted to leave Pippa to her own devices when they saw her success. If her new employers seemed shocked that she would lower herself to the eye level of the child, Pippa paid them no mind.

According to Mr. Helsden's letter, she did not think that would be the case with this family. They loved each other deeply and were desperate to improve Miss Rebecca's situation. She could hardly imagine any of them treating children as inferiors. Those families, Pippa knew from experience, would struggle far more to correct their child's behavior. A firm hand was not the same as a cruel or unfeeling one.

"Good afternoon, Miss Rebecca," Pippa started, keeping her voice low and measured. She tilted her head to the side to maintain her view of the girl's confused face, encouraging eye contact without forcing it. "I am Miss Philippa Seymour. Starting today, I will be your new governess. What do you think of that?"

Wedging herself deeper into the corner, Miss Rebecca twisted her head away. She mumbled something that sounded vaguely like a rather cutting insult that just escaped Pippa's hearing. No matter. Pippa had been called far worse. She had even been slapped, kicked, punched, and bitten more times than she could count.

Pippa leaned forward, angling her ear toward Miss Rebecca. "Pardon me? Would you repeat that?"

Panic flashed across the girl's face. "I shouldn't.... Mama will be very cross."

"Do not worry about your mama for now," Pippa said gently, hoping that Lady Helsden would catch her hint and remain quiet. "This is between us. And in order for me to do my duty to the best of my ability, I would like to know what you think of my presence here in your home, among your family."

Miss Rebecca narrowed her eyes at Pippa and turned her body away, as if trying to disappear into the seam where the two walls met. "I said I think you should get back in your carriage and drive all the way to Liverpool and get on a boat to America and never return."

Pippa nodded, feeling the tension growing behind her as Miss Rebecca's parents and brother watched. She ignored that. For now, her only concern was Miss Rebecca and laying a foundation. "Would you believe me if I said I do understand your feelings?"

"You are not cross?" the girl asked, eyeing Pippa with a healthy dose of suspicion.

"Not in the least," Pippa chuckled. "Having some stranger come into your home and spend hours every single day with you is quite a change from your usual—especially if you keep repeating those early steps over and over with a new person. You never properly become acquainted or adjust to the situation. That can be quite frustrating, yes?"

Curiosity smoothed Miss Rebecca's furrowed brows and pursed lips. Her shoulders shifted ever so slightly, turning her upper body back toward Pippa. She still had many walls that Pippa would need to carefully rearrange into a brick path leading to a positive future and peaceful relationships. For now, even this minuscule indication of interest—of trust—was enough. Miss Rebecca nodded her agreement.

"In truth, Miss Rebecca, nothing you are feeling is wrong or bad or silly—whether it is about my presence or changing into a different dress. We do not always have control over how we feel in any given situation. It is how we work to understand those feelings and how we express them to others that are far more important."

Miss Rebecca's bright blue eyes flashed from Pippa to her mother and back again. "Are you going to make me wear the new dress?" she grumbled, her hands still entangled in her skirts, ready to raise the alarms once more.

"Would that not be nice, darling? It is just here on your bed. At least come take a look at it," Lady Helsden offered quickly, seizing the opportunity to make her point. Unfortunately, it was the incorrect point.

Pippa could not blame her. What many people assumed to be the core of the argument was actually only the very surface of it. Oftentimes, whether between disgruntled parents and children or spouses or friends or even strangers, the cause of the argument masked the true, far simpler issue. This fight was not about the dress. Over time, Pippa would discover the heart of the matter for Miss Rebecca, the reason why she resisted such instruction so fiercely.

"If you do not mind, Lady Helsden, for now I think it best if we set aside the dress," Pippa suggested over her shoulder.

Lady Helsden, a mirror image of her youngest child, glanced longingly at the dress sprawled across Miss Rebecca's bed. "I suppose…. If you think it best," she relented.

"Indeed. It seems like everyone could use a few moments to catch their breath and collect their thoughts," Pippa continued. Without meaning to, she caught Mr. Helsden's eye as he lingered beside his mother and father. He offered her such an amazed smile that Pippa felt a rush of heat under her skin, starting from her cheeks and slipping down the back of her neck.

Praying that the feeling would subside quickly, Pippa returned her attention to Miss Rebecca. She noticed the girl's eyes transfixed on someone behind her. Her mouth twitched up in a reluctant smile. Certain she knew the cause, Pippa threw another glance over her shoulder. Mr. Helsden mouthed something to his sister, words of encouragement or comfort or perhaps simple nonsense just to ease her frayed nerves.

These two siblings shared a special bond, one of understanding and patience. After all, Mr. Helsden had been the one to write to Pippa and beg for her assistance for Miss Rebecca's sake as much as for the rest of their family. Pippa had seen the opposite far too often. In families with one exceedingly troublesome child, their siblings often regarded them with annoyance at best and complete disdain at worst. Thus they all became her charges in a sense.

Pippa did not reform disobedient children. She reformed

fractured families pushed to their limits and brought them together again under the banner of mutual respect and harmony.

Perhaps that would not need to be the case with the Helsdens—at least not as far as Mr. Helsden was concerned. He was just as invested in Miss Rebecca's improvement as their parents. He wanted to be involved in the transformation process. So, Pippa decided, she would involve him.

"Mr. Helsden, would you mind—"

The gentleman anticipated Pippa's request before she could complete it. He rushed forward and offered a hand to Pippa—a light, gentle hand despite its generous size. After helping her to her feet, Mr. Helsden dropped to one knee before Miss Rebecca. How he had known that Pippa wanted him to take her place, she could not begin to fathom.

As Pippa turned to Sir Arthur and Lady Helsden, she caught Miss Rebecca burrowing herself in Mr. Helsden's arms from the corner of her eye. The demands of the day had overstimulated the child, her tantrum sapping her of energy.

With a safe place now within reach, she allowed herself to deflate. Mr. Helsden easily pulled Miss Rebecca onto his lap, a surely uncomfortable position given her age and size. Yet he uttered not a single word or look of complaint. He instinctively understood what others needed and happily provided it.

"It is such a pleasure to make your acquaintance, Miss Seymour," started Lady Helsden, her sharp eyes showing signs of weary tension around the corners. "I am Lady Helsden and this is my husband, Sir Arthur. You have already met our eldest, Mr. Jasper Helsden, and…I am sure Rebecca has left quite a first impression."

The governess offered a graceful curtsy to her new employers. "Thank you, Lady Helsden, Sir Arthur. I am thrilled to be here."

Lady Helsden huffed a wry laugh. "Surely you jest."

The baronet rested a calming hand on the small of his wife's back. "We truly cannot say how sorry we are that you had to be introduced to us in such a fashion," Sir Arthur offered with a kind, apologetic smile that looked very much like his son's.

"As you saw, our dear Rebecca possesses some difficult behaviors—namely her temper and disobedience—that have been plaguing our family for several years now." He spoke quietly, keeping his voice low so the girl would not overhear and likely spiral into another fit.

"There is no need to apologize," Pippa insisted, hoping to ease the distraught parents' shame. "I love what I do, so I do not mind jumping right into work."

"You clearly have a gift," said Lady Helsden, a little of her stiffness melting away as she watched Mr. Helsden embrace and comfort his youngest sibling. The girl had fallen into silence, her breathing steady and her color returned to its normal slightly rosy hue. "Thank you for coming on such short notice, Miss Seymour. I am sure it is no mystery why we are at our wits' end."

Pippa nodded. "I am sure you have done your very best to help your daughter. And unfortunately, not all governesses are equipped to manage such situations. I only happened to fall into it myself when the little boy in my second family proved to be quite an energetic handful who was loath to listen to any instruction. He also had a habit of pulling at hair—his own and other's—when he did not get his way.

"I am happy to report that when I left, he was just as energetic as ever, though he found far better outlets for it. The last letter I received from them informed me that he is quite an accomplished horseman with numerous wins under his belt."

Both parents raised their brows, impressed. "Goodness,

that would be a wonderful outcome for our Rebecca," Sir Arthur sighed. "We do not wish to change her completely, you see. We only hope to help her regulate her emotions in a more positive way."

"Certainly," Pippa agreed. "That is exactly the sort of attitude that will take us far on this journey. Not all families realize at first that each child is unique, and those traits should be encouraged and molded rather than banished. Trying to force your child to be someone they are not never works well in the end. So we are already making progress."

Sir Arthur and Lady Helsden glanced at each other, a glimmer of hope in their eyes. Pippa peeked over her shoulder to find Mr. Helsden eyeing her with a reassured smile of his own, Miss Rebecca's head tucked under his chin.

"Why don't you settle into your rooms and rest from your long travels? You were not meant to really start until tomorrow, after all," said Lady Helsden.

"Allow me to escort you, Miss Seymour," Mr. Helsden offered eagerly. "Rebecca, I must go see that your new governess finds her way to her rooms and approves of her accommodations. I will not be gone long."

Miss Rebecca mumbled something unintelligible. Her tone carried no anger or fight. Mr. Helsden disentangled himself from the girl and guided her toward their parents. She peered up at them, her round eyes bashful and contrite.

Pippa watched, interested to see how Lady Helsden and Sir Arthur would react to the child's silent apology. To her immense relief, they smiled at each other and then their daughter. Lady Helsden wrapped an arm around Miss Rebecca's shoulders while Sir Arthur stroked her tousled hair.

"Shall we?" Mr. Helsden asked when he returned to Pippa's side, his head tilted, a wavy lock of black hair drifting across his forehead.

"Yes, that would be lovely," Pippa said, clearing her throat and trying to ignore the way her heart fluttered at that look.

Mr. Helsden led them out of Miss Rebecca's room and back into the hallway. She followed, a pace behind and off to the left, forcing her gaze over her surroundings and absorbing none of it.

Soon enough she would grow used to the future baronet's presence. Once she became accustomed to her new situation and focused all her energy on her work, Mr. Helsden would fade into the background.

Though they would share a roof for many months, they would not have much reason to spend any significant time together. Pippa only had to wait. Then, this strange feeling in her chest that longed to walk beside Mr. Helsden, if only to feel their arms brushing against each other, would evaporate into an ephemeral mist.

"Here you are, Miss Seymour," he announced when they reached the end of another hall on the floor above. "I hope you will find everything to your satisfaction. Of course, if you find something amiss, please do not hesitate to let us know. We are so happy you are here and want to make your stay as comfortable as possible."

The earnest smile he wore as he opened the door to Pippa's rooms sent her heart fluttering again. She ignored it. "Thank you, sir. That is very generous. I am sure I shall be perfectly content."

Pippa dropped her eyes to the wood floor as she slipped past Mr. Helsden into the room. It was a tighter fit than she had calculated. Her shoulder brushed against his chest ever so faintly. She knew she would wonder later if she had only imagined the sensation. Pippa turned to face him once more, expecting to exchange farewells.

"Miss Seymour," the gentleman started, his eyes locked on Pippa.

"Yes, Mr. Helsden?"

"I know I have said it before, and perhaps you are already tired of hearing it, but thank you for coming. Truly. And thank you for your assistance earlier. It is rare that Rebecca cools from such an outburst so quickly. I pray that our time together will be fruitful. Though, if I may be so bold, it already seems it will be."

Praying that her cheeks would not go as red as her hair, Pippa offered Mr. Helsden a polite smile. "A governess never tires of hearing about the difference she makes in her charges' lives, so I greatly appreciate your kind words. It will help on challenging days. And I can assure you, sir, that any challenge can be overcome. It shall be a fruitful endeavor indeed, I will make sure of it."

Mr. Helsden nodded, his own smile turning into an almost boyish grin that made Pippa want to reciprocate. Such an expression, however, would not be appropriate for a governess—even if she had no plans to impress Society herself. Her students would learn proper manners from her example, and her employers would expect to see the proof of her own genteel breeding in all her actions. Even if she had a feeling that Mr. Helsden would not mind.

"I have every confidence in you and Rebecca. Now I shall bid you farewell for the time being. Do ring if you have any questions or require any assistance."

The man bowed, turned on his heel, and strode down the hall. Pippa watched for a moment, peering around the doorframe. With his back to her, she allowed herself that optimistic grin she had suppressed into politeness. Mr. Helsden walked with his head held high, a little bounce in his step.

Pippa closed her new bedroom door and leaned her back against it. She always vowed to do an excellent job when she arrived at a new assignment. This time, with a hand over her dizzying heart, Pippa vowed the same not only for the child who needed her help—but for Mr. Helsden as well.

Something inside her longed to prove him right, to exceed his expectations, to bring that same happy bounce to his step every day.

CHAPTER 3

The early December chill nipped at Pippa's exposed cheeks and eyes, her wide-brimmed bonnet doing little to shield her from the brisk breeze. She huffed with every step she took, breath forming little clouds and boots crunching along the dormant grass. At least the sun blazed bright in the pale blue sky above, warming the large walking party exploring the quaint grounds of Goddard House.

The entire Helsden family and several Harcourts, including the cousin staying at Goddard, marched across the generous lawn toward a small now barren garden on one corner of the property. Pippa had instructed Miss Rebecca to remain by her side for the time being.

"What did you think of the story you last read, Miss Rebecca?" Pippa asked, taking the opportunity to continue lessons outside the schoolroom.

Miss Rebecca peered up into the sky. "It was interesting."

Pippa nodded thoughtfully. "In what way?"

"It had a dog in it. I like dogs. My Aunt Harriet and Uncle Jonas have a great big dog that my cousins Felix, Ezra, and

Margaret get to play with every day. I asked Mama if we could get a dog, but she says they are too messy."

"Very good," Pippa continued, bracing herself against a particularly harsh gust of wind that made Miss Rebecca giggle rather than flinch or pull her mantle tighter about her, as many others did. "What about the other characters? Did anything strike you about their actions?"

After a moment of thought, Miss Rebecca chattered away about the story, chosen by Pippa when she learned of the girl's interest in adventure and heroism. She had been with the Helsden family for just about two months now. Thanks to Mr. Helsden's comforting presence and readiness to lend a hand, Pippa and Miss Rebecca had made much more progress than Pippa had originally anticipated. After one particularly spectacular tantrum about a month ago, Mr. Helsden had sought Pippa out and revealed something Miss Rebecca had told him about struggling to understand why adults made her do certain things.

Ever since, Pippa had been mindful to explain the reasoning behind her decisions and instructions. Even if her charge still disliked the action itself, she was more likely to follow through without much more than a few grumbles. The tantrums had not completely disappeared, however, for which Pippa was selfishly glad. She needed more time to effect long-lasting change.

"Wonderful, Miss Rebecca! Why don't we continue the lesson later? Go enjoy yourself," Pippa suggested when Miss Rebecca lulled into silence.

The girl grinned up at her, a delightfully endearing and increasingly common habit that Pippa would soon have to train into subtlety. Miss Rebecca bounded away, running after a cluster of cousins, aunts, and uncles.

"Aunt Caroline, might we return to the house? It is a bit too chilly for my taste," said Miss Hannah Harcourt, one of the Attwood Manor cousins. The young lady unabashedly rubbed her hands up and down her arms for warmth, little caring to maintain proper decorum despite her debut in Society looming just around the corner. Pippa had quickly come to learn that this loving family preferred to relax the rules when in each other's company.

"Yes, Mama, do you want poor Hannah to freeze to death before she has the chance to prance about for the *ton*?" added Master Sidney.

Lady Helsden laughed and shook her head. "You both are far too dramatic. No one will be freezing to death. Besides, the snow will start in earnest any day now and then we really will not be able to enjoy any exercise out of doors. We must take advantage while we can."

Pippa silently agreed. She found the cool air invigorating, and she loved seeing Miss Rebecca running about so happily with Sir Arthur, Master Sidney, and her uncle Mr. Dalton Harcourt. She looked exactly as she should, like a girl enjoying herself and expending some pent-up energy.

Amiable conversation drifted over to Pippa on the next gust, a familiar voice rising above the others, full of warmth. She glanced to the left, spotting Mr. Helsden with his mother on one arm and his sister on the other. Miss Colette had taken Miss Helsden's other arm, the four chatting and joking together, carefree and content.

A pinch of longing forced Pippa to look straight ahead once more and return her attention to her charge, now running large circles around Sir Arthur. This was a family outing. Pippa was not family. She could not simply join their conversation to hear Mr. Helsden speak, to listen to the gentle sway of his voice. She should have been perfectly happy to walk with Miss Rebecca or by herself, as she usually did.

Never before had Pippa so desired to be part of such a

pleasant gathering. She glanced over to that group again. It was not her fault this family was so inviting with their light-hearted laughter and companionable manners. After Pippa's first assignment as a governess—just a few weeks after she had lost her own home—she had vowed to never feel this ache to truly belong in a household again.

That road would only lead her to pain. She had endured enough of that already after losing her beloved father when she was just a girl of ten, watching her mother remarry, and living under the shadow of her stepfather and step-siblings, who all seemed to think her nothing more than a nuisance and a drain on their finances.

As far as Pippa was concerned, she had all the family she needed in her students and the parents who relied on her to return harmony to their homes.

"Miss Seymour!"

The call jolted Pippa out of her melancholy reverie. She refocused on her surroundings only to find that her eyes had drifted to Mr. Helsden's group once more. Miss Colette smiled over her shoulder at the governess. Pippa flushed. She must have been staring.

Miss Colette waved to Pippa with her free hand. "Miss Seymour, come join—"

"Look, look!" cried Master Duncan, thankfully drawing everyone's attention to himself. "Cousin Hayes here says I cannot do a cartwheel. I aim to prove him wrong!"

With all eyes on him, the boy grinned madly and stretched his arms out to the sides and high up over his head, preparing his body for a miraculous feat.

"Duncan, no!" Lady Helsden moaned, though she could not hide her own smile as her middle child performed a clumsy cartwheel, almost slipping on the brittle grass.

Master Duncan leapt up and threw his arms out wide. "Ta-da!"

A chorus of laughter filled the air. Once again, Mr. Helsden's rose above them all, not because it was louder than anyone else's—that distinction belonged to his gregarious uncle, Mr. Harcourt—but because, against all reason, it was the one Pippa wanted to hear most.

Before she could chastise herself for such a ridiculous and needless thought, an equally unwanted ache returned. Pippa looked out at the lawn, scattered with cheerful Harcourts and Helsdens.

This was what a true family should look like, she could not deny that. The possibility of such a lovely, picturesque scene had been stolen from her long ago by Father's death and Mother's second marriage to a greedy man who had wanted nothing to do with his new daughter. He had tossed Pippa out of his home at the first opportunity, forcing her to seek employment as a governess wherever she could.

At least she had been blessed with love for her profession early on, even if it meant she would forever stand on the outside of familial happiness, always looking in. Governesses had no business finding marriages for themselves. Their sole purpose was to prepare their young ladies to attract appropriate suitors, or young lads to transition to tutors and boarding school.

Many governesses, Pippa knew, eventually became lower tier members of the families they worked for since most remained in their posts from their charges' toddling days all the way to their debut in the marriage mart. It was not the same as true acceptance, yet it was still more than Pippa would ever enjoy given her tendency to move on to the next family in need after only a few months or a year. Most of the time, she had no qualms about the path she had taken. On days like today, however—

"Miss Seymour! Look at what I found!"

Pippa shook those thoughts away once more as Miss

Rebecca trotted across the lawn toward her. She beamed up at Pippa, breathless and eager, loose curls bouncing around her face. Pippa smiled back, her dark memories dissipating under the power of Miss Rebecca's sheer joy.

"What have you got there?" she asked, noting the girl's one clenched fist.

Miss Rebecca turned her hand over and slowly uncurled her fingers to reveal a rock resting atop her palm. "It looks just like a rabbit, does it not?"

"My goodness, it truly does!" Pippa laughed. She leaned closer for a better look, providing her charge's discovery with ample attention and admiration. "A brilliant find, Miss Rebecca."

"I think I should like to keep it," Miss Rebecca mused, smiling down at the rock in her hand as she turned it this way and that.

Pippa's heart soared with hope. Under those deep-rooted behavioral issues existed such a sweet, intelligent, charming soul. Pippa was more determined than ever to ensure Miss Rebecca could find ways to feel this happy and carefree every day.

"Well now, what's all this excitement?" asked that lovely voice. Pippa and Miss Rebecca turned to find Mr. Helsden striding toward them, dark waves windswept, cheeks and nose reddened by the chill.

"I found a rock that looks like a rabbit! No, do not hold it that way," Miss Rebecca giggled as her older brother took up the rock and narrowed his eyes at it. "Here, like this. See? Those spiky points are the ears, these little indentations are the eyes and nose, and those curvy shapes at the bottom could be its little feet."

"Ah!" Mr. Helsden cried with a delightfully charming smile. "I do indeed recognize it now. Excellent discovery, sister!"

He pressed the rock back into Miss Rebecca's palm. She peered up at Mr. Helsden and her governess, a playful glint in her eyes.

"Would you like to know a secret?" she asked under her breath, gesturing for the two adults to lean closer. Pippa and Mr. Helsden shared a curious glance and bent forward. "I did not really discover it. I stubbed my toe on it! When I searched around in the grass to scold the culprit, I found this and almost thought it might be a baby rabbit until I picked it up. Do not tell anyone, though. I would rather be thought of as a sharp-eyed explorer."

Pippa bit the inside of her cheek to keep from bursting into laughter when she caught Mr. Helsden's bemused grin from the corner of her eye. Miss Rebecca truly was a wonderful, eloquent girl with quite a colorful imagination. Unfortunately for Pippa, she did have to seize the opportunity for a lesson. That was her first duty as governess, no matter how joyful or entertaining her charges' antics might be.

"Now, Miss Rebecca, I would not advise picking up baby animals of any sort," Pippa said, a giggle escaping despite her best efforts.

"Miss Seymour is correct, dear girl," offered Mr. Helsden. "Adorable as they are, wild critters can carry all manner of diseases or bugs that we do not want crawling all over us. Or, when caught off guard, they could even scratch or bite. It is best we leave them to themselves." The gentleman glanced around and leaned down even further, bringing his mouth to Miss Rebecca's ear. With a conspiratorial air, he added, "But luck was on our side this time, eh?"

Miss Rebecca nodded eagerly and smiled down at her treasure once again.

"You know, I have just had an idea," Mr. Helsden continued, straightening to his full height, several inches taller than

Pippa. He gripped his chin in his fingers, tapping at his jaw with his fingertips. "Why don't we take your rabbit rock home with us and perhaps paint it to look like a real rabbit?"

The girl's eyes widened and her mouth fell open. Pippa fixed her with a stare and raised a brow. Miss Rebecca caught on and snapped her mouth shut, though Pippa did not yet have it in her to correct Miss Rebecca's beaming smile.

"Yes, that would be so very fun! Surely painting must be better than embroidery," she scoffed. Pippa cleared her throat, fighting her own smile. Miss Rebecca nodded and repeated in a more polite tone, "I mean, surely painting must be better than embroidery."

Pippa nodded her approval at the vocal correction, even if the content of Miss Rebecca's words still lacked finesse. They had plenty of time to improve upon that. Leaving Miss Rebecca to bask in the triumph of the discovery and her exciting new plans, Pippa turned her attention to Mr. Helsden.

"What a lovely idea, sir. Creative and engaging while still developing a crucial skill," Pippa said.

Mr. Helsden's eyes grew round as well, quite similar to his sister. Though they possessed rather different temperaments, Pippa could not deny the family resemblance between these two.

"Is that so? Well, thank you, Miss Seymour," he mumbled in that sweet, winsome way of his. He even followed it with a shy smile and a deepening shade of red on his cheeks, a habit Pippa had noticed far too often over these past two months. How such a charming, handsome young man could find so many reasons to be bashful, Pippa had not a clue. That only added to his many endearing qualities.

"I will go and show the others," Miss Rebecca announced, pride shining in her eyes. Without waiting for an official dismissal, she dashed away toward the nearest group of walkers.

"I must confess I have been taking inspiration from you, Miss Seymour," Mr. Helsden whispered as they fell into step together, trailing after the rest of the Helsdens and Harcourts.

Pippa looked over at the future baronet. He stared straight ahead, eyes desperately roaming the wintery landscape. "How so?" Pippa asked.

"I have been observing how you interact with Rebecca—generous with praise while gentle yet firm with instruction," he continued. "I have encouraged my parents and siblings to do the same, and it has been making a world of difference. You truly have made more progress with Rebecca in these past two months than any of the previous governesses managed in half a year's time or longer."

A warm blanket of pride and satisfaction settled over Pippa. She hardly felt the cold anymore, in no small part thanks to Mr. Helsden's presence by her side. He always felt so warm, so welcoming whenever he was near. During those stretches when they did not see each other for days save for passing in the hall or entering one room just as the other left, she found she missed that comforting familiarity that had no right to feel so intimate.

"I greatly appreciate you saying so," Pippa replied. "There is still much work to be done yet since Miss Rebecca still has multiple tantrums every week. At least we can enjoy one full day without one, or very minor and easily resolved ones. I am quite confident she is well on her way to moving beyond these issues, though she is still reluctant to share with me why she behaves this way."

"Your skill is truly astounding, Miss Seymour. I have every faith in your abilities."

Mr. Helsden smiled at her, his genuine confidence apparent. Heat raced up the back of Pippa's neck. It was her turn to look straight ahead, ignoring her walking companion. She could feel her fair skin blazing and offered a prayer of thanks for the biting chill. Everyone looked as red as she did, and some even more so.

"How are you enjoying the area?" Mr. Helsden asked after a moment of pleasant silence. Before Pippa could answer, his expression fell and he turned to her with a painfully apologetic frown. "Forgive me, Miss Seymour, for asking such a foolish and insensitive question. Of course I should know that you have precious little time to take advantage of the grounds or the village."

Pippa giggled, covering her mouth with a gloved hand just in time to keep from looking completely silly and ill-mannered. "You need not fret so much around me, Mr. Helsden. I hardly think you could say anything to seriously offend or wound me. In fact, I find it very kind that you would ask after me. Would you perhaps…." Pippa paused and shook her head with another awkward laugh, hoping desperately that Mr. Helsden would abandon the topic.

"Would I perhaps?"

Pippa's heart sank. She lowered her head and glared at the browning grass crunching beneath her walking boots. Why did Mr. Helsden always inspire her to speak before she thought? Pippa had never had such problems holding her tongue. In fact, she prided herself on her ability to pause any of her initial reactions to a situation, consider how a proper lady should respond, and act or speak accordingly. Why must Mr. Helsden bypass all her ladylike training?

"I am afraid it was rather impertinent so, if you do not mind, I think I should refrain," Pippa confessed in an embarrassed whisper.

When Mr. Helsden did not respond, Pippa dared to

glance at him from the corner of her eye. He watched her with a patient, understanding smile.

"If you are allowed to claim that I cannot say anything to offend or wound you, then you must allow me to claim the same," he chuckled.

That small sound rippled through Pippa like a pebble dropping into the still, empty surface of a lake that had been untouched for years. It settled far below, the aftereffects still pulsing gently.

"Of course, if you would rather not, I quite understand. I did not mean to pry. Goodness, you must think me in need of a governess. I have been so rude," the gentleman rambled, nervously fiddling with the button of his black coat.

This time Pippa did not worry about hiding her laughter. It had been far too long since she felt so light, so accepted. All her past families had treated her with kindness and respect, but never anything precisely like true equality. Not like Mr. Helsden.

"Remember our new agreement, Mr. Helsden? You have not been rude in the least. In fact, I was going to ask if you would perhaps like to accompany me around the area when we both have an opportunity?"

Mr. Helsden's expression transformed into wonder and excitement. Pippa's heart quickened in response. "Yes, I would like that very much."

"Sidney, stop it!"

"You stop it! Just show me!"

At the sound of a heated debate, Pippa and Mr. Helsden both turned their attention further afield. Up ahead, Miss Rebecca stood in a defensive stance against Master Sidney who was trying to pry her hand open.

"Sidney, leave your sister alone," Lady Helsden called.

The boy only gritted his teeth and tried harder. "Why? She showed everyone else her little rock, so why not me?"

"You are trying to steal it!" Miss Rebecca cried, her voice cracking with desperation. "It is not your rock and you cannot take it from me!"

"Rebecca, this is nonsense," retorted Master Sidney. "I only want to have a look. I swear I will return it!"

Unconvinced, Miss Rebecca continued to struggle against her older brother, her eleven-year-old strength no match for a growing fourteen-year-old lad.

When the furious, unintelligible shouting began, Pippa knew she had very little time to act. She marched forward, sending a cautionary glance to both Lady Helsden and Sir Arthur. They stayed back, watching nervously.

Miss Rebecca and Master Sidney seemed prone to antagonizing each other. When Pippa had first arrived, it had been severe. She had had a frank conversation with Master Sidney, after obtaining permission from his parents, and encouraged him toward greater kindness and understanding for his sister. Like Miss Rebecca, the boy had improved remarkably.

Unfortunately, even a little brotherly teasing or a simple request could still send Miss Rebecca into a fit of rage. She clearly did not believe Master Sidney's innocent intentions to return her beloved rock and reacted accordingly.

"What seems to be the problem here?" Pippa asked, giving both children a hard stare.

"Sidney is going to take my rock!"

"Rebecca is being selfish!"

They both answered at the same time, their frustrated shouts overlapping in an angry burst. The siblings glowered at each other, Master Sidney towering over Miss Rebecca's diminutive frame. She refused to retreat, the fire in her eyes never shrinking.

Pippa had to admire it. Perhaps one day Miss Rebecca would learn to channel that fierce determination in a healthier direction. For now, Pippa needed to focus on keeping the youngest Helsdens from brawling right there on the lawn.

"Miss Rebecca," Pippa started, turning to give the girl her full attention. "Do you remember the calming steps I taught you?"

The girl stared up at Pippa, dismayed. "How can I be calm? I must protect what is mine! My brainless thief of a brother—"

"Stop," Pippa demanded, holding a hand up. Miss Rebecca fell silent immediately. When she had to, Pippa left no room for argument or resistance. "No matter how we feel, we do not needlessly insult another. It serves no purpose and will not make you feel any better in the end. Apologize to your brother."

Miss Rebecca jerked her head in the other direction. "Sorry, Sidney," she mumbled from the side of her mouth. When they progressed a little further, Pippa would push for a better, more genuine apology. It would suffice for now.

"Now, do you remember the calming steps?" Pippa repeated, shooting a warning glance at Master Sidney before he could gloat.

The girl nodded reluctantly. "Breathe in slowly, hold for five seconds, breathe out slowly."

"Good, I would like you to practice it now."

Pippa waited. Miss Rebecca grumbled and scrunched her nose, shifting her weight from one foot to another. Pippa continued to wait. Her students quickly learned that the governess' patience could outlast them in any stalemate, and they would soon grow bored of their own defiance. Miss Rebecca was no exception. After a few long moments, Miss Rebecca's chest rose, paused, and fell, her breath puffing in little clouds of warmth, even if her face remained contorted in displeasure.

THE NECESSARY LESSON

"Now, Master Sidney," Pippa continued, turning to the boy. "Why did you wish to see Miss Rebecca's rock?"

At least the boy had the sense to look mildly ashamed. He peered down at the tips of his boots as he answered, "She showed it to everyone else. I wanted to see, too. But she keeps insisting I will steal it, even though I promised I would not."

Pippa nodded slowly. "Miss Rebecca, why did you want to avoid showing your rock to Master Sidney when you showed it to everyone else?"

Miss Rebecca shot a withering glare at her brother. "Because I knew he would try to take it from me and run away with it."

"Why did you think that would happen?"

"Because Sidney is always pestering me! He teases me and snatches my things and makes me jump for them!"

"Master Sidney, is this true?" Pippa asked in a grave tone.

The boy rolled his eyes. Pippa inhaled sharply. She had not been expecting such an open display of disrespect from him. Before she could reprimand, Master Sidney continued.

"Of course you would take her side," he spat. "All Rebecca does is ruin everything. She takes everything so seriously. Jasper and Amelia and Duncan are never cross with me because they know I am only playing. Why must Rebecca always be doted on when she's nothing but horrible?"

"That is enough," growled Mr. Helsden. Pippa spun around. She had not realized he had been by her side the entire time, watching respectfully until Master Sidney crossed the line. "You heard what Miss Seymour told Rebecca. Insults are not constructive."

"But—"

"Thank you, Mr. Helsden," Pippa interrupted, offering a grateful smile to her assistant. "Your brother is right, Master Sidney. We know this situation is difficult for you as well. I promise you that whatever happens with Miss Rebecca, you are a valued and loved member of your family. It might be hard to feel that at times, but it is a fact that cannot be changed regardless of the situation. And, as you know, we are all working to achieve a better balance. Now, will you tell Miss Rebecca why you did not like that she shared her discovery with everyone but you?"

The boy sighed and lowered his head. He shuffled around to face Miss Rebecca. She still refused to acknowledge him with anything less than a seething scowl.

"It hurt my feelings that you left me out, Rebecca. I felt that perhaps you did not think I deserved to see it. I know I have not been the best brother, but I swear I had no intentions of taking it from you, nor will I do that in the future. Perhaps my teasing and games are not to your liking. I am sorry, sister."

Pippa and Mr. Helsden shared an impressed glance at Master Sidney's mature and humble response. They quickly returned their attention to Miss Rebecca, awaiting her reply with bated breath.

Miss Rebecca shrugged, hiding the rock behind her back. "Well, I do not think you deserve it. You have been mean to me in the past and I do not feel like forgiving you, even if you apologize."

"Rebecca," Mr. Helsden said in quiet warning. "That is not how we behave as a family. We love each other, even when we make mistakes. Can you not see that Sidney is genuine? Can you give him another chance to improve, just as he has done for you?"

The girl glanced up at Pippa, an excellent sign that she was softening and finally allowing herself to seek and accept guidance from the adults in her life. Pippa nodded her agreement with Mr. Helsden's wise words. The admiration she had long since felt for the young man only burned brighter. He had such a natural talent with these children.

After a torturously long moment, Miss Rebecca nodded. Without looking at Master Sidney, she turned to face him. "I forgive you, brother. I hope you will forgive me as well. Would you still like to see it?"

Relief crashed over Pippa. She grinned first at her charge, then at Mr. Helsden. He had played a vital role in nudging Miss Rebecca away from the edge of a terrible outburst. He grinned back, just as relieved and proud of the children's progress.

Master Sidney nodded and held out a hand. Still a touch reluctant, Miss Rebecca surrendered her rock to his care.

"Why don't you two come over here and let us have another look?" called Master Duncan from his group of companions, waving at his two younger siblings.

"Yes, tell us how you plan to paint it, Rebecca," added Miss Helsden, her arm looped through Master Duncan's. They offered grateful smiles to both Pippa and their oldest brother. When Pippa glanced around, she found the rest of the family looking on with similar expressions of relief and appreciation.

With the problem solved and both children interacting happily with their other siblings and cousins, everyone resumed their walk—including Pippa and Mr. Helsden. A comfortable silence permeated the air between them, a bright ray of afternoon sunlight spilling down from the clouds to bathe them in a triumphant glow.

A jolt of inspiration from the heavens struck Pippa to her core, her eyes widening.

"You look quite thoughtful, Miss Seymour." Mr. Helsden's voice, so close to Pippa's ear, made her start. When she turned her head, she found herself almost nose to nose with the gentleman. He had leaned in close so as not to be overheard.

"Do I?" she mumbled with a self-conscious chuckle.

"Would you care to share? Am I allowed to ask that under our new agreement?" he asked with his own nervous smile.

Pippa bit her bottom lip. She really had backed herself into a corner with that declaration. But did she really mind? Her heart yearned to open itself for him. Against all her better judgment, she did just that.

"Well, I had another unusual request to make of you, if you do not mind," she started slowly, eyeing him from her peripheral vision to gauge his reaction. If he seemed even the least bit irked, she would rescind and concoct some flimsy excuse to explain it away.

Mr. Helsden only appeared intrigued. "By all means. Whatever it is, I shall do everything in my power to bring your request to fruition."

"Even if you have not yet heard the request?" Pippa asked, tilting her head to one side.

"Even so." Mr. Helsden nodded with dramatic solemnity.

Pippa bit her lip again, this time to suppress a foolish smile. What an odd man he was to blindly accept a favor from an almost complete stranger.

"If you insist, then."

"I am afraid I do," said Mr. Helsden, his smile gently encouraging.

"I thought—and please do not feel obliged to agree—I thought that perhaps you could act as my assistant with Miss Rebecca," the words spilled from Pippa. There was no returning now. Mr. Helsden arched one brow and scrunched his mouth to the side in thought.

"You see," Pippa continued, "I would normally never dream of asking such a thing of the family. It might seem that I am not confident in my capabilities as a governess. However, Miss Rebecca responds so well to you. I noticed it immediately upon my arrival. She clearly adores you, and for very good reason."

"For very good reason?" Mr. Helsden repeated, his voice low and almost surprised. The redness of his cheeks deepened once more.

Embarrassment flamed through Pippa, threatening to match his. She prayed he would not ask her to enumerate those reasons. There were far too many, most of them exceedingly humiliating to admit to a man she hardly knew —a man she had no business noticing such things about.

"Of course. You are such a positive influence for her, the picture of an adoring older brother," Pippa offered, returning the focus to Miss Rebecca, where it should remain. "She trusts that you see and accept her for who she is, even when she is not at her best. In my experience, the other family members start to alienate the difficult child. She knows, no matter how frustrated the others become, you will never turn away from her."

Mr. Helsden nodded slowly, his gaze falling to the lawn, a line appearing between his thick brows. Pippa groaned internally. She had gone too far. Their silly little agreement to take no offense had been nothing more than the facade of a polite promise made on a cheerful, carefree day.

It had meant nothing real, just as it should have. Pippa had been all too eager to misinterpret it, to fabricate a deeper meaning that only existed to her. How dare she seek assistance from the son of her employer? She should have been able to manage this duty on her own—and if she could not, then she no longer suited this profession.

"Forgive me, I should never have—"

"I accept."

Those two simple words shocked Pippa into stillness. She

paused and stared wide-eyed at Mr. Helsden, who continued a few steps beyond. He turned and smiled.

"You accept?"

"Of course I do. I am more than happy to help in any way I can. I love Rebecca, and I love my family. At present, my most earnest desire is to see all of us happy and harmonious. You have already brought us a long way toward that goal in such a short time. If there is anything I can do to assist, then I shall gladly accept your offer, Miss Seymour."

The tension inside Pippa deflated until she thought she might drift into the sky. "Thank you, Mr. Helsden," she sighed. "I must say, you are rather a remarkable gentleman."

He glanced down at his feet, his expression bashful. "I do not know about that. But I do trust that we will work together wonderfully, Miss Seymour."

Pippa's spirit lifted in anticipation of both Miss Rebecca's progress and her future proximity to Mr. Helsden.

"I could not agree more."

CHAPTER 4

Jasper's temples pulsed as he made his way down the hall, leaving behind the schoolroom and its occupants. He rubbed at his forehead with forefinger and thumb, marveling at the difficulty of the full-time responsibility of managing a rowdy child. It had only been a few days since he had started his new task of assisting Miss Seymour with Rebecca's instruction, and he already felt completely overwhelmed. How Miss Seymour handled it on her own, he had no idea. His admiration for the governess had grown tenfold since.

The soothing notes of a familiar pianoforte piece drifted down the hallway. His nerves only increased the closer he came to the music room. Pausing just outside the open door, hidden from view, Jasper took a deep, steadying breath.

"Cousin, how lovely to see you!" Colette greeted the moment Jasper stepped foot beyond the threshold. "I have missed your presence during the day. You are always so busy until dinner."

Mama looked up from her chair by the window. Amelia did the same, her fingers stilling over the pianoforte keys.

"He has been helping Miss Seymour with Rebecca, remember?" said Amelia. "He has always been Rebecca's favorite, though I could not tell you why. You would think she would be more bonded to her only older sister." The young lady shrugged with a disappointed frown.

"Shrugging and frowning are impolite, Amelia," Mama chided.

Amelia heaved a sigh, another one of their mother's least favorite expressions. "I know, dearest Mama. It is only Jasper. I doubt he will gossip to my future suitors about me making faces now and again. That is for family only, and only when they deserve it."

"Yes, daughter, but what if you forget—"

"Mama, I have a request to make of you," Jasper hurried.

Amelia mouthed a silent "thank you" to her brother. He had no doubt spared her several minutes of lectures on ladylike behavior, the importance of putting one's best foot forward when out amongst the *ton*, and how perilously easy it was to make minor mistakes that could compound to damage one's reputation forever.

The closer Amelia and cousin Hannah, just a month younger, came to debuting, the longer and more impassioned Mama's lessons became—never mind the fact that both had benefited from the tutelage of the finest governesses who had drilled these matters of utmost importance into their young minds for years.

"And what might this request be?" Mama asked, folding her hands neatly in her full azure skirts.

Suddenly aware of the three pairs of eyes on him, Jasper quickly crossed the room to Mama's chair. He angled his back to his sister and cousin and lowered his head.

"I thought that perhaps Miss Seymour could be excused from her duties tomorrow. She has been working so very hard and surely deserves a day of rest. After spending these past few days in the schoolroom and witnessing firsthand all that she does, I thought it would be a kind gesture to show how thankful we are," he mumbled, rushing the words out in the hopes that it would be too garbled for Amelia and Colette to hear.

Mama narrowed her discerning eyes at her eldest child. Jasper swallowed, the faintest sheen of sweat gathering at the nape of his neck. Clearly she suspected something deeper behind Jasper's reasoning. If he confessed that he would be spending Miss Seymour's day off with her to accompany her around their corner of Somerset, surely everyone would misinterpret his intentions and tease him mercilessly. Nor did Jasper know how Mama would feel about the heir to the baronetcy doing something that looked suspiciously like courting a governess—even if he explained that courtship was the last thing on either of their minds at present.

"Yes, I do think you are correct, dear Jasper," Mama finally said, though the intrigue did not leave her eyes. "Miss Seymour has indeed been such a blessing to us. The poor girl could use some rest. We must do everything in our power to keep her happy if we do not want to be abandoned to Rebecca's wild whims once more."

Jasper exhaled a breath of relief, nodding eagerly. "Precisely, Mama, precisely."

"Just a moment. Why all this hushed conversation? What is happening?" Amelia prodded.

Steeling himself for further interrogation, Jasper turned to face his sister, perched on the edge of her bench and peering through the open top of the pianoforte.

"It is nothing terribly interesting, sister," Jasper offered with a strained smile. "Surely not as interesting as that lovely piece you were just practicing."

"It is not quite so charming when you have listened to the same few measures for the last hour," Colette chuckled.

Amelia pouted at their cousin. "Practice makes perfect, as Mama always says. You know, you could stand to practice, too, Colette. Don't you wish to make your debut at some point in the future?"

"I think not." Colette shook her head with a wry smile. "What does the daughter of the examiner of plays need with a debut? Society has never been inclined to pay me much mind, and I cannot say I am bothered by that fact."

Jasper's sister, younger than Colette by only a few months, deflated. "Really, cousin, how do you expect to find a husband? Besides, you are still the granddaughter of a baron."

Colette shot Jasper a bemused glance. With Amelia's debut just around the corner and dreams of finding her perfect match swirling around her mind every second of every day, the young lady could hardly fathom how anyone else might not harbor the same desires.

She even found Jasper rather odd for not securing a match in his first two Seasons, no matter how ardently he reassured her that he did not mind waiting for the right woman and, more importantly, the right circumstances. The present situation within their family did not exactly lend itself to carefree courting.

"There are many other ways to find husbands, Amelia," Colette replied with a nonchalant shrug that earned her a raised brow from Mama.

"Of course there are, my lovely niece. Perhaps you aim to catch his attention from across the street with your uncontrollable shoulders?" the older woman added with a good-natured and perfectly restrained laugh.

"One can only hope, Aunt Caroline."

"Well, I suppose I should excuse myself before things take

a nasty turn in here. I know all too well how passionate you ladies become when the topic of the marriage mart arises, and I am afraid I do not have the stomach for it," Jasper teased.

He only made it half a step before a prim cough interrupted him.

"Now, now, brother," said Amelia. Her lilac floral skirts rustled as she rose from the bench. "I do not think I received an answer to my earlier question."

Jasper's stomach hollowed. Of course he should not have hoped to escape the music room without a little more prodding. He turned back to face Amelia, catching Mama's eye in the process and desperately trying to convey his pleas for rescue.

Mama offered an almost imperceptible nod. "Our darling Jasper has just had the most wonderful idea. He suggested that we allow Miss Seymour to take a well-deserved day away from her duties tomorrow. He has seen for himself how difficult it is to not only manage Rebecca's temper but ensure she is receiving the proper education as well."

Amelia's ever active imagination snatched onto the perfectly normal explanation. Her eyes grew wide.

"Is that so? How thoughtful indeed." She tapped a finger against her chin, a smile spreading. "Still, I cannot help wondering if perhaps there is more to this generous request than you are letting on, Jasper."

"No, no, I can assure you there is nothing untoward—" Jasper sputtered as his nerves spiked. A droplet of sweat broke free and slid down his neck, pooling under his stiff collar.

"Of course not," Colette offered with a light laugh. "Really, Amelia, do you not know your brother at all? He is a complete and utter gentleman to everyone he meets. I am certainly not surprised that he would champion Miss Seymour's mental and physical health. He would do the same for anyone."

Catching Jasper's eye, Colette subtly nodded toward the door. His escape had arrived at last. While his sister and cousin argued over his intentions and even his very nature, Jasper seized the opportunity and quit the music room.

He fanned himself with a hand as he made his way back to the schoolroom, which had also once served as a nursery during their younger years. He had hoped his heart would resume its normal pace by the time he returned. No matter how many times Jasper told himself that Colette was correct, that his family simply liked to poke fun with harmless assumptions—especially where two young single people were concerned—that stubborn thing in his chest remained completely oblivious.

Until he opened the schoolroom door. As soon as Jasper's eyes landed on Miss Seymour and Rebecca, seated at the large table in the middle peering at an open book, his anxieties and uncertainties melted into insignificance. Jasper slowly and quietly crossed the room, careful not to disturb the pair.

Let them all speculate. It would not be the worst thing in the world for them to imagine that such a wonderful woman might possibly be interested in a simple, average man like Jasper, or that he might be taken by her incredible poise and talent. Even if none of that were true, Jasper knew he would not trade this opportunity for anything. It was an honor to watch an expert in her element. It was an honor to play even a small role in his sister's transformation.

"*J'ai onze ans*," Rebecca mumbled, her brows knitted and mouth puckered in a deep frown.

"Almost," said Miss Seymour. "*J'ai onze ans*. Try again, a little firmer and with a more nasal tone on the last word."

"J'ai onze ans," Rebecca tried again, with little improvement, before groaning in frustration. "I cannot do it, Miss Seymour. This is silly. Why must French be such a silly language?"

Just as Jasper settled into the chair opposite them, Rebecca's fingertips started digging into the leather cover of her lesson book. She gripped it in one hand, raising it up over her head. Jasper tensed, prepared to catch it before its delicate pages could crash to the ground, or at least try. He never had been a very sporty or agile man, not like his Uncle Dalton or his older cousin Hugh or even his own younger brothers.

"Miss Rebecca," said the governess, just a touch of sternness in her voice. She eyed her charge with a calm, impassive expression. To Jasper's relief, Rebecca paused and glanced at Miss Seymour. "Your calming steps."

After a moment of disgruntled deliberation, Rebecca inhaled a deep breath, her face still contorted. It smoothed slightly with the next breath, and still more with the next. Each time, she lowered the book a little until she finally returned it to the table.

"Very good," Miss Seymour offered with a gentle smile, pride in her lovely eyes. "Even when we are upset and frustrated, we mustn't throw things. We talk about them instead. You said you think French is a silly language. Why is that?"

Jasper and Miss Seymour exchanged an amused glance when Rebecca pouted thoughtfully, as if privately enumerating the faults of the French language.

"I suppose it is not. But then that means I am the silly one," Rebecca confessed, her narrow shoulders drooping. "I simply cannot make it sound as lovely as you do, Miss Seymour. No matter how hard I try or how many times I repeat."

Miss Seymour reached one hand over to cover the girl's,

forcing her to release the lesson book from her grip. Rebecca peered up at her governess, eyes round and imploring. Jasper marveled at the vulnerability his stubborn sister showed to Miss Seymour, only vaguely aware that he was staring.

Rebecca never liked being told she was wrong or that she could not do a particular thing. Yet somehow Miss Seymour had worked her way behind those defenses and encouraged Rebecca to confront uncomfortable feelings and consider other perspectives. Warm pride welled up in Jasper's chest for both of them. He had never expected to hear Rebecca admit she might not know everything or that she might need help. Miss Seymour was responsible for bringing about that incredible transformation, and in just two months. It was a miracle if Jasper had ever seen one.

"You are not silly, Miss Rebecca. At least not for this," Miss Seymour added in a conspiratorial whisper. The girl struggled to maintain her glum demeanor, a small smile fighting through.

"Learning a new language—in fact, learning anything—is difficult by its very nature. We are pushing ourselves past unfamiliarity and down the long road to proficiency, and perhaps even mastery. But it is a long road indeed, one that requires patience with ourselves. As long as you come to your practice and lessons and put your best effort forward—even if you stumble or feel worse off than you were yesterday—you can still consider that progress. So, shall we try again?"

Rebecca frowned. "For how much longer?"

Once again, Miss Seymour and Jasper happened to catch each other's eyes. They both chuckled, Miss Seymour politely covering her mouth behind her hand. What a shame it was, Jasper thought to himself, that he could not hear what her true laugh sounded like—all for the sake of propriety and providing a proper example.

"Let us finish this page and then we can pause for lunch," Miss Seymour suggested.

Sitting up straighter with an almost eager smile, Rebecca took up her lesson book once more and flipped to their current page. She situated it between herself and the governess so they could both see.

A moment later, they sank back into the lesson as if there had been no near disastrous interruption. Jasper watched and listened, perfectly content to enjoy their company and observe their interactions. Rebecca did not complain again, though she continued to make faces when she fumbled over the unfamiliar pronunciation rules.

"Well done, Miss Rebecca!" the governess cheered. She cupped the back of Rebecca's head in her hand and pulled the girl into her side for a brief hug of triumph. Rebecca grinned up at Miss Seymour, pride finally overriding frustration. "Go play while we wait for lunch to be delivered."

Rebecca need not be told twice. She never needed to be told twice when it came to play. Miss Seymour hardly finished her sentence before Rebecca was out of her chair and striding straight for the corner where her dollhouse waited. Jasper and Miss Seymour laughed again, a little louder this time.

Miss Seymour excused herself and rose from the table. Jasper did the same, following on her heels to the other corner with the service bell like a nosy dog. When she turned around, she jolted and pressed a hand to the high neckline of her simple emerald gown. Jasper jumped as well, surprised by how close he had actually come. They stood almost toe to toe.

"Forgive me, I did not mean to frighten you," he started with an awkward chuckle.

"Not at all." Miss Seymour smiled and waved an elegant

hand. "I did not hear you behind me. It seems you can be quite silent when you wish it."

Jasper gave a bemused shrug. "Yes, that is what everyone says. I have a habit of sneaking up, though I assure you it is entirely unintentional. My older cousin Beth—she lives in Oxfordshire with her husband and son—used to despise it so because she startles very easily."

"Indeed?" Miss Seymour asked, eyes widening in surprise. "How odd. I cannot imagine despising anything about you."

Heat coiled up the back of Jasper's neck, his breath freezing in his lungs. It was only polite, lighthearted conversation and nothing more. He forced air back into his body with a ragged inhale.

"I—Is that so? I would certainly say the same of you," Jasper mumbled, averting his gaze from her kind countenance. If he became this flustered by a simple compliment, how would he survive these next several months working in such close proximity with Miss Seymour? He must become accustomed to it, and quickly.

"You rang, Miss Seymour?" called a footman at the schoolroom door.

"We are ready for lunch to be brought up, Humphrey. Thank you."

And thank heaven for Humphrey, Jasper thought. The interruption provided a much-needed moment for Jasper to gather his wits and get to the point.

"I have good news, Miss Seymour. You have a day of rest tomorrow should you want it. I spoke with Mama earlier and she approved. I thought I might take you around the grounds of Attwood Manor since you have not yet had an opportunity to see much of them. Of course, if you would rather spend your free day doing anything else, I completely understand. I am afraid it was rather presumptuous of me to assume you would wish to spend it with me. You should spend it however you choose—"

"Then you are in luck," Miss Seymour said, raising her voice over Jasper's anxious ramblings. "I do, in fact, wish to spend it with you on a sightseeing excursion. It was my idea in the first place, remember?"

Relief washed over Jasper, slowing his erratic heartbeat. He did remember that, of course. Yet facing the situation, facing the unfairly pretty Miss Seymour, was an entirely different story altogether. In the last few days since that conversation, Jasper had half convinced himself that Miss Seymour must have changed her mind. She would be mad not to. Why would she choose to walk about the area with him when she could do any number of vastly more exciting things?

"Please do not feel obligated," he muttered under his breath, still unable to look Miss Seymour in the eyes.

"Do not fret, Mr. Helsden. I have been quite looking forward to our outing." The quiet cheer in Miss Seymour's voice echoed inside Jasper's mind, lifting his spirits. He dared to lift his eyes as well. Her smile conveyed only genuine anticipation. Had she indeed been looking forward to it as much as Jasper?

"I have come to know you best out of everyone I have met here so far," she continued, her gloved fingers fidgeting around each other. "I feel perfectly comfortable walking and talking the day away with you."

Jasper exhaled, another wave of relief loosening his stiff shoulders. "Excellent. Shall we meet in the foyer after breakfast?"

"Certainly."

"Lunch is here!" cried Rebecca from the other side of the room.

Once again, Jasper and Miss Seymour started, their heads

whipping around to find two footmen filing into the schoolroom bearing trays full of sandwiches, cold meats, tea, and the necessary allotment of sweets to encourage Rebecca into her afternoon lessons. It was Miss Seymour's hope that they could soon do away with such bribes, though until Rebecca's temper stabilized a little more, she suggested they take all the help they could get.

CHAPTER 5

Following a mostly sleepless night, Pippa found herself walking on Mr. Helsden's arm—a less than subtle suggestion from Miss Helsden—around the grounds of his grandparents' home.

A light dusting of snowfall crunched under their walking boots. Thanks to the bright late morning sun, her nerves, and the heat radiating off Mr. Helsden, Pippa hardly felt the cold, even when it whipped by in a short-lived gust. Nor did she hear the constant chatter of Miss Helsden and Miss Harcourt walking just ahead of them, huddling together for warmth and lost in their own conversation.

Silence stretched between Pippa and Mr. Helsden. They had only just reached the eastern lawn, the grand house towering behind them. She peered around the landscape with a content smile, enjoying the companionable silence between them. Indeed, though the purpose of this outing was to introduce Pippa to the area, she found she did not require any conversation—a fact Mr. Helsden seemed to understand instinctively.

Another biting breeze nipped at them, kicking up the tails

of Mr. Helsden's thick winter coat and the hem of Pippa's simple dark green mantle. Without thinking, she burrowed herself deeper into Mr. Helsden's side. Her shoulders rose up around her ears as she let out a breathless laugh that drifted off into the crisp air.

Blood rushed to Pippa's ears when she realized what she had done. She quickly righted her posture and smoothed her expression, praying he would think nothing of it.

Perhaps she should not have allowed Mr. Helsden's sister to talk them into walking arm in arm like some courting couple. It was not necessary, after all. Pippa was only a governess. Yet Mr. Helsden had agreed, saying the thought of letting her walk alone in this chill did not sit right with him. A gentleman through and through.

Pippa felt Mr. Helsden's attention on her from the corner of her eye. Anxiety wrestled with the calm exterior Pippa had just resumed. She could sense something curious in his gaze, something curious about her—and there were things she did not yet wish to reveal to him, or anyone, for that matter.

"If you do not mind, Miss Seymour, I would like to become better acquainted with you," he started slowly, a slight hitch in his voice.

Pippa's heart softened. The poor man always seemed so nervous whenever he spoke, even if they had reached a friendly agreement, as if he could not bear the thought of making her uncomfortable.

She pulled her eyes away from the barren gardens in the distance and looked up at Mr. Helsden from beneath the wide brim of her hat, trimmed with lace and fabric flowers to match the color of her mantle.

"I do suppose I know much more about you than you do about me," Pippa said, returning her gaze straight ahead. Her eyes remained unfocused, sorting through a lifetime of memories, choosing what she could or should divulge.

"Only if you wish to share, of course," Mr. Helsden added quickly.

Pippa glanced at him, a bemused smile tugging at her lips. Goodness, he was quite endearing. "I know, Mr. Helsden. I greatly appreciate your commitment to ensuring my comfort. Not everyone always considers that."

She allowed her words to trail away as she looked down at the dormant grass, valiantly peeking up between clumps of slowly melting frost. That was already more than she had ever told anyone else. Would it be too much? Perhaps he was not expecting to hear of the harsher realities that accompanied her profession, only the favorable moments.

"They do not?" he asked gently.

"I should not have—I am not sure it is appropriate to discuss," Pippa muttered despite the tender interest in his voice. Her fingers subconsciously curled tighter into Mr. Helsden's coat sleeve, desperate for something to ground her, to reassure her that she had not made a terrible misstep.

After all, if Mr. Helsden deemed her inappropriate for any reason, he would report to his parents and, with Pippa's entire livelihood in their hands, they could decide to send her on her way—with or without a reference. She would be doomed, even worse than when Mr. Clark had thrown her out. Those early households had been accepting of a fresh governess. Now, after several years, new families would expect glowing recommendations to support her own claims of her skills and abilities.

Mr. Helsden did not seem the type to cause trouble over trifling matters, yet could Pippa really afford the risk she was taking by opening up to him, regardless of how earnestly her heart cried out for it?

"Please do not fear judgment from me," Mr. Helsden whispered. "I wish to hear what you have to say, the good and the bad. If I may be so bold...."

"You may," Pippa laughed quietly as relief flooded her from head to foot, her proper posture relaxing ever so slightly. When he spoke so gently, she could hardly imagine any negative outcomes to anything. He could set the entire world to rights just with that sweet voice.

"I hope by now that we might consider ourselves...friends?"

Pippa's reserved smile grew wider. "That would be wonderful, Mr. Helsden. Henceforth, we are not only colleagues of a sort, but friends as well."

"Then do continue," he suggested, sharing an encouraging smile. "I am always more than happy to lend an ear to a friend."

Another long moment of silence filled the space between them, a space that seemed to grow smaller by the day—for better or worse, Pippa's flustered mind could hardly fathom. She would save that introspection for some other time. For now, her heart fluttered about in her chest, eager to accept Mr. Helsden's reassurances and finally give voice to some of the thoughts she kept buried beneath her exhausting schedule.

"Not every family is as kind and accepting as yours, Mr. Helsden," Pippa started with a slow exhale.

Mr. Helsden's brows furrowed as if he could not fathom any family being any less loving and caring as his own.

"They all treat me professionally, of course. But that does not matter to me as much as the children. As long as I am making a difference there, I am perfectly content," Pippa continued. Mr. Helsden only nodded and occasionally hummed thoughtfully, allowing her the space she needed to find the words she needed.

"My previous family, for example, had three darling boys —and, of course, one who most would never dream of calling a darling in a thousand years. At first their parents preferred to remain in the background, simply watching and waiting for improvement. But, eventually, I managed to pull them all together and turn their fourth boy into as much of a darling as his brothers."

As Pippa relayed more stories from her past assignments, Mr. Helsden absorbed every word, the setting of Attwood Manor fading away for both of them. Even from the corner of her eye, Pippa could see a myriad of expressions passing across the gentleman's handsome face, from shock to gloom. His kind heart could hardly fathom how some families failed to treat Pippa with the minimum respect she deserved for the work she did.

Pippa, on the other hand, had long since come to accept the fact that for most families, she was more of a tool than someone who could ever become a true companion if given the opportunity. The Helsdens had already proven themselves unique in that regard. Particularly Mr. Helsden. No one had ever asked to spend time with her outside of her working hours.

"And what of…." he started after Pippa's words faded into silence, his own query dying on his full lips.

Pippa peered up at him, curious. Mr. Helsden chewed on his bottom lip, clearly deliberating. "Yes, Mr. Helsden?" she prodded gently after another long moment of his pensive silence.

He cleared his throat and gave a small smile. "And what of our little corner of Somerset? What do you think so far?"

Disappointment pinched Pippa's chest, surprising her. Just a few minutes ago, she had been so determined not to reveal anything about her life before her governess days. He seemed on the verge of asking. Only now did Pippa realize just how difficult it was to keep holding that in when she felt so certain that if anyone would understand and empathize, it would be Mr. Helsden.

Perhaps one day, when they grew closer—

Pippa shook her head to banish that impulsive thought. They had no need to grow closer beyond the necessity of helping Miss Rebecca. That was her ultimate goal—her only goal. What clouded Pippa's past was none of Mr. Helsden's concern, nor would it ever be.

"Miss Seymour, are you well?" Mr. Helsden asked, peering down to see her face, searching for some sort of illness or injury.

"Yes, yes, quite," Pippa said with an awkward chuckle. "Just a bit cold out today."

"Indeed it is, especially with this indecisive breeze. Just when I think it is gone for good, it comes flying past us again," Mr. Helsden sighed. Seemingly unawares, he brought his other hand over Pippa's where it rested upon his forearm, rubbing back and forth to spark some warmth.

He only sparked an internal panic and a wildly buzzing heart. Pippa appreciated the gesture, though. She stared at his comforting hand as it continued its ministrations.

With a jolt, Mr. Helsden realized what exactly he was doing. His hand froze around Pippa's, his eyes as round as the bright white sun above. He snatched it back to his side and glanced nervously to the two young ladies walking ahead, as did Pippa.

It would not do well to set such a casual example for young ladies so near the precipice of emerging into Society. Luckily for both Pippa and Mr. Helsden, his sister and cousin remained oblivious to their other companions.

"As I was saying, this area is so lovely and charming," Pippa continued, unable to hide the flustered strain in her voice. "Quite idyllic."

Before either of them could decide if they should drop the moment or address it—and what it might mean—head on,

Miss Harcourt pulled away from Miss Helsden and whipped around with an eager smile on her face. Miss Helsden turned as well. Had they done that mere moments ago, they would have caught the governess and Mr. Helsden engaged in rather familiar behavior bordering on intimate. While Miss Harcourt might have the sense to politely ignore it, Miss Helsden had already shown too much suspicion for Pippa's comfort. She had no doubt the girl would read into it as far as she could—likely already considering them on the verge of marriage.

Pippa's heart hammered as the two ladies approached.

"Since we just passed through the gardens—and I am sorry, Miss Seymour, that you could not see them in their full spring and summer glory—I thought we might venture to the cottages and pay a visit to cousin Helen," Miss Helsden suggested. "I have only seen the new baby a few times since I arrived. If Helen is agreeable, of course. I am sure she is busy enough minding the little one and managing the cottage that we might prove more of a nuisance than she can accommodate at the moment."

Mr. Helsden nodded enthusiastically, just as happy for the distraction as Pippa. "We could certainly stop and ask, and accept gracefully if she rejects our visit."

"Goodness, Helen has been so busy since becoming mistress of the second Corbyn Cottage," Miss Helsden added, looping her arm through her cousin's once more and leading them down another path that branched off from the main garden. "Her husband, Miles, is unofficially the head gardener of Attwood," she said over her shoulder for Pippa's benefit. "Since they live more modestly than Helen's upbringing, she has had to learn how to do all her own cleaning and cooking—and how to raise a newborn without the aid of a nurse!"

Pippa gave a sympathetic smile. "That does sound like

quite a challenge indeed, though I am sure if she is related to you all, she is more than up to the task."

If anyone could understand the great upheaval Mrs. Corbyn's life had recently undergone, it would be a governess, formerly a lady of some rank and a comfortable situation who had found herself in need of employment. Though Pippa still had the advantage of servants at her beck and call, not all of them treated women in her position with much courtesy.

That was not the case at Goddard House. The same could not be said for Pippa's previous homes. Even with the assistance of servants—begrudging or otherwise—Pippa still had to work to earn a living that could sustain her. That was no small feat for a well-bred woman who was accustomed to some degree of luxuries.

Her first few months had been such a struggle to adjust that Pippa had found herself on the verge of quitting and crawling back to Mr. Clark's home to beg for mercy. Until her first charge had finally smiled for the first time since Pippa's arrival, showing her how impactful her presence could be when given time.

Surely Mrs. Corbyn had experienced a similar shock. At least she still had her family nearby to offer support and shower her with the love she needed to encourage her through the challenges of her new life.

"How wonderful that Mrs. Corbyn can remain on the grounds so near her loved ones," Pippa said as the row of quaint cottage homes, reserved for the more prominent grounds and household staff, came into view. They stretched out down a long lane, each one boasting a small stonework home, a fence, and a modest lawn and garden.

"We are very fortunate indeed," Mr. Helsden agreed, his eyes landing on cheery Miss Helsden who would make her debut on the other side of winter, fall in love, marry, and relocate to her husband's home, wherever that might be.

Pippa watched his heart sink, almost feeling his conflicted emotions as if they has sprung from her own mind. If she knew just one thing about him by now, it was that he loved his family more than anything. With that love came the desire to see them happily settled despite the melancholy realization that, one by one, his siblings would make their own ways in the world.

"She might not go very far either, you know," Pippa whispered, leaning into Mr. Helsden's side and tilting her head up, her nose almost brushing against his jawline. "But if she does, there are always letters and carriages."

Mr. Helsden smiled and nodded, his gaze falling to the gravel path, a touch of optimism fighting against his gloom. "You are certainly correct, Miss Seymour. It will just be so very strange without her at Goddard House. I am not entirely sure how I will manage losing a sister—never mind how I will manage when it comes time for my own future children to find their paths."

Pippa's hand, still clutching his forearm, loosened just enough to offer a gentle pat. She ignored the lightheaded sensation attempting to derail her steady demeanor, forcing away images of little ones who looked like Mr. Helsden. It had been a very long time since this pang of longing had afflicted her—the longing for children who truly belonged to her. And the fact that it followed on the heels or Mr. Helsden's statement was not lost on Pippa.

She pushed it all deep down into the furthest corner of her heart. She could not afford to chase such thoughts and feelings. Never. There was no place for them in her life now.

"You will find a way," she said quietly. "It may not be easy, but only think of the wonderful happiness and love on the horizon for Miss Helsden—and your little Helsdens—that will fill their lives. Parents who want the best for their children, even if it causes them difficulty and heartache, are the best parents any child could hope to have."

There it was again, that reserved curiosity that colored Mr. Helsden's sweet eyes. Perhaps, had they not been at the Corbyns' fence gate, he might very well have finally opened the door to Pippa's past.

She would never know what he might have done or how she might have responded. The cottage door swung open just moments after Miss Harcourt's knock.

"Visitors! How lovely!" Mrs. Corbyn cried, true joy writ large on her face. "Do come in and warm yourselves. I am preparing dinner at the moment, if you do not mind."

The group filed into the cottage, a welcome heat wafting to them from the kitchen on their left and a fire crackling in the hearth in the main room on their right. The ladies removed their hats and hung them upon hooks beside the door. Pippa gazed about the cozy cottage, the familial atmosphere warming her from the inside out.

"Might we see little Josiah?" Miss Harcourt inquired.

"Certainly, but you all must promise that you will spend some time with me in the kitchen." With a smile, Mrs. Corbyn threw a mostly clean rag over her shoulder and returned to her dinner preparations.

"Right this way!" an unfamiliar voice called from the main room.

The four visitors found Mr. Corbyn laying flat on his stomach atop a thick rug, chin propped up by his fist, bringing him eye level to Master Josiah. The baby sat with a plump pillow against his back to steady him as he developed the necessary muscles to one day sit on his own. He swayed and cooed as he turned his head to inspect their guests.

"Why, good afternoon, you handsome little lad," Miss

Harcourt whispered, grinning from ear to ear as she dropped to one knee.

Taking this as an invitation, Master Josiah allowed himself to fall onto his hands and crawl with all his might toward his first cousin once removed. Everyone laughed when he stopped several inches away from the lady and reached out a chubby hand, a spot of drool dribbling down his chin. Alas, he was still not the best judge of distance. Miss Harcourt happily scooped him into her arms and stood, positioning him on her hip.

"Quite a charming thing, is he not?" Mr. Corbyn asked, standing and brushing the dust off his front. Pride shone in his kind eyes as he smoothed the unruly blond hair on the back of his son's head. "I will see if I can handle dinner preparations for a while so Helen can enjoy some time with you all."

When he disappeared into the hallway, Pippa and Miss Helsden took the opportunity to converge on the baby. Miss Helsden pinched his cheeks while Pippa whispered many sweet compliments, her heart swelling as the baby smiled up at them. Mr. Helsden hung back with a content smile, watching the others dote on the newest addition to the family.

"Your son is an absolute darling, cousin!" Miss Harcourt cheered as Mrs. Corbyn slipped into the cozy main room with a tray of tea and plain cakes. Before Pippa could act, Mr. Helsden rushed forward to relieve her of the burden and set it down on a slightly wobbly end table.

"He is when he gets at least six uninterrupted hours of sleep at night and a nap mid-morning—or when we have company," the new mother chuckled, her eyes no less loving for the dark circles beneath them. "He somehow already seems to know how to behave in front of company. Yet when it is just Mama and Papa, Josiah knows no shame and will find himself a mess to dig into if we turn our backs for even half a second."

"Sit down, Helen, and allow me to serve," Mr. Helsden offered, a hand on his weary cousin's shoulder. Pippa kept her eyes on the baby, suddenly quite aware of Mr. Helsden's proximity in this small room. Still, she could not help smiling at his genuine, thoughtful gestures—always so willing to help in any way he could.

"At one point in time, my pride might have compelled me to deny you," Mrs. Corbyn said with a deep sigh as she eased herself into a handsome if a little threadbare chair in the corner. "But these days I will accept any help that is foolish enough to cross my path."

"I can take him, Miss Harcourt," Pippa offered as Mr. Helsden prepared the tea, extending her arms out to young lady and Master Josiah. "Take advantage of the fire and the tea."

"What of you, Miss Seymour?" Miss Helsden asked as she accepted a cup from her brother.

Pippa felt his eyes on her, the small hairs at the nape of her neck lifting. "I should like to spend some time with Master Josiah. I hardly ever get to work with such young ones."

The baby settled the matter himself when he reached for Pippa, babbling excitedly at the stranger. Miss Harcourt transferred him and Mr. Helsden handed his cousin a cup. The two younger ladies settled themselves closest to the fire while the gentleman took the seat beside Mrs. Corbyn.

Pippa sat across, nestling Master Josiah onto her skirts. She bounced her legs up and down, jostling the grinning baby on her knee. For several long, blissful moments, Pippa lost herself in the simple joy this brand new life represented. With his attention so wholly on her, nothing else seemed nearly as important as keeping Master Josiah's smile on his chubby face.

The main room filled with merry conversation ranging from life in a cottage to Mr. Corbyn's plans for the spring planting to Miss Rebecca's slow yet steady improvement. All the while, Pippa managed to ignore Mr. Helsden's side of the room. She had learned very quickly that merely looking at the man while holding a baby would send her thoughts spiraling to that dangerous place.

Instead, Pippa focused on blowing air against Master Josiah's small fists to create a humorous sound. The baby laughed with abandon, inspiring Pippa to join, marveling at his simple happiness.

"Allow me, Miss Seymour. You really should have some tea to warm you up."

Pippa started at the sound of Mr. Helsden's voice just inches away. Master Josiah had so thoroughly captivated her that she had not even noticed the man cross the room.

"Are you sure?" Pippa asked with just a hint of disappointment.

"Certainly," he insisted, a strange strain around his eyes. "I am quite revitalized myself. Besides, whenever Josiah is near, the ladies always keep him to themselves. I hardly ever have a chance to dote on my precious little cousin."

Pippa could hardly blame him for that. Unfortunately, some men could hardly care less about their own children, let alone the children of their siblings or cousins. Not so for Mr. Helsden. His eyes shone with love as he smiled down at Pippa and Master Josiah. Her breath caught in her throat, unprepared for the exhilarating shiver that raced down her spine at that look.

"Very well then. Thank you, Mr. Helsden." Pippa nodded and stood, adjusting Master Josiah in her arms.

Mr. Helsden opened his, and for one wild moment, Pippa

longed to settle herself into that welcoming embrace. She suppressed the thought as best she could and passed the babe to Mr. Helsden's care, her hands brushing ever so slightly against his chest.

As soon as she pulled away, the moment disappeared. Master Josiah straddled Mr. Helsden's hip, his short fingers clutching the thick fabric of his uncle's black winter coat. Pippa took his vacated seat and quickly turned her attention to Mrs. Corbyn, asking about her favorite recipes to make and which were the most difficult for her to learn.

Try as she might, Pippa could not keep her traitorous eyes from wandering to the chair she had just occupied. It was impossible not to appreciate the way Master Josiah bounced himself up and down on the gentleman's lap, clumsily clapping his hands together. It turned to sheer torture when, a few minutes later, the little one slumped to one side and burrowed himself into the crook of Mr. Helsden's arm, asleep in an instant.

"Helen, should I bring him to his crib?" Mr. Helsden whispered as loudly as he dared. Pippa took the opportunity to return her full attention to that achingly sweet scene.

"Good heavens, no! That is, if you do not mind letting him rest on you for a while? I must confess I lost track of time. This would be about the time for his usual afternoon nap, and if he is woken he will not return to sleep easily. I hope to spare your ears of that nightmare."

Mr. Helsden nodded and the other ladies chuckled quietly. "It would be my honor," he said under his breath. His gaze filled with warm contentment and love as he stared down at the precious babe, just as he might someday in the future with one of his own—a future so far out of Pippa's reach it almost cracked all the resolve she had built over these past five years.

"Miss Seymour, have you ever been to Somerset before?"

Mrs. Corbyn asked just as a sudden and urgent knock struck the front door.

Everyone in the living room jumped in their seats. Poor Master Josiah stirred in Mr. Helsden's arms, rubbing his fists against his contorted face, a cry building up behind his pouting lips.

Mr. Corbyn darted out of the kitchen to answer as the baby let out a pitiful wail. The voice of a familiar servant wafted to Pippa in the main room. She shot a nervous glance at her walking companions while Mrs. Corbyn collected Master Josiah from her cousin and rocked him in her arms with quiet shushes and reassurances.

"Mr. Helsden, Miss Seymour," the footman started when he burst into the main room, Mr. Corbyn peering around him with concern.

Pippa and Mr. Helsden both shot to their feet. "Yes, Harold?" asked the future baronet.

A cold weight settled in Pippa's stomach. Since Harold had only addressed herself and Mr. Helsden, he could only surmise that something must be amiss with Miss Rebecca.

"I am afraid Miss Rebecca is in a terrible state," the servant continued, his breathing hard, hair windswept, and cheeks red. "She discovered that you and Miss Seymour had gone out without her and she is…it is not good. Sir Arthur and Lady Helsden sent me in the gig to find you."

Mr. Helsden's strong jaw tensed. "We will come at once. Helen, Miles, I pray you will forgive us for this sudden exit. Amelia and Colette, you may continue the walk without us if you wish."

"Not at all," Mrs. Corbyn insisted, speaking over her son's frustrated sobs. "Best of luck, Jasper, Miss Seymour."

Thanks to his long legs, Mr. Helsden quit the cottage in just a few purposeful strides. Pippa followed right behind him and nearly bumped right into his back when he hesitated at the fence gate, the gig on the other side.

"Harold, what of you?" he asked, spinning around on his heel as Pippa hastily tied the ribbons of her bonnet under her chin, one arm poking out awkwardly as she clutched Mr. Helsden's top hat under it. Pippa looked between the two men, admiration temporarily overriding her panic. Even amidst this alarm, Mr. Helsden still took the time to look after his staff.

"Take the gig, sir," Harold answered. "I will make my own way back after I see if there is anything I might do for Miss Helsden and Miss Harcourt while I am here."

"Good man," Mr. Helsden said with an appreciative smile as he snatched Pippa's free hand and hoisted her up into the gig. She hardly had any mental space left to process the feeling of his gloved fingers around hers, the way they seemed to fit so well together.

Pippa scooted all the way over just in time. Mr. Helsden flung himself in after her and snatched up the reins, flicking the horse into the fastest trot he could risk given the damp and icy grounds.

"Wait, your top hat!" Pippa cried as they reached the end of the cottage lane in record time.

He only spared a quick glance at her lap and returned his eyes to the road ahead. "Hold on to it for me, if you do not mind," he answered. Pippa was glad he had rejected when she saw the way the rushing wind tousled his dark wavy hair.

Despite her pounding heart and racing mind wondering what kind of trouble Miss Rebecca was causing now, Pippa felt the tug of a smile longing to break through. He looked just like a hero racing to the rescue, his gaze urgent and his jaw firm.

"I must say, Miss Seymour, is there ever anything that

slips your mind?" Mr. Helsden chuckled, glancing at her once more.

The icy air stung Pippa's eyes as she looked down at his top hat, a strange sort of pride she had never experienced before spreading through her chest.

IN WHAT FELT like the blink of an eye, Jasper turned the gig onto the long drive leading to Goddard House. He heard Rebecca's screams over the churning of the wheels and the horse's hooves. Harold was right. This was not good.

He pulled the gig to a stop, his eyes landing on a heap of yellow skirts on the lawn surrounded by Mama and Papa. Another footman and a maid lingered nervously behind them, unsure of what they could or should do. Jasper leapt from the gig, his boots kicking up a fine cloud of dust.

Before he could turn to assist the lady, a blur of dark green rushed past him. Not quite believing his eyes, Jasper whipped his head back and forth between the now empty gig and the lawn. Miss Seymour was already almost halfway to the scene, hands lifting the hem of her gown, leaving Jasper dumbfounded at the speed of her action.

He almost chuckled. He should not have been surprised. The governess had proved many times over by now that she had no qualms about abandoning ladylike manners when her charges needed her.

Jasper jogged along behind Miss Seymour, effortlessly catching up thanks to the ease of movement provided by his trousers. The fact that Miss Seymour could run at all while encumbered by layers of skirts and a mantle was no small feat. Mama and Papa, kneeling beside a hysterical Rebecca, looked up at Jasper and Miss Seymour, gazes strained and distraught.

"What happened? Is she hurt?" Miss Seymour demanded as she dropped to her knees before them. A few bright red curls framed her face, complimenting the robust pink coloring her cheeks and the tip of her nose. Jasper did the same, the dampness of the grass seeping through his trousers, his heart thundering in his ears. Even after all her tantrums, Jasper had never seen Rebecca quite like this, her hands tearing at the grass and face deep red. Nor had he ever heard such terrifying, almost inhuman screeches.

Mama rose and took a few steps back, pressing a bare hand to her mouth as she squeezed her eyes shut, as if that could block out this terrible display.

Papa heaved a deep sigh, a strong arm still wrapped around Rebecca's shoulders despite how little good it seemed to do. "She asked us not long ago when you and Miss Seymour would return, and when we said you might be gone the entire day, well…. Needless to say, she was not thrilled about that. She thought you would only be gone a little while. We just caught her trying to sneak out of the house to follow after you."

"You betrayed me, Jasper! You, too, Miss Seymour! You said you would always be with me!" the girl cried, her raw throat cracking. Her eyes blazed with fury as she tore another clump of grass from the lawn and flung it toward them. Without a breeze, some of the blades fell limply from her hands while others, slick with melted snow, clung to her palms.

A guilty lump rose in Jasper's throat. He exchanged a remorseful glance with Miss Seymour. It must have been too early to make a big change in her daily routine, even if it was only for one day. Now she appeared to have regressed to a worse state than when the miracle governess had arrived. It had been too much for Jasper to hope that they could achieve even a fraction of normalcy so soon.

"My darling Miss Rebecca," the governess started, a hitch in her voice, "I am so terribly sorry. It was not at all our intent to deceive you. I understand now that we were not as clear as we should have been with our plans for the day."

"You *lied* to me...."

Rebecca's strangled whimper tore at Jasper's heart. Never before had he wanted to retreat, to run as fast as he could in the first direction his eyes set upon...and never look back. If he did, he would have to face the pain and disappointment he had unknowingly caused his sister. If this was the price he paid for trying to enjoy an outing on his own—for suggesting to Miss Seymour that they could have some sort of relationship apart from Rebecca—Jasper could hardly consider it worth it.

That thought tore at his heart, too, especially when he saw the regret beneath Miss Seymour's incredible patience and understanding. But nothing was worth this.

"We did not mean to, Miss Rebecca, I promise," Miss Seymour continued, tentatively reaching for one of the girl's hands. When she did not flinch or fold in upon herself, the governess wrapped her fingers around Rebecca's. The poor dear had not even thought to don gloves before trying to run after them.

"Of course we did not, sister," Jasper added. Following Miss Seymour's approach, he also carefully held out a hand and cupped Rebecca's cheek. "We said that we would always be with you, and that is still true. But perhaps we need to better explain what that means?" His eyes darted to Miss Seymour, seeking guidance. Just like on that first day, she smiled with admiration and gratitude.

"Could we go inside, warm ourselves, and talk about this?" Miss Seymour suggested.

After a grand and entirely vulgar snort, which inspired Mama to pass her youngest a handkerchief, Rebecca nodded.

Her head remained bent as Jasper, Miss Seymour, and Papa helped her to her feet, her energy almost completely depleted.

As they turned Rebecca back toward Goddard House, Papa's large hand on the back of her head, Mama caught sight of the deep stains marring the lovely yellow dress.

"Good heavens," she groaned under her breath as she followed after her husband and daughter, a few tendrils of hair framing her weary face.

Jasper slid an arm around Mama's waist. She instinctively let her head fall to his shoulder for a moment. "None of that right now, dear Mama," he whispered. "It will not do her any good. Perhaps the laundry maid can remove the stain, and failing that we could send it to Attwood to see what they can do there."

"You are right," Mama sniffled. "Instead, I should be saying 'Good heavens, you and Miss Seymour can certainly make miracles out of a horrible situation.' Nothing we said or did would calm her in the slightest. In fact, it seemed to make matters worse more often than not."

"I believe, despite this tantrum being rather severe, that it will become easier and easier for us to pull her back from them —and eventually for you to do the same. She feels she has been deeply wronged, and perhaps she has been, in truth," Miss Seymour, on Mama's other side, admitted with more than a hint of self-reproach in her voice. "That is not an easy thing for any child to process, thus the intensity of the outburst. But, thanks to the progress we have made, they will not be as long-lasting."

"I pray you are right," Mama sighed, rubbing at her temple.

Once inside Goddard House, Miss Seymour quietly asked her employers to give them some time and privacy. After Mama and Papa retreated, she led Rebecca toward the downstairs sitting room. Jasper closed the door behind them as Miss Seymour removed her mantle, laid it across a chair, and motioned for Rebecca to sit, then moved her own chair closer to her charge.

"I am afraid we must have it out now, Miss Rebecca," the governess started, her tone still even and patient, as Jasper pulled up another chair.

"What do you mean?" Rebecca grumbled, avoiding eye contact and drawing her shoulders up by her ears, the last remnants of her surly energy.

"You must tell me why you become so upset in these instances, as well as you can express it."

Head still lowered, Rebecca glared up at Jasper and Miss Seymour. Seeing their understanding expressions, her own features softened into that anxious, insecure child Jasper often noticed after these particularly difficult fits.

"I do not know, it just happens."

"Try your best. When you were out on the lawn and said that we betrayed you, what were you feeling?" Miss Seymour prodded.

Rebecca shifted in her seat, no doubt smearing wet grass on Miss Seymour's mantle. "I felt angry…and hurt."

"Why?"

The girl stared down at her hands clasped in her lap, shoulders rounded as if she longed to disappear. "Because you left me behind even though you promised to always be with me."

"But Miss Rebecca, even if I or your brother or anyone else spends some time away, that does not mean they will never return. In fact, enjoying time for ourselves can refresh us and make us more appreciative of the people waiting for us at home. Even when we are away, we still cherish you deeply."

"How can you cherish me yet abandon me for an entire day?" Rebecca demanded.

Miss Seymour fell into silent thought as she pondered Rebecca's question, never for one moment looking as though it was an absurd or childish fear. Jasper looked on in quiet amazement, stunned by Miss Seymour's ability to coax these answers out of Rebecca. Even he had never gotten this far with any of his queries.

"Your loved ones will always cherish you even if they are not physically near," the governess continued. "Say, for example, your mama wishes to take a trip to visit your Aunt Anna or Aunt Harriet. She may be away for a long while, but I know she will always be thinking of you, wondering how you fare, writing to you. Nothing can diminish your family's love for you no matter where they go or for how long. Love follows us wherever we go, and the ache we feel during separation—even if only for a day—makes the reunion that much sweeter. We know that we can go out into the world because we are confident that their love is following us, too. Does that make sense?"

After a few sniffles, Rebecca gave a reluctant nod. All the while, Jasper continued to stare at Miss Seymour, her words filling him with such comfort, ringing true to the depths of his heart.

"Can you tell me why you feared we would abandon you?"

"Because...with so many people around here and at Attwood Manor, I sometimes feel like I get lost. I am afraid that if I do not find some way to draw attention, everyone will forget about me. Or that everyone has already forgotten about me because they do not care for me. So the things and people I love will be taken away by others. It already feels like that is happening since everyone is always telling me to do this instead of that, or stop doing this...as if they cannot stand who I am and must poke at me until they like me better," Rebecca mumbled.

The peace Jasper's heart had just experienced at Miss Seymour's words shattered with Rebecca's. He curled his hands into fists where they rested atop his knees, his stomach twisting into guilty knots. No child should ever feel that their existence was unwanted, that their family's love came with conditions they could not understand yet must strive to meet lest that love be ripped away. That certainly had not been their intention in the least, but it had happened regardless—all without any of them realizing it.

"Dearest Rebecca," Jasper gasped, heartache and shame squeezing his chest so tightly he thought it might cave in on itself, "I am so, so sorry we have made you feel this way."

She turned her gaze to Jasper. To his immense surprise, her smile was soft and thoughtful—certainly not bitter and angry as Jasper had expected. For a moment, she looked older and wiser than her eleven years.

"Do not apologize, Jasper. I know you always see me. You always make sure to see everyone around you." Rebecca leaned forward and did her best to cover Jasper's large hand with her small one.

Something was strange about this picture, the youngest sibling comforting the oldest, yet Jasper could not help feeling anything short of pride in Rebecca. The road might still be long ahead of them, but there was true growth in this moment, true development of the wonderfully kind heart hidden beneath defenses they once thought impenetrable.

"Thank you, sister, but I do still feel I owe you an apology. We all do. I hope you know that we love you to the depths of our hearts," he mumbled around the clog of emotion in his throat.

Rebecca dropped her gaze. "I think I do. I love you all, too, even though sometimes I do not act like it."

"Well, now that we understand each other a bit better, perhaps we can all make improvements together. What do you think of that?"

"Only if everyone else is not terribly sick of me. Perhaps I should be sent away to a girls' school," Rebecca sighed, starting to pull her hand away. Jasper caught it and held on tight.

"Of course they are not, my dear. Frustrated, yes, but not a single one of us would ever wish for you to be gone. We need you here, in our home, Rebecca."

Rebecca only nodded and adjusted her hand in Jasper's to intertwine their fingers.

Triumphant and relieved, Jasper dared to glance over at Miss Seymour. He had rather commandeered her lesson. When he found her eyeing him with interest—and something else Jasper could not identify—heat prickled the back of his neck. He quickly returned his attention to Rebecca.

"I will send for tea," Miss Seymour suggested, crossing to the bell on the other side of the room.

"Come here, you silly girl," Jasper chuckled, holding his arms open.

Still without looking at him, Rebecca slid off her chair and clambered ungracefully onto Jasper's lap. She was growing too fast for this to remain practical for much longer, yet Jasper did not mind. The child desperately needed the reminder that she would always have a place in her older brother's arms. He pulled her into a comfortable embrace and settled his chin on her head.

Miss Seymour waited by the door for the tea to be delivered, allowing the siblings a much needed moment of peace. When the maid set the tea tray down on a nearby table, Miss Seymour wordlessly set about preparing a cup for Rebecca, who returned to her own chair with a mumbled apology regarding the state of her governess' mantle.

Confident that Rebecca would not burst into tears if he left his spot, Jasper joined Miss Seymour at the table and insisted he make his own cup while she tended to hers.

"I feel so wretched for poor Rebecca," he whispered as he stirred a lump of sugar into the warm liquid. "I never thought she harbored such pain. How ignorant we all were to her suffering."

While his eyes followed the circular motion of the spoon, his mind thought back on countless outbursts in the past, countless teasing remarks from siblings and cousins, countless exasperated scoldings from Mama and Papa. Every example—and those only the ones he could immediately recall—was like a dagger in his heart. Every incident must have unwittingly acted as yet another confirmation to Rebecca that her own family saw her as a nuisance to be dismissed, wished away, forgotten.

A gentle hand, familiar and thrilling all at once, settled on Jasper's upper arm. He broke eye contact with his tea and glanced at Miss Seymour.

"You feel so wretched because you love so deeply, Mr. Helsden," she said with a reassuring smile that, for one wild moment, Jasper longed to lose himself in. "I can assure you, however, that feelings such as these are actually quite common for children—especially young ones who come from large families. But that simply means that Miss Rebecca loves you all so much that she is terrified of losing any of you."

"Pardon me," Rebecca's small voice called.

Miss Seymour snatched her hand away from Jasper's arm. They both spun around to face the girl. "Yes, Miss Rebecca?"

"I am quite tired," she replied, covering a generous yawn with her hand just in time.

The governess returned her cup to the silver tray without taking a single sip, without even a hint of complaint. "I am sure you are. Shall we make our way upstairs and have a nap? Bring your cup here first."

Rebecca nodded and obeyed, carefully placing her half-full teacup beside Miss Seymour's. Wrapping an arm around the girl's shoulders, the woman led them toward the door. Not knowing what else to do, Jasper followed.

When he opened the door for them, Miss Seymour sent Rebecca through first. She paused, eyes darting as she deliberated. After a long moment, she finally looked up at Jasper.

"Thank you, Mr. Helsden."

Already feeling the dreaded color rising to his cheeks, Jasper coughed and shrugged. "I am always happy to help."

Miss Seymour stifled a giggle that Jasper so desperately longed to hear. "I also meant to thank you for the lovely day. I hope we might repeat it again soon."

Before Jasper could formulate a response, Miss Seymour quit the sitting room. He stared at the empty doorway, mouth still slightly ajar.

Perhaps they could develop some sort of relationship apart from Rebecca after all.

CHAPTER 6

*G*entle flurries of snow wafted past Pippa's small window through a bleak February sky. She pulled her shawl tighter around her shoulders, her rooms comfortable yet chilly on the top floor of Goddard House.

She would have to shed the shawl before making her way downstairs to begin her day with Miss Rebecca. For now, she clung to the warmth as she played a game she'd kept in her memory since childhood. Her eyes caught on one particular snowflake and followed it through twists and turns until she lost sight of it. Perhaps she would suggest it to Miss Rebecca later when the girl inevitably grew antsy from too many days spent indoors.

The quick knock at the door snapped Pippa out of her reverie. There was only ever one reason anyone knocked on her door. She rushed across the cozy room, expertly dodging the bed frame hidden under her thick blankets that had caught her shins on more than one occasion in her early days at the Helsdens' home.

"Letters for you, Miss Seymour." The strict housekeeper

shoved several folded sheets into Pippa's eager hands with a stiff nod before hurrying off to attend her many other duties.

"Thank you, Mrs. Fuller!"

Heart rising with anticipation, Pippa settled at her writing desk, situated before the single window. She quickly lit a candle, more for warmth on the other side of the slightly frosted glass than for light. She snatched up the small stack of letters and thumbed through them, ignoring the names of past families who wrote on occasion to inform her of her previous charges' progress and ask after her. Touching as those letters always were, Pippa was looking for something else.

Finally, toward the bottom of the pile, her eyes landed on the wonderfully familiar handwriting she had been searching for. Smile stretching from cheek to cheek, Pippa set the others aside and carefully popped the seal of this special letter.

"My dearest daughter...." the letter began.

Pippa traced her mother's precious words, words she received far too infrequently. But there was nothing either she or Mother could do about that.

These were her stepfather's rules. Mother could only write to Pippa once a month.

Of course, Pippa could write as often as she wished, but Mother could only respond once. In fact, early on in her governess days, Pippa had written to Mother every few days, updating her on the adventures, challenges, and triumphs of her new life. Based on Mother's single response, Pippa had guessed that Mr. Clark had withheld most of Pippa's correspondence save for whichever letter he deemed best. Thus, Pippa now distilled her news to a single letter every month, just as Mother did.

Icy dread filled Pippa's veins the further she read, her eager smile quickly turning to dismay. She reread several sentences, just to be sure she had not misunderstood. Upon multiple scans, Pippa could not deny the truth in Mother's elegant yet rushed handwriting. She gripped the bottom corner too hard, the paper crumpling in her fingers.

According to Mother, Mr. Clark had run the family—*their* family, as Pippa no longer considered herself part of it—into financial issues. Though Mother did not go into detail regarding the nature of said issues, Pippa could not help suspecting that years of reckless gambling had finally caught up to her stepfather. Mr. Clark hoped to remedy the situation by selling off a small portion of their land.

"Good heavens," Pippa muttered, letting the page drift from her fingers down to the desk. She lifted her head and stared out the window, unable to focus on a single snowflake no matter how hard she tried.

She knew Mr. Clark had never been adept at managing his money. He had married Mother, a comfortably wealthy widow, just weeks after her official mourning period ended, promising to love and look after her and Pippa. By the time his true intentions started showing through—to use Mother's funds to feed his numerous unsavory habits and banish Pippa at the first opportunity, keeping the Seymour money for himself and his own children—it was far too late.

If he had finally come to the decision to sell land, Pippa dreaded what that meant about the state of the Clarks' finances. Many men who found themselves in difficult positions would exhaust all other options before parting with any of their land, land that might have been in their families for generations.

Fear wrapped a cold hand around Pippa's heart and squeezed. Mother was already treated as a lesser being by Mr. Clark and his adult children from the marriage that had left him a widower. If the situation really were that dire, what would become of Pippa's beloved mother?

Pippa's eyes darted to the inkwell on one corner of her desk and then to the small clock on the other corner. Responsibility warred with love until logic finally won out. With a heavy sigh, Pippa forced herself away from the writing desk.

As much as she longed to answer Mother's worrisome letter right away, Pippa had work to do. Even if she sent a letter that morning, it would not go out into the post until the following day and take at least a few days to travel to the Clarks' home. It would do Mother no good at this precise moment.

"We have encountered a spot of trouble, I'm afraid...."

"Fear not, darling, I believe Mr. Clark has plans to sell just a small portion of his land and all will be put to rights, I am sure of it...."

Mother's message haunted Pippa as she made her way downstairs to the schoolroom. Her looping letters, usually a comfort to Pippa, burned behind her eyes as she paced up and down the far wall while waiting for Miss Rebecca to finish her breakfast with the rest of the family. Half-formed solutions presented themselves to her, each dismissed in turn as folly.

Realistically, what could Pippa hope to do for Mother now? Whatever hole Mr. Clark had dug, she doubted her modest governess wages could fill even a quarter of it. And no future families would wish to hire a governess with her mother in tow. Not that Mr. Clark would be inclined to let his wife travel all over England without his watchful eye to monitor her every move—not unless it benefited him somehow.

"Good morning, Miss Seymour!"

That bright, melodic voice banished the dark clouds crowding Pippa's mind in an instant. She paused and looked to the door to find Miss Rebecca bounding toward her with a cheery smile.

"Good morning, Miss—" Pippa wheezed as her charge nearly slammed into her, wrapping her arms around Pippa's middle and squeezing tight. "I see someone woke up on the right side of the bed today. Or perhaps the cook served your favorites for breakfast?"

Miss Rebecca released her governess from a surprisingly strong grip and took her seat at their worktable, still smiling. "Honey cake and hot chocolate!" she cheered. "But you know, Miss Seymour, you always say there is no such thing as a right or wrong side of the bed. We must choose peace and happiness in every moment of the day."

Pippa stared as the girl pulled out a lesson book and flipped through it, briefly reviewing past lessons. Her pride almost completely eclipsed the worry that had been eating away at her since the arrival of the letter.

"Yes, Miss Rebecca, that is correct. Well done," Pippa mumbled in awe as she took the seat beside her eager student.

"Thank you, Miss Seymour. Now, I believe we left off… here." Miss Rebecca reached the page she had been looking for and pointed to it with anticipation shining in her eyes.

One crucial thing Pippa had learned about Miss Rebecca was that the girl threw herself wholeheartedly into everything—whether it be tantrums or studies that appealed to her. Over these past four months, Miss Rebecca had found more of the latter to direct her energy toward, though she still fussed when it came time for French.

They had made remarkable progress—even for Pippa's skills. Though Miss Rebecca was still not quite at the place Pippa wanted to see, she had made leaps and bounds toward it once they discovered the root of her behavior.

When Pippa had explained her findings to the rest of the

family, they adjusted their attitudes accordingly. She had no doubt their willingness to examine their own actions and change for the better helped push Miss Rebecca along much faster than most of Pippa's past students.

The Helsdens understood their family could only function at its best—especially when one of them faced such heart-wrenching internal struggles—when they all worked together and lifted each other up.

"Blast, I see you have started without me!" another wonderfully familiar voice called from the door. Pippa and Miss Rebecca both looked up to greet Mr. Helsden. "Forgive my tardiness, ladies. You know how Duncan gets when he discovers a new interest. I am afraid he rather cornered me after breakfast to provide me with painstaking detail over his piquet win against Papa last night. I fear for the wallets of the *ton's* gentlemen when he comes of age if he keeps this up."

"You have arrived just in time, as a matter of fact," Pippa said, gesturing to his usual seat.

With a sheepish smile that highlighted the kind lines at the corners of his dark eyes, Mr. Helsden hurried across the schoolroom.

When his gaze met Pippa's, her anxieties and concerns melted into the background. They were still there, yes...but when Mr. Helsden was near, all things seemed a little more bearable.

PLODDING notes and frustrated huffs filled the otherwise silent music room. After a particularly discordant tone, Jasper peeked over the top of his book. He saw Rebecca shake her head and square her shoulders. Miss Seymour put a comforting hand on her back, a silent encouragement.

Jasper returned his eyes to the page and scanned it up and

down. His brows furrowed. None of this looked familiar. He had clearly absorbed nothing. It was difficult to maintain focus on something as tedious as a book when Miss Seymour was in the room. That was quite an accomplishment on her part considering Jasper was the most enthusiastic reader in his family, matched only by Uncle Patrick, Colette's father, who read day in and day out as the primary examiner of plays in London.

"Yes, you were very nearly there! Excellent, Miss Rebecca!" the governess cheered, offering a muted clap. Jasper looked up again. The pride and enthusiasm shining through her expression did things to him that should not have been possible, not with Rebecca still a long way to go toward refining her temper and manners.

"I swear I will get it just right next time," Rebecca grumbled.

"I am sure you will, dear."

Jasper's heart fluttered when Miss Seymour brushed the back of Rebecca's head, something like love in her eyes. Then again, he supposed she must love all her students. She could not possibly be as effective as she was without at least some love for these children.

What else did she love? Who else did she love? Pondering those questions proved far more entertaining than whatever he had been trying to read. Still holding the book up to at least give the appearance of interest, Jasper gave himself over to watching them over the pages and trying to puzzle out the mystery of Miss Philippa Seymour.

Even after the time they had spent together, Jasper hardly knew anything about her. The vast majority of their time was occupied by working with Rebecca or talking about Rebecca. They did not have much energy to give to exploratory or even idle conversation.

She also might not care for her employer's son digging

into her past, not that Jasper would use anything he discovered against her. Perhaps, despite their earlier agreement and the strange level of comfort they had found themselves in of late, there were still some things Miss Seymour could not trust Jasper with.

No matter how many times he told himself that that was perfectly normal for their situation, the thought still stung. He foolishly deluded himself into expecting more from their professional friendship, through no fault of Miss Seymour's. Jasper's silly heart was the culprit.

"There! What did you think, Miss Seymour?" Rebecca called, bouncing on the pianoforte bench.

Miss Seymour smiled down at the girl and gave another round of applause. "Wonderful indeed, Miss Rebecca. Try it again."

The girl deflated, then straightened her spine when she felt Miss Seymour's gaze on her. "Must I?" she whined. "I might not be able to do it right again."

"You might not, but there is nothing wrong with that. We only improve our skills when we practice them diligently, no matter how many times we get it wrong or right," Miss Seymour said, every word filled with patience and kindness. "You might miss notes next time, and the next, and the next. But soon enough, you will play right more often than not, until any mistakes become exceedingly rare. Do not give up now just because it continues to be difficult. It will not always be that way, but it will if you stop practicing out of frustration and then try again some time later. You will always find yourself in the same place—at the beginning. We do not want that, do we?"

Jasper grinned, hidden behind the safety of his book. Miss Seymour truly was a brilliant woman. None of his childhood governesses or tutors had ever explained the concept of practice in such an eloquent yet understandable way.

"Very well then," Rebecca sighed.

When she put her fingers back to the keys—indeed missing a note here and there—Jasper could not help noticing a change overcome Miss Seymour's expression. The first few times, he thought he'd imagined it, or that she disliked the cold, gloomy, snowy day. Yet there it was again.

Curiosity stirred inside him once more. There was something unusual about her this afternoon, her normal undercurrent of quiet contentment clouded by...something. If she was troubled, Jasper wanted to do everything in his power to ease her burdens—even if that meant prodding more forcefully than usual.

"There, another perfect practice," Rebecca announced with a triumphant nod. "Now may I please stop?"

Miss Seymour's eyes darted in Jasper's direction to the clock above the fireplace. For a flash of a moment, he thought they also landed upon him before returning to Rebecca.

"You may," the governess agreed. "You did wonderfully, Miss Rebecca. You persevered even when it was difficult, and I greatly admire that."

"Thank you, Miss Seymour!" Rebecca leapt up from the bench and strode across the room to Jasper, snatching the book out of his hands and snapping it closed.

"Miss Rebecca!"

"Forgive me, brother, Miss Seymour," Rebecca mumbled. She returned the book to Jasper. "I got a bit too excited."

"Indeed you did, but for good reason, it seems?" Jasper asked, raising a brow.

"Did you hear, Jasper? I still make mistakes, but I think I am much improved since we started the piece last week." The words tumbled from his sister's mouth, the exhilaration of achievement making her breathless.

"I did hear, and I am so very proud of you. You get better

every single day. Mama and Papa will be so thrilled to hear of your progress."

Jasper stood, set the book down on his vacant seat, and gave Rebecca a generous hug that lifted her off her feet and elicited a squeal of laughter. As soon as he released her, she marched of her own volition toward the music room door, ready to return to the schoolroom for afternoon lessons with a spring in her step.

Side by side, Jasper and Miss Seymour followed her lead down the hall. Jasper watched his youngest sibling with an amazed smile. At least now they could get through a lesson with a few whines instead of outright tantrums more often than not.

That was all thanks to the woman walking beside him. He glanced at her from the corner of his eye. She wore an expression that perfectly mirrored his own, a contented pride.

"Would you retrieve your French lesson book and your writing utensils, Miss Rebecca?" the governess instructed when they arrived at the schoolroom.

Rebecca whirled around to face them. "Must I do French right after pianoforte?"

Miss Seymour chuckled. "Yes, you must. That is our schedule."

The girl pursed her lips together as if deliberating between accepting her fate and causing a ruckus. Jasper held his breath and only released it when she huffed and trudged off to the bookcase in the corner of the room. After her conquest of the pianoforte, suffering through French—her other enemy—would likely inspire more grumbles and perhaps even a minor fit.

Miss Seymour took a step toward the table in the middle of the room. Without thinking, Jasper's hand shot out and closed around the dark blue sleeve covering her wrist. When her head whipped around in shock, vibrant red curls bouncing, Jasper dropped it as if she had stung him.

"Is something wrong, Mr. Helsden?" she asked hesitantly.

"N-No. Well, perhaps, but not with me," he stammered, clearing his throat with an uncomfortable chuckle. "I was wondering if you...that is, if perhaps something was wrong with you?"

"Is there something wrong with me?" Miss Seymour asked, tilting her head to one side. Her bright blue eyes flashed with a teasing glint.

Jasper gasped and desperately waved his hands in a placating manner. "Goodness, no, of course there is nothing wrong with you. In fact, you are rather— What I meant to say is, are you well?"

The governess giggled quietly, muffling the sound behind her hand. How Jasper longed to pull it away, to hear her laughter unbridled and crystal clear! But he had already been far too forward—and promptly made a fool of himself. He would have to be forward once more if he hoped to obtain any answers to the inner workings of Miss Seymour.

"Do I seem unlike myself today?"

"A bit, yes. Sometimes. Not all the time," Jasper admitted.

Miss Seymour looked down at the polished hardwood floor. Her eyes flickered back and forth as if struggling between wanting to confide in him and wondering if it would be appropriate, her fingers twisting into the fabric of her skirt.

"I am asking as a friend, Miss Seymour," Jasper offered. "Whatever you say will stay between us as friends."

The governess glanced up, reading his expression for a silent moment. Jasper hoped she would find reassurance there. His heart sank when she looked over her shoulder toward Rebecca, already seated and waiting at the table. Of course now was not the best time to have such a conversation, if there was any to be had at all.

"Miss Rebecca, I will be there shortly. For now, could you start with quiet reading?"

She turned back to Jasper, relief under her tight smile. "Thank you, Mr. Helsden. I received a letter from my mother this morning that has been weighing on me heavily. I have been able to put it out of my mind for the most part, but sometimes it returns without any warning."

Jasper listened intently as Miss Seymour shared the contents of the letter. She had never mentioned any blood relatives or step-family before. In fact, she had been so tight-lipped about that subject that Jasper had started to wonder if she was an orphan.

As much as he longed to ask more questions about her mother and stepfather, Jasper knew that would be best saved for another time. Based on the way she spoke of them, Jasper suspected the history there carried pain for her.

Indeed, the longer she spoke, the clearer her worry became. She continued to fidget with her dress while her words spilled out in a panicked rush. Jasper frowned, his mind turning over this unsettling information and heart aching for his friend's obvious distress.

"Do you really think it could be that dire?" Jasper asked quietly when Miss Seymour finished.

The governess sighed and released her skirts from her anxious grip, already defeated.

"It is unfortunately very possible. My stepfather, you see, has never been the most responsible man even though he already had children of his own by the time he married my mother. I was too young at the time, but now I believe that he saw her as an easy catch, someone who would be none the wiser when he took advantage of her. What kind of man does such a thing? What kind of man preys on a still-grieving widow and makes promises he never intended to keep?" she demanded, voice shaking. Her bottom lip trembled and her beautifully bright eyes glared at Jasper imploringly, desperate for answers she knew he could not provide.

"Forgive my harshness, but that is no man at all," Jasper growled, his hand curling into a loose fist at his side. His entire being, raised from his earliest days with the knowledge of his responsibility not only to his family but to his fellow man, bristled against Mr. Clark's cruel and selfish actions. Miss Seymour nodded her agreement.

"Could that, perhaps, have anything to do with why you became a governess?" he continued, daring to take the opportunity now that she had opened up.

He prayed he was wrong.

Miss Seymour swallowed and broke eye contact, her expression blank as she stared at the floor again. "It is. He threw me out on my own as soon as I was old enough. He thought supporting me was a waste. Nothing I or Mother said—no matter how desperately we pleaded—could change his mind. Now he only allows Mother to write to me once a month. Any more than that and I suppose he thinks she will start missing me and beg him to take me in again."

"How awful," Jasper mumbled, horror twisting his stomach. Desperate to provide poor Miss Seymour with some solace, he dared again. Careful to angle himself away from Rebecca's line of sight, he reached out and took her hand in his. He held it loosely, prepared to let go at the first sign of resistance.

She did not pull away. Instead, she smiled up at Jasper, melancholy touching her expression.

Jasper stared back, shocked into silence by her passionate and heart-wrenching confession. A hollow sadness filled his chest. How did a woman who had suffered so much pain still possess any shred of optimism and kindness? That, even more than her skills as a governess, spoke volumes of the character Jasper had so longed to learn more about.

"I became a governess out of necessity, yes, as most governesses do. But I have come to love my profession from the bottom of my heart," she said, truth ringing loud and clear in every word.

"That is plain to see in everything you do."

Miss Seymour peered over her shoulder again. Rebecca diligently mouthed the French phrases from her lesson book, brows knitted over her button nose that occasionally scrunched in distaste.

She turned back to Jasper, joy seeping back into her smile. "I would not trade it for anything. In my eyes, family is everything."

"Indeed it is," Jasper nodded.

"And this is all the family I need—these children who look to me when others are on the verge of giving up on them."

Jasper nodded again, a strange mixture of bittersweet admiration seizing his heart. He gently returned her hand to her side.

If he had any faint hope that Miss Seymour could possibly one day—

No, Jasper told himself. That path only led to heartache. He had known all along that Miss Seymour was dedicated to her profession.

"Thank you for sharing that with me, Miss Seymour," he said, his voice a whisper. "Perhaps your mother's next letter will bear more positive news. And I am very glad that, despite your circumstances, you were able to find the happiness that you so rightly deserve in your life."

Miss Seymour smiled, an unidentifiable emotion flitting through her eyes. "Thank you for listening, Mr. Helsden. I do feel better for it, and I pray you will be right. Ah, I just had a thought."

"Tell me," Jasper urged.

"Since we are leaving for London next month, could you provide me with the address of our residence? I would like to include it in my response to my mother so she will know where to send her next letter."

"It would be my pleasure. Now, if you do not mind me saying, I believe you have a pupil over there who is about to die of boredom." He subtly pointed around Miss Seymour toward Rebecca, who sat with her head craned all the way back, long hair spilling down the back of her chair.

Miss Seymour turned around, laced her fingers together, and cleared her throat. Rebecca sat straight as a pin, the faintest blush coloring her full cheeks. At least now she had the sense to be embarrassed when caught doing something she knew her governess would not approve of.

"Is quiet reading time over?" she begged. "If I must do French, I would rather do it with you than alone."

"As you wish, Miss Rebecca," Miss Seymour chuckled.

Rebecca grimaced. "I did not say I wished it."

Over her shoulder, Miss Seymour said, "Alas, I must go where I am needed."

"Indeed you must," Jasper agreed, his treasonous heart sinking into depths he had not realized could exist.

She was right, after all. After she deemed Rebecca improved enough to return to the care of a normal governess, Miss Seymour would move on to the next family. Surely there was no shortage of parents on the verge of tearing their hair out and children who struggled for one reason or another to make sense of their oftentimes rigid and confusing world.

Jasper followed after Miss Seymour and resumed his usual seat, waiting in the wings to offer advice or additional examples to Rebecca or intercept an oncoming outburst. The two ladies dove right into the lesson. Jasper forced himself to watch, to recognize just how wonderful Miss Seymour really was at what she did.

Despite the heavy conversation they had just shared, her eyes lit from within as she guided her pouting charge through the French lesson.

She truly loved her mission now, even if she had been forced into it years ago. Who was Jasper to convince her otherwise?

CHAPTER 7

Miss Rebecca had made marvelous progress with Pippa's aid at Goddard House. The road to London had threatened to undo it all.

After a particularly fearsome fit on the steps of their modest townhouse, Pippa and Mr. Helsden had finally managed to convince her to at least continue it from the comfort of her temporary bedroom. Kind Mr. Helsden had offered to wait with Miss Rebecca until she calmed down, encouraging Pippa to escape, settle into her own room, and rest from the long days of travel.

Pippa had done just that, sinking into a two-hour nap, her body eager for proper rest after dozing off in the carriage and making do with crowded and noisy inns. Refreshed, Pippa wandered through the townhouse and came across Lady Helsden, who directed her toward the new schoolroom before rushing off to meet with the housekeeper.

She stood in the doorway, luggage in hand, looking around the room. It was smaller than the one at Goddard House, but they did not need even that much space. The recently dusted and polished table would do perfectly for their lessons, and the bookcases lining the far wall and a chest in the corner would house all the materials they would need.

Since no one had any plans to explore London or entertain company, Pippa took advantage of the restful quiet of the townhouse and flitted about the schoolroom, setting up for tomorrow's lesson. This would be almost the entirety of her scenery for the next several months until the Season ended and they returned to Somerset.

A knock at the door pulled Pippa's attention away from the stack of lesson books she situated on the shelves. She turned, prepared to assure whichever staff had come to inquire after any further needs that she had everything well in hand. Her eyes widened, heartbeat quickening, when she saw Mr. Helsden standing just inside the doorway.

"Has Miss Rebecca calmed down?"

"She is fast asleep," the gentleman answered with a relieved sigh. "I passed Mama in the hall and she mentioned you were in here getting everything prepared. Do you require any assistance?"

Pippa glanced to another large stack of books on the table, waiting to line the shelves. Normally she would have insisted that she could manage on her own, but the toll of travel made her move slowly, her muscles aching from the bumps along the road and the lumps in the inns' beds.

Mr. Helsden did not wait for an answer. He hurried across the room and snatched up the entire remaining stack, books piled high, his chin resting on the top volume. Pippa forced herself to return her attention to the task at hand—and away from the easy strength he displayed, lean muscles straining against his tight coat sleeves.

"Thank you," she said when he took up a spot beside her. "But are you not tired? You should go rest now that Miss Rebecca is settled."

Balancing the stack of books in one arm, leaning them against his broad chest, Mr. Helsden shrugged with the other shoulder. "Yes and no. I always find that, no matter how exhausting the travel, the nerves and anticipation of arriving will not allow me to sleep until nightfall. So, why not make myself useful? Besides, it seems to me you are not resting either. How would you like these organized?"

"I am putting the French books on this shelf, histories and geography can go there, and mathematics there," Pippa suggested. "I did rest very well, as a matter of fact. I slept nearly two hours. I cannot say I remember the last time I did that during the day. But it was just the thing, and now I have at least enough energy to prepare the schoolroom today instead of rushing tomorrow morning."

Long, elegant fingers slipped the first book into its spot on the shelf, fingertips brushing along the spine. Pippa tried not to notice that either, or wonder how those fingers would feel brushing against her cheek or the back of her hand. If her heart beat any more erratically, Mr. Helsden was sure to hear it. Perhaps the travel had addled her brains after all.

Yet ever since the arrival of Mother's last letter and the way he had listened to her so thoroughly and seemed just as invested in the trials of her life, Pippa's feelings toward the gentleman had undeniably shifted—even if she tried to deny it at every turn.

She had always thought him sweet, gentle, and understanding. That was just his nature. It had nothing to do with her specifically. So why had his consideration and sympathy on that day made her breathless? Why did his presence ever since send her heart into a flurry and her stomach into knots?

If it meant what she thought it meant, it simply could not be borne. Soon enough she would gather her mental composure and remember what it was like to have a real friend, not just someone who extended friendliness alongside a monthly allowance.

"Are you happy to be in London, Miss Seymour?" Mr. Helsden asked. His warm eyes scanned another title, located its proper spot, and darted to her.

Pippa could only smile at the book in her hand as she nestled it between two other volumes. "Well, I do not plan on doing almost anything while in town. Unless Sir Arthur and Lady Helsden arrange outings for the entire family, in which case I will accompany Miss Rebecca. But I suspect we will be spending the majority of our time in here."

"Yes, of course," Mr. Helsden mumbled, that now familiar and unfairly charming stammer in his voice.

"I do not mind it," Pippa continued, eager to reassure him. "London has its attractions, certainly, but I am perfectly content to spend all my days in the schoolroom or the music room or wherever else my charges and I might enjoy lessons. Perhaps Miss Rebecca will benefit from experiencing a little more of the world and the many unexpected scenarios that might crop up, but in her case I would not advise too much of it right now lest we push her too far beyond her limits."

"Yes, of course," Mr. Helsden repeated.

The governess dared a glance at the man by her side. "I do very much hope that you will enjoy yourself. I am sure there are many exciting opportunities and adventures for a young man in London."

"I would enjoy myself more if you could come out with us properly...."

Pippa's hand stilled, the book teetering precariously on the edge of the shelf. She dared not glance again. She was not sure what she hoped to see, and how she would feel if she actually saw it.

"Of course, it is such a shame to come all this way and not be able to take advantage of what this great city has to offer," he continued, rushing the words out as he shelved several more volumes in quick succession. "It almost seems cruel to me that you should remain cooped up in here while the rest of us entertain ourselves amongst the *ton*."

The anxious curiosity swirling inside Pippa did not diminish. She had heard his words, but she had also heard the genuine melancholy beneath his forced casualness. At least, she thought she did.

If she were truly honest with herself—a terrifying prospect on its own—she could not help hoping that meant he might see her as more than a friend, more than the governess teaching his sister.

Soon, he would have a full schedule of dinners, card parties, balls, carriage rides—and courtships. They might only have time to greet each other in the hall before Pippa and Miss Rebecca sequestered themselves in the schoolroom and he went out to his next appointment.

She would squeeze the life out of that hope later. For now —just for now—could it hurt to indulge a little?

"Fear not, Mr. Helsden," Pippa replied. "I am sure I will see enough of London to satisfy. And I do not regret missing out on all the marvels of the *ton*. I have heard enough stories to make me wonder how anyone dares throw themselves into it year after year. I suspect one must have a strong constitution for it, as you do."

Mr. Helsden paused, just one more book left in his hand. He half-turned to Pippa, leaning against the shelves.

"I dare say you have the strongest constitution of anyone I know, Miss Seymour. To overcome what you have…. Surely you could survive gossiping matrons and tedious dinners with people you hardly know. And your grace and manners would outshine them all."

A lump rose in Pippa's throat, her heart hammering in her ears. "You are very kind for saying so," she mumbled.

Just like that, Pippa knew that even a little indulgence could not be tolerated. It fanned the flame of her hope to terrifying heights when he said such sweet things, when he looked at her with such kindness in his eyes.

She was just about to make some excuse to quit the schoolroom when hurried footsteps echoed up the hallway. They turned at the same time to find Sir Arthur walking right past and then backtracking. He paused in the doorway.

"Ah, Jasper, I was just looking for you. Do you have a moment to join your mama in the drawing room? She is looking over tomorrow's schedule and she wants to know if you have already made any plans that could potentially conflict with hers before she starts answering invitations. Can you believe it? Dozens of invitations already, and we have only just arrived."

"I will be there shortly. I am almost finished here," Mr. Helsden answered. Sir Arthur continued on to his next mission.

"Lady Helsden must be quite popular," Pippa marveled. She had spent Seasons in London with previous families and had wondered how any of them kept abreast of their many engagements. Lady Helsden seemed to occupy a league of her own, a particularly impressive feat for the wife of a baronet.

"Indeed," Mr. Helsden sighed with a bemused smile as he placed his last book. "It is quite a burden for her children to bear, though I think Amelia will rise to the challenge nicely. I cannot say the same for myself, however," he chuckled.

Pippa laughed as well and shook her head. "I wish you luck, Mr. Helsden."

"Thank you, I shall need it," he nodded. "Well, let the madness begin."

THE NECESSARY LESSON

THE BAROUCHE SLOWED to a stop against the pavement under a patch of shadows from the overhanging tree branches. The famed Gunter's Tea Shop stared at Pippa from across the street. She had heard so much about the place, yet had never been invited or allowed to visit. Her mouth watered at the prospect of all the delightful treats within. Even Mr. Helsden, seated across from her, could not quite distract her from her anticipation.

Miss Rebecca felt much the same. The girl struggled to keep herself from bouncing in her seat. Pippa could not blame her. She might have done the same at Miss Rebecca's age, even if half the *ton* walked or rode past and might have scoffed at such distasteful behavior. How could they begrudge a child the thrill of a delicious dessert?

"Here we are!" Lady Helsden called from another carriage. "My favorite place in all of London."

"It's mine, too!" cried Master Sidney as he leapt down from the carriage his parents and other brother occupied.

"Really, Sidney, must you announce that to the entire street?" Miss Helsden hissed, leaning across Mr. Helsden. "Oh, Colette! Here we are!"

Immediately forgetting her own reprimand, the young lady raised her voice to catch the attention of four vaguely familiar figures walking down the opposite side of the street toward them—the Harcourts who lived year-round in London.

"Must you announce that to the whole street, Amelia? We are rather hard to to miss," Mr. Helsden teased, gently elbowing his sister in the ribs.

Pippa peered up and down the cluttered road at the several other carriages lining up behind and ahead of theirs. To celebrate their first trip to Gunter's of the Season, Lady Helsden had made it a family affair. Even much of their extended family Pippa had yet to meet had accepted her invitation and now parked their own carriages along the street. In fact, most of the street looked to be their party.

"Sidney, return to the carriage at once. I could not stand to see you run over," Lady Helsden instructed. "We cannot all possibly go inside, so we will send our men with our orders."

"Well? Are you excited?" Mr. Helsden asked as footmen descended from several carriages and came around to the open sides.

"Of course she is! Who wouldn't be excited for Gunter's?" Miss Rebecca cheered, the last two weeks of outbursts and stubborn disinterest in lessons disappearing under the bright promise of sweets.

Pippa laughed and tapped Miss Rebecca's knee, a gentle reminder to mind her volume when in public. "I am terribly excited, though I fear that after hearing so many wonderful things, I will find myself disappointed."

The girl's head whipped around. She stared at her governess with horror. "You mean this is your first time at Gunter's?"

"It is. You see, I have never had time or reason to go. But I am glad I have the privilege of sharing my first experience with such lovely company."

"Heavens!" Miss Rebecca exclaimed under her breath. "How did you survive all these years without Gunter's, Miss Seymour? It is the only reason I like coming to London."

Laughter surged through Pippa's chest at the girl's scandalized tone. She clamped down on the inside of her cheek to keep it at bay.

"I am sure after I have my first ice, I will be asking myself the same thing."

"Since this is something of a special occasion," Mr. Helsden started, his eyes falling to his lap, "I would like to buy you as many ice flavors as you wish, Miss Seymour."

Miss Rebecca and Miss Helsden eyed their older brother

with very different expressions—the former with jealousy and the latter with deep intrigue. Pippa bit the inside of her cheek again, this time in the hopes that the pinch would distract her senses enough to keep her face from going red.

"Sir, madams, what ice flavors would you like?" a footman asked, appearing so suddenly in Pippa's peripheral vision, partially obscured by her bonnet, that she nearly jumped.

"Chocolate, please!" Miss Rebecca said.

"Lavender for me, please," Mr. Helsden requested.

"I would prefer jellied fruit, thank you," added Miss Helsden.

All eyes turned to Pippa.

Miss Rebecca leaned into Pippa's side. "You should try the parmesan flavor," she whispered.

"Allow Miss Seymour to choose what she likes," Mr. Helsden interrupted, grimacing slightly at the mention of Miss Rebecca's suggestion. "Whatever and however much she likes," he added, his earnest gaze returning to Pippa once more.

"I will start with the orange flower for now, thank you," Pippa said. She had asked Lady Helsden the day before for a list of ice flavors and prepared her answer ahead of time. "And thank you, Mr. Helsden, for the generous offer."

The gentleman gave a small smile, looking both relieved and anxious at the same time. Pippa's heart ached. She had missed that endearing expression these past two weeks. Mr. Helsden had been so busy they had hardly had any time to share more than a few quick pleasantries.

"Tell me, Mr. Helsden, Miss Helsden, how has your Season been thus far?" she asked.

Miss Helsden took the lead, brimming with excitement and wonder as she regaled her audience with as many tales as she could recall. She seemed to hardly care that her younger sister peered over the side of the barouche, far more interested in watching carriages go by, or that her brother had likely been present for most of these stories.

Pippa could hardly blame the young lady. Everything was so fresh, everything was still to be discovered. Had life turned out differently for Pippa, perhaps she might have been just like Miss Helsden if she had been able to make her debut five years ago.

Of course, Pippa would have liked to hear more of Mr. Helsden's experiences. He seemed content to listen to his sister, only occasionally adding a forgotten detail or clarifying some social connection for Pippa.

"The ices are coming!" Miss Rebecca cheered, cutting off her sister mid-sentence. She did not seem to care, her attention turned toward the footmen as they carefully picked their ways across the busy street with shining silver trays in their gloved hands.

"They look…different than I expected," Pippa whispered, more to herself than anyone else. She leaned forward around Miss Rebecca and narrowed her eyes. Could that possibly be right? Did anyone else notice anything odd about these highly anticipated desserts?

When she turned to see if anyone else looked as puzzled, Pippa found Mr. Helsden already watching her, more interested in her reaction than the ices.

"A little strange, are they not?"

"Are they supposed to be strange?" Pippa inquired, glancing at the footman's tray once more. "That one looks like…a swan. And is that—good heavens, is that a pineapple?"

Mr. Helsden laughed, the timbre a deep, rich rumble that took Pippa by surprise. "They are indeed meant to look strange. That is part of the fun. They use molds of all different shapes to form the ice. At least it is not so hot yet that half the thing will be melted before it reaches us."

With Mr. Helsden's assistance, the footman distributed

their unusually shaped treats. Miss Rebecca grinned as she snatched hers, lifting it up to eye level and examining every detail.

"Look, mine looks like a platter of cheese," the girl giggled. She wasted no time in scooping up her first bite.

Pippa stared down at her own pumpkin-shaped ice, turning it this way and that to appreciate its ridges and even the delicate leaves carved into the top. Mr. Helsden was correct. The shape of the thing was just as exciting as the taste, no doubt.

Before Pippa could verify, a commotion by the other carriages distracted her. The other Helsdens had climbed down, ices in hand.

"Come, my precious family, let us walk, enjoy our sweets, and acquaint ourselves with one another," Lady Helsden announced.

The message flowed down the long line of carriages and their occupants descended upon the pavement. Mr. Helsden exited their barouche first, helping each lady down in turn. Miss Helsden hurried off to greet her other family members who might not have heard her exciting debut stories.

"Miss Seymour, may I walk with my cousin, Margaret?" Miss Rebecca asked.

Pippa peered down the street to see a family of five she had not officially met yet toward the end of the line. Based on the name Miss Rebecca cited, Pippa knew them to be the Drakes. "Certainly, but do not wander too far. Stay within my sight."

The girl nodded enthusiastically and strode with purpose toward another child about her age with bright blonde hair and rosy cheeks. They hardly looked part of the same family tree, yet they greeted each other with warm smiles and a squeezing hug.

Pippa and Mr. Helsden started down the pavement as the

rest broke off into constantly shifting groups, drifting in and out of conversations. The gentleman introduced her to various members of his extended family as they went, including his Aunt Anna and Uncle Noah and their grown children as well as his Aunt Harriet and Uncle Jonas, their twin sons, and Miss Rebecca's favorite cousin, Margaret. Though Pippa had always been adept at remembering names and faces, all these aunts and uncles and cousins and even a few first cousins once removed had her head swimming. She made a mental note to ask Mr. Helsden for a proper lesson later.

With introductions out of the way, Pippa opened her mouth to finally ask after her friend until someone else called his name.

"Jasper! And— Oh," Miss Colette faltered when the pair turned to her.

Pippa pasted on a smile, praying it would mask her disappointment. She had grown quite fond of Miss Colette over the winter and had forgotten until it came time to travel that she had her own home in London and would not be staying with them during the Season.

"Please join us if you wish, Colette," Mr. Helsden offered, his generous smile a little tighter than usual.

Was he, too, disappointed by all these interruptions and distractions? Was he just as eager to hear about Pippa's life these past couple weeks? Not that she had been up to anything exciting, yet the thought that he might want to hear it regardless buzzed in her chest.

Miss Colette gave an apologetic nod. "Perhaps later. I was actually looking for cousin Beth. I wanted to ask her all about her new little girl."

With a suspiciously pointed look, the young lady disappeared into the crowd of her family. Pippa and Mr. Helsden were alone—as alone as they could be under the circumstances—once more.

"You were about to say something, Miss Seymour?" Mr. Helsden asked. He scooped a spoonful of ice from his swan-shaped treat and stopped it halfway to his mouth.

"Mr. Helsden, are you well?" Pippa tilted her head back a little further to see better under the wide brim of her hat.

"Your ice! Drat, we have been so occupied with all these conversations that you have not even had your first bite yet."

Pippa's brows raised as she peered down at her treat, the pumpkin slowly losing its shape despite the cool spring air. She and Mr. Helsden seemed to notice the issue at the same time. They both gasped as their eyes locked onto a dribble slipping down the side of the ice, just seconds from spilling over the side of its container and onto Pippa's finest pair of white gloves.

Mr. Helsden reacted first. His hand shot forward and, with his spoon, he scooped up the dribble and a chunk of ice. They stared at it for a moment and breathed simultaneous sighs of relief.

"Thank you," Pippa said. "I must say I have not the faintest clue about removing ice stains from silk."

"Here, why don't you try it now?"

Pippa froze in the middle of the pavement. At least they had found themselves at the back of the group, and the other Londoners had chosen to give their large party a wide berth, so there was no one to run into her. Mr. Helsden paused as well, one corner of his mouth pulled down in a curious frown.

A moment later, his eyes widened almost to the size of Pippa's ice pumpkin. He had just offered to feed her right here on the street—and with his own spoon, no less.

"Forgive me! How utterly inappropriate," he groaned,

looking as though he wanted to fling the spoon into the street.

Laughter burst from Pippa, laughter she had been stifling since her arrival into the Helsden family's life—into his life. She had never met someone who made her want to laugh so much with his endearingly embarrassed quirks.

She could contain it no longer. Right there, with Mr. Helsden's family all around and the eyes of the *ton* hiding behind every corner, the governess lost herself to a fit of laughter.

And why shouldn't she, Pippa wondered? Why shouldn't she share her joy at this sweet, strange little moment that had broken her carefully cultivated wall of propriety?

She had almost recovered when Mr. Helsden's laughter joined hers. His shoulders shook, a lock of wavy black hair falling across his forehead. There was no way she could stop now, not when she saw his mirthful grin through her own watering eyes.

When their laughter finally died away into breathless chuckles, cheeks aching and sides splitting, they found a few heads turned in their direction, the strangers annoyed and the family amused.

Still, Pippa could not bring herself to lower her head in shame. Those few seconds had been the happiest she could recall in many, many days of mundane routine and demanding challenges.

"Why don't you have that bite and I will have the next?" she suggested, motioning toward his still upraised spoon.

He nodded and ate the dollop of orange flower ice, his full brows arching in pleasant surprise. "I do not think I have ever tried orange flower, now that I think about it. Lavender has been my favorite since childhood, and usually once I find something I like, I never deviate from it. But this orange flower is absolutely heavenly. You must try it at once."

Pippa need not be told twice. She took up her own spoon and scooped a generous pile onto it. A gentle, sweet flavor overcame her senses as the ice melted on the back of her tongue. She gasped, eyes wide. "Heavenly indeed! I must say I quite understand Miss Rebecca's shock earlier. How did I live my entire life without this?"

The gentleman chuckled and ate another bite of his own ice. "I am glad it exceeded your expectations. My earlier offer still stands, you know. I would be happy to buy you as many flavors as you like when we return this way. Try them all, if you like. Except perhaps for the parmesan. I am afraid Rebecca was trying to prank you with that suggestion."

With a sigh of contentment, Pippa eagerly took another scoop. "Perhaps I could try a bit of your lavender. Like you, I often prefer to find something I like and then keep to it. Perhaps that is why I wear so much green." She glanced down at her plain walking dress, a deep forest shade overlaid with a white floral pattern.

"It certainly suits you," Mr. Helsden agreed, his eyes traveling up and down her figure in a way that sent delicious shivers down Pippa's spine. "It provides a lovely contrast to your hair and fair complexion."

"Thank you," Pippa mumbled, stuffing another bite of ice into her mouth to busy herself as they resumed their walk, now well behind the rest of the family.

"Here, try some of mine," Mr. Helsden offered, tilting his head toward the melting swan in his hand.

Pippa nodded, avoiding eye contact, and snatched a small serving from one of the wings with her own spoon. "Mm! I must say, I do believe we chose the two best flavors on Gunter's menu," she chuckled, a few crystals of ice still dissolving on the back of her tongue.

"Ezra!" Miss Rebecca's voice cried in annoyance, jolting both Pippa and Mr. Helsden out of their dazes.

The girl clutched her ice closer to her chest, a shoulder lifted around it protectively, as a young man Pippa assumed to be cousin Ezra Drake, son of their Aunt Harriet and Uncle Jonas, strode away with a scoop of Miss Rebecca's ice and a teasing smile.

Every muscle in Pippa's body tensed, ready to leap into action. Miss Rebecca still struggled with her temper when it came to sharing. She clung fiercely to what was hers, including the people she loved—save for when they tried to steal from her.

Just as Miss Rebecca took two stomps toward her older cousin, Miss Colette swooped in and wrapped an arm around her shoulders. She spoke too quietly for Pippa to hear, but it seemed to work. Miss Rebecca's scrunched expression slowly smoothed back into her usual sweet, open countenance. Of course, it helped that Miss Colette offered a large scoop of her own ice to the girl.

"Thank goodness," Mr. Helsden exhaled, relief washing over his face.

The relief only lasted a moment, turning quickly into discomfort. Pippa looked ahead once more to find Miss Colette peering at them over her shoulder wearing a small, encouraging smile that seemed to convey more than a simple desire to allow them a break—almost as if she hoped they would continue taking advantage of this rare time together.

"How has Rebecca been doing with her lessons?" Mr. Helsden asked. When Pippa glanced up at him, she noticed the tips of his ears had gone slightly red. He must have sensed something strange in his cousin's expression as well.

Eager to leave that behind, Pippa latched onto the new topic of conversation. "The change of scenery was quite overwhelming for her at first, especially with everyone being so busy and guests constantly coming in and out of the house. It certainly caused a few outbursts, though none as severe as the ones she used to have when I first arrived. But she has slowly been settling into the rhythm of London life."

"Good, very good. I worried that perhaps it would still be too much for her. She has never much liked the Season. In fact, one of her governesses quit in the middle of the Season a couple years ago because Rebecca...well, you know how she used to be. But the thought of leaving both of you in the country—"

Mr. Helsden cut himself off, surprised by his own near confession—though confession of what exactly, Pippa dared not imagine. They both busied themselves with more bites of ice. Being new to the experience provided Pippa with a much-needed respite from these strange feelings storming inside her, from the strange atmosphere pulsing between them. At least for those few seconds when she indulged in that sweet orange flower, Pippa could set all that aside and simply enjoy the wonderful flavor.

"What of your Season?" Pippa forced herself to ask with a forceful swallow. "How have you been enjoying it?"

The gentleman's expression eased as he let out a rueful sigh. He teased the tip of his spoon into his ice absentmindedly as he thought back on the whirlwind of the past two weeks, gaze unfocused and so weary that Pippa's heart sank for him. Such a busy lifestyle must not have been easy for a gentle, serene man like Mr. Helsden.

"I must admit this Season feels even more frenzied than my previous two combined. I did make many new connections, and even a few firm friends that I have been enjoying spending time with."

Pippa nodded. That did not surprise her. Mr. Helsden's good-natured spirit, though sometimes self-conscious, was certainly not unfriendly. In fact, Pippa thought him one of the most amiable people she had ever met. It seemed only right that, in this bustling city filled to the brim with the *ton*, his kindness would draw others to him from far and wide.

"It already feels like an entire Season has been squeezed into these past two weeks. Mama has kept my schedule full of dinners and balls and walks about Hyde Park. I swear, she must know all of the *ton* personally. She has already introduced me to a dozen young ladies and encourages me to add my name to every dance card that still has an empty line," he continued, shaking his head with a wry smile.

Despite his obvious overwhelm and discomfort with the whole thing, Pippa's stomach could not help twisting into painful knots.

She knew how to dance in theory, though she almost never had any opportunity to practice with a real partner. Most families brought in a dance master to teach their children, and Pippa would help them sharpen their skills in between lessons. She would not have been surprised if Mr. Helsden proved to be an excellent dancer. Surely his genteel partners were just as talented.

Mr. Helsden elaborated on a few of the more interesting events he had attended thus far—from a dinner where a poor young lady's gigot sleeve caught on a sharp corner and tore, resulting in her fleeing from the room in tears, to a dance where one of his partners was dismayed to learn that his handsome older cousin, Mr. Hugh Harcourt, had married a few years ago.

Why did her chest burn with jealousy when she knew she would never have a place in a ballroom? What did he discuss with his partners while he danced with them, walked with them, courted them? Surely things far more interesting than his younger sister's lessons and behavior. That was about all Pippa had to offer.

The bitter realization tainted the flavor of her long-awaited treat. Even the shadows from the trees lining the pavement chilled her. She stuck her spoon in the ice, her appetite evaporated.

She had gone too far in fancying herself an equal to Mr. Helsden when the only thing they had in common was their mutual desire to discover and heal Miss Rebecca's problems. Here in London, he could find company that suited a wide variety of interests. How could Pippa compete with that? In fact, there could be no competition from her unsuitable starting point.

"Of course, if I am honest," Mr. Helsden added, his voice low and hesitant, "I find I much prefer this—a relaxing conversation with my friend, someone with whom I feel completely at ease."

In an instant, Pippa's mood and heart lifted, soaring right into the bright blue sky above. She could not resist looking at him from under her hat to see if he felt what she did. His dark brown eyes, so soft and sweet, returned Pippa's fleeting hope.

"I am glad," she whispered, mind swimming with his words. No doubt they would echo all the rest of the day and especially when she laid down in her bed and tried to sleep. "In fact, I quite agree."

Even if sleep did not come and left her groggy the next day, Pippa would not mind reliving this moment over and over again.

"Good," Mr. Helsden sighed with relief. "At least we know we have each other in this mess."

Every fluttering heartbeat rang with a growing truth. He enjoyed her company on a more intimate level than just two people brought together by trying circumstances. Perhaps he even had affections for her—true, deep affections.

CHAPTER 8

"Mama, might I ask you a question?" Jasper asked as he peered into the morning room. His mother sat by the window, embroidery in hand. The early mornings were her only opportunity to indulge in any of her favorite hobbies, the rest of the day given over to conveying various family members from one event to the next.

She glanced up with a calm smile. "Of course, son. Come in."

Jasper crossed the room, looking over his shoulder to ensure none of his siblings—especially curious Amelia—happened to walk by. Mama waved to the chair across from her and Jasper took it, perched on the edge.

"Is something wrong, Jasper?"

"No, not precisely," he mumbled, fidgeting with the light tan fabric of his trousers where they bunched at the sides of his knees.

"Are you wondering why I have kept your schedule so busy?" she pried, gaze never leaving the cottage scene she diligently stitched.

Jasper jumped, his spine straight. He eyed Mama with wonder and a tiny dose of fear. "How did you know what I was going to ask?"

Her piercing eyes flashed up, accompanied by a mischievous smile. "A mother always knows these things, darling. To answer your question, I thought you might need a little boost in finding a lady. I know you tend to be on the reserved side like your father. You make and keep friends very well, but when it comes to ladies—well, I only want you to have the best advantage. It is already May, after all, and your past two Seasons did not prove very fruitful for courtships. But now you have more connections and I am always expanding our circles, so we simply need to utilize them."

A dejected sigh escaped Jasper. Intrigued, Mama lowered her embroidery hoop to her lap and looked at him fully.

"I do appreciate that very much, Mama, but you know I am not in much of a rush. I know the right woman will come along at the right time," he offered, hoping that she would not read the rest of his thoughts with her powers of motherly wisdom. Jasper could no longer deny that that woman was much closer than Mama realized—if his hopes and suspicions proved correct.

Of course, knowing him, Jasper would not have been surprised if he had somehow terribly missed the mark and completely misinterpreted Miss Seymour's speech and manner. Yet that little voice in the back of his mind, growing stronger by the day even when he did not have time for so much as a glance in the governess' direction, whispered that he had not gotten it wrong this time. Miss Seymour was fond of him. Every fleeting look, every hitched breath, every warm word confirmed it.

"I have every faith that she will," Mama agreed, her normally sharp and discerning eyes softening. She leaned forward and laid her hand over Jasper's, encouraging him to relax and cease his fidgeting. "I pray for it every day, for all my children. I only hoped to use my vast network of acquaintances to expedite the process. Is it too overwhelming? Should I pare down your engagements a tad?"

Jasper mustered a small smile. "That would be nice, I think. Besides, I have been neglecting my commitment to help Miss Seymour with Rebecca. She seems to be managing well enough on her own, but I know Rebecca responds positively to my presence."

Mama frowned. "You know that is not really your responsibility, Jasper. It is very kind of you to want to help. You have always had such a heart for it. But during your Season, you must prioritize—"

To Jasper's surprise, Mama paused, her mouth still slightly ajar and eyes wide. His mother was one of the most eloquent and self-assured people he knew. She always knew just what she wanted to say. Stopping in the middle of a sentence was not at all her norm.

"Mama? Are you unwell?" He turned his hand palm up and wrapped his fingers around hers, concern hollowing out his stomach. He realized a second too late what had just dawned on her, an excuse springing to the tip of his tongue.

"Ah, I see now," she mumbled before Jasper could explain. He knew well enough by now that Mama would not be fooled by flimsy excuses. His heart stuttered before leaping into a frantic gallop.

She had finally discovered the truth. But how would she react? Jasper had tried hard not to ponder that. He remembered the tales of her romantic love story with Papa—the daughter of a baron and the son of a baronet, best friends since their infancies.

Papa had been in love with Mama for years, yet Mama had had her sights on a future of luxury and a title to match —until she realized that none of her suitors could meet her expectations, no matter what they offered. Her heart already belonged to her dearest friend, even if he did not possess the trappings of wealth she thought she wanted.

Jasper had no doubt of their enduring love and happiness. That had been the model for his own desires in a marriage, as well as the examples he grew up surrounded by in his grandparents and his aunts and uncles, and now some of his own cousins. Still, he could not be sure that Mama would not prefer a much more advantageous match for her children, even if she had chosen a less conventional one for herself.

As he had told his mother, Jasper had never worried about finding love for himself someday. He had trusted heaven's perfect timing. Then, Rebecca's behavior became so unbearable that Jasper had no other choice but to act as a pillar of support for his parents and his other siblings.

Since Miss Seymour's arrival, Jasper had started to think that heaven's perfect timing had worked in a rather mysterious and unexpected way by bringing her into their lives to solve two problems at once—Rebecca's tantrums and Jasper's dreams.

"Are you telling me that you miss spending time with our governess?" Mama asked quietly, a hint of awe in her voice.

Jasper lowered his head. He could not bear to see the disappointment or judgment in her eyes. He could not bear to watch when she told him that a governess would not suit him, that he could surely find a love match with a lady of more appropriate social standing.

"Yes," he said so quietly he was not sure Mama would hear.

Instead of any of those things Jasper feared, she simply laughed. When he dared to glance up, he saw only amused shock in her expression. She caught him eyeing her nervously and lifted his chin with her free hand, encouraging him to look at her boldly. Jasper offered his best approximation, his stomach still slithering with anxiety.

"Fear not, my dear. I happen to think Miss Seymour is absolutely lovely and charming. In fact, why don't we invite her for a big family luncheon tomorrow at your grandparents' townhouse? As a guest, of course."

∽

"BETH, WESTON, THERE YOU ARE!" Mama called before the butler could announce her niece and nephew. She and several other family members flocked to the drawing room door to greet one new arrival in particular.

"Please forgive our tardiness," Beth sighed, smiling down at the fussing bundle in her arms. "This one had to change her dress just as we were leaving."

"Everyone, we are pleased to introduce you to our daughter, Wilhelmina," Weston announced with a flourish. "Big brother Ernest is still processing her entrance into our lives," he chuckled as he settled a hand atop his shy five-year-old son's dark red hair.

The drawing room of Lord and Lady Welsted filled with chuckles and soft coos as everyone took turns admiring the baby. As eager as he was to greet his cousin's new little miracle, Jasper contented himself with hanging back, catching snippets of the others' observations, and keeping an eye on Miss Seymour from his peripheral vision.

She craned her neck to see around the small crowd of Harcourts, leaning to one side and brushing against Jasper's shoulder. "How lovely," she whispered. "You all must be so thrilled. I am afraid I feel a little like an intruder during such a special moment, the very first time a new baby is introduced to the whole family."

Jasper did not hide his smile from her or from anyone

else. The joy of the day, of having Miss Seymour by his side as a guest, easily won out over any nerves. Besides, the baby would certainly distract his more suspicious siblings and cousins.

"You are already like family to us, Miss Seymour. It only seemed right that you should enjoy this day with us."

"I am glad you think so," the governess said with a small smile that hid what Jasper thought to be an undercurrent of hopeful anticipation.

Thankfully, Jasper did not have to come up with something clever or insightful to follow up with. Movement to his left caught his attention. His cousin Hugh and his wife Charlotte approached from the corner they had been hiding in.

Jasper had been curious about that. It was not like them to remain removed from the excitement, yet they had seemed quite wrapped up in some interesting discussion of their own—perhaps something to do with the center for workers' rights they had established not long after Charlotte had relocated to England permanently. Jasper had no doubt it was a difficult operation to run which required their constant communication with their manager back in Somerset.

He exchanged a curious glance with Miss Seymour. She, too, seemed to notice the strange air around them as Hugh leaned down to whisper something in Beth's ear. Beth, daughter of Aunt Anna and Uncle Noah and the oldest of the cousins, whipped around to stare at Hugh and Charlotte in wonder. The others clustered around her started nudging them to share their secret conversation. With a grin, Beth eagerly nodded to Hugh and Charlotte.

Miss Seymour's head tilted to one side. The light pouring in from the window behind them turned her blue eyes into deep jewels. "I wonder…."

"Wonder what?"

Hand in hand, Hugh and Charlotte strode to the middle of the room, looking about at most of their large family gathered there—only missing Helen and Miles in the country and Uncle Patrick, overloaded with work since his assistant examiner had recently taken another opportunity elsewhere.

"No, I do not wish to say lest I am embarrassingly wrong," Miss Seymour chuckled. "I shall keep it to myself for now, but I promise to tell you after the grand reveal."

"Everyone," Hugh started, his bright voice booming through the drawing room. Jasper tore his attention away from Miss Seymour's beautifully thoughtful expression, curiosity overpowering him. "Well, almost everyone. But since enough of you are here, Charlotte and I would like to announce that we are expecting! Theresa is to be a sister!"

The room erupted into such enthusiastic cheers and applause, the glee already elevated thanks to little Wilhelmina's presence, that Jasper swore he felt the floor tremble. Perhaps Miss Seymour had felt it, too. With a surprised laugh, drowned out by the celebratory noise, she shrank into his side.

Instinctively, Jasper wrapped a protective arm around her shoulders, little caring if anyone else saw, though he was certain they were all too busy rushing at Hugh and Charlotte to notice. How delightful that she could share in this marvelous moment with them all! His chest flooded with warmth, spreading out into every inch of his body. It truly did feel like she belonged here—with him, with his family.

"Bravo!" Uncle Dalton, Hugh's father and the future Baron Welsted, shouted at the top of his lungs. Even quiet and proper Aunt Winnie was so overjoyed that she did not bother scolding her husband for his volume.

"*Félicitations*," added Rebecca, inspired by the atmosphere to utilize her growing French skills. Though she did not much like change, she was always happy to hear of a new cousin.

"*Très bien*, Rebecca!" said Aunt Eloise, a native of France. Rebecca, peering between a mass of people, flashed a proud smile at Colette's mother.

"Wonderful, absolutely wonderful!" Grandmama, the current Lady Welsted, stepped away from the commotion. She pressed a hand, slightly swollen with arthritis, to her chest, tears in her eyes. "A new great-grandchild right here, and another on the way!"

Grandpapa joined her, looping his arm around her much like Jasper had just done with Miss Seymour. Grandmama fussed with her fluffy sleeves so she could rest her head against his shoulder. "How blessed we are!" the baron sighed with utter delight.

In a flash of imagination, Jasper's mind stretched far, far into the future—to a day when he and Miss Seymour looked just like his grandparents, just as thrilled to welcome the news of a grandchild or great-grandchild of their own.

"Perhaps we will be celebrating you soon, son," Papa whispered into Jasper's ear, appearing as if out of thin air, never one to flock toward a scene. He rested a hand upon Jasper's shoulder and gave an encouraging squeeze, his wise eyes darting to the arm around Miss Seymour's shoulders.

It took everything in Jasper not to flinch in surprise and tip off Miss Seymour to a conversation he was far from ready to broach. Or perhaps, even worse, she would think Papa meant Jasper had found a lady amongst the *ton* he had set his sights upon.

"Perhaps," Jasper muttered under his breath with a strained smile.

Papa nodded, always so calm and knowing, and finally made his way toward the happy couple occupying the center of the room. He approached Mama from behind and pulled her into his arms. The baronet lowered his head and pressed his cheek to his wife's—yet another mirror of the future Jasper longed for.

Before he could completely lose himself in that still farfetched fantasy, a piercing wail cut through the joyous racket. All heads turned toward Beth and Weston, now seated in a pair of chairs by the fireplace. A tiny arm shot out from the blankets, flailing as the baby screamed in discomfort or displeasure or a combination of the two. Ernest scrambled into his father's lap and buried his face into Weston's chest.

Miss Seymour rushed forward, instinct taking over. Jasper's arm fell limply to his side, a coldness seeping into him where she had just been.

"Allow me, Mrs. Quincy," the governess offered, keeping her voice low so as not to agitate Wilhelmina further.

"My apologies, Beth," Hugh called with a sheepish smile. "I forgot in all the excitement that our celebrations might disturb your little one."

Beth smiled thankfully at both Miss Seymour and Hugh. "Thank you, Miss Seymour. Do no fret, dear Hugh. I am so very pleased for you and Charlotte!"

"There is no need to exert yourself, Miss Seymour," Charlotte added, crossing the room toward the new center of attention, her words lilting in a faint American style. She put one hand on Miss Seymour's shoulder and used the other to cup Wilhelmina's cheek. "We brought our nanny, who is staying with Theresa in the nursery. Wilhelmina can join them there."

"I do not mind, really," Miss Seymour insisted gently. "I am trained in infant care as well, though since I usually mind older children, I do not have many opportunities to practice it. At the very least, allow me to bring her to the nursery."

Despite the overwhelmed happiness still buzzing through the room, Jasper's heart sank. He had been hoping to spend the entire luncheon with Miss Seymour—and that she could enjoy a much-needed rest from her duties.

As Beth transferred the baby into Miss Seymour's arms, offering a few instructions and a small leather trunk, Jasper felt a rush of air speed toward him. Jerking in surprise, he whipped his head around to find Colette materialized at his side. Last he had seen, she had been one of the many surrounding cousin Hugh and his wife to offer hearty congratulations.

Jasper bit his lip to keep from groaning. Why must his family always sneak up on him when he was at his most vulnerable? He bit too hard when Colette jabbed him in the ribs with a bony elbow, the faint metallic taste of blood assaulting his mouth.

"You should go help Miss Seymour," she whispered urgently, her eyes flashing toward the door where the lady in question had just exited, babe in one arm and luggage in the other.

Jasper pondered this for a moment, his heart torn. "I do not know anything about caring for babies, cousin. I was too young and squeamish when Rebecca was born to have much interest in learning."

Confident that no one would notice her lapse in decorum, Colette lifted a shoulder in an impatient shrug. "Well, now you are older and possess a stronger stomach."

"I would not want to get in her way," he added, looking to the door again. What if he did the wrong thing and made an even bigger mess of the situation? He could happily hold a newborn in his arms for hours—until they started crying, at which point he usually handed them back to a parent or an experienced aunt or uncle.

The young lady rounded on Jasper with an exasperated sigh. "I say this with all the love in my heart, Jasper, but are you dense?"

The bluntness of her words shocked him into realization. His eyes widened. Colette was giving him an excuse to remain near Miss Seymour—even if it meant stepping outside his comfort zone into something he knew nothing about. At least he could carry whatever new knowledge he gained from this experience into the future when he became a father. Perhaps with such an experienced and caring woman like Miss Seymour, these early days of parenthood would not be so intimidating.

Jasper hurried from the room, throwing a quick explanation over his shoulder and giving no one any time to question him. Miss Seymour paused at the bottom of the stairs at the end of the hall. Just as a footman stepped forward to offer assistance, Jasper broke into a trot.

His footsteps echoed down the hall, drawing their attention. "Miss Seymour!" he called, slowing before the governess and the footman. "Here, let me take this." Miss Seymour did not resist when Jasper's hand wrapped around hers and slipped under the handle of the leather case bearing Wilhelmina's necessary items. She shifted the baby, cradling her in both arms, and Jasper nodded a dismissal to the footman.

"Thank you," the governess said. "But I am afraid we will have to take a detour into another room when we get upstairs. I believe she is in need of a diaper change."

With a hand on the small of her back, Jasper guided Miss Seymour and the baby up the steps and into the first room they could find. Miss Seymour wasted no time, rushing toward the coffee table in the middle of what appeared to be an infrequently used sitting room. Matching her step for step, Jasper quickly snatched the empty vase and trinkets atop the table and stowed them beside the sofa, safe from their rushing feet.

"Would you open the trunk? Mrs. Quincy informed me it

contains a blanket. We should lay that over the table before we change her," Miss Seymour instructed, bouncing the whining baby in her arms.

Kneeling down on the ground, Jasper worked like lightning to throw the clasps open and dig around in the case until his hands grasped a soft fold of fabric buried beneath other essentials. He pulled it out and threw it over the coffee table, looking up at Miss Seymour for his next task.

To his amazement, Miss Seymour made such quick work of the diaper change that Jasper's stomach hardly had time to turn at the less than pleasant experience. As soon as Miss Seymour finished pinning the fresh cloth around Wilhelmina's bottom, the baby's furrowed brow smoothed, her irritated whimpers subsiding into sleepy gurgles.

"There we are," Miss Seymour sighed. "That feels much better, doesn't it? Thank you for all your help, Mr. Helsden," she added, scooping up the baby and turning to Jasper. "You once again prove yourself to be an invaluable assistant."

Jasper chuckled, heat bubbling under his skin. "I appreciate the compliment, but I am afraid I had very little to do with all that. It was all your expertise and skill."

"Still, having a calm presence nearby—and someone to hand me things—helps immensely." She offered Jasper a generous grin, relief aglow in her lovely eyes.

"Was I calm?" Jasper mused as he packed up the case of baby items. "I felt rather panicked, I must admit. I was terrified I would hand you a washcloth instead of a diaper. They do look rather similar, in my defense."

"I would have never guessed," Miss Seymour said, one brow arching up, impressed. "You held yourself together very well."

A dizzying rush of pride swelled through Jasper's chest until he remembered the question that had popped into his mind just as Colette encouraged him to follow the governess.

"Miss Seymour, is something the matter? I hope you do not mind my saying that I thought you looked a bit…eager to quit the drawing room."

The governess looked down at the baby in her arms and pushed back a fold of the blanket to reveal more of her sweet face. Fuzzy dark hair like Beth's was just starting to sprout in patches around her delicate head. The corner of Miss Seymour's mouth twitched up in a melancholy smile.

"Well, I thought I would bring Miss Wilhelmina to the nursery and perhaps remain there, where I am most suited," she confessed, voice so low that Jasper had to take a step closer to hear properly—not that he ever minded being this close to Miss Seymour.

"May I ask why? Do you feel uncomfortable around us?"

"Of course I do," she sighed. "Though it is not any of your doing, I assure you. Everyone has been so wonderfully kind and welcoming that I almost forgot I am a governess. I know Sir Arthur and Lady Helsden arranged this luncheon and invited me as a guest, but it still feels a little strange to dine so intimately with my employers."

"What if…I wish for you to be there?"

Jasper's words hung between them for a long moment. For once, he did not try to take them back or explain them away. It was true. With each passing day he found it harder to hide it. He had even started wondering what might happen if he stopped hiding it, if he was completely honest with himself and with Miss Seymour?

"You do?" She inhaled sharply, surprised and perhaps a touch enthralled.

"I do. I can only imagine how odd this must feel, and I certainly do not wish for you to do anything against your will. But I think you will find that my family is extremely generous with their friendship and love. Not a single one of them think you less worthy of dining with them because of your profession."

Miss Seymour looked down at Wilhelmina once more, considerations flashing behind her eyes. "I suppose," she finally said. "It is only my own self-consciousness that is standing in my way. Then why don't we bring this one to the nursery and return to the luncheon?"

"I would like nothing better." Jasper grinned, staring in dumbfounded triumph until Miss Seymour glanced to the trunk with a chuckle. He snatched it up and moments later, they found themselves in the nursery, bursting with toys, cribs, and small beds for any number of great-grandchildren to hide away and nap or expend their playful energy.

By the time they returned to the drawing room, everyone had settled back into the usual flow of conversation. Jasper and Miss Seymour slipped in undetected just as Mama announced that they could move into the dining room. The rest of the luncheon passed amicably, Miss Seymour conveniently seated to his right. Jasper would have to thank Mama for that later.

Slowly, she relaxed and lit up as she eased into casual discussions with Jasper's various family members. All the while, he watched and listened, a happiness he had never known before overwhelming all his senses, tinged by a cloud of regret.

Jasper wished so desperately that Miss Seymour could have known the love of a family like this…but perhaps she still could—if he could find the courage to make it so.

CHAPTER 9

Just a couple weeks after the successful luncheon at Lord and Lady Welsted's townhouse, Pippa found herself on another excursion with the Helsden family.

Hyde Park bloomed with bright green foliage and pleasant conversation as members of the *ton* took advantage of the perfect spring weather. Families, friends, and courting couples walked or rode past the Helsdens' happy picnic shaded by a canopy on the large lawns beside the Serpentine. Several of them offered greetings to Lady Helsden and even a few to Sir Arthur, who Pippa had learned was much like his eldest son in his reserved yet undeniably friendly manner.

Of course, Pippa was acting as governess today, though Lady Helsden had reminded her to do her best to enjoy herself. It was too fine a day to let it go to waste, she had said.

Pippa agreed. Though she sat prim and proper on one corner of the large blanket, gloved hands folded in her lap, she could not help absorbing the family's infectious joy. Master Duncan and Master Sidney chased Miss Rebecca around the lawn while everyone else nibbled on sandwiches and tarts and sipped tea, a low hum of conversation ever present.

She particularly enjoyed hearing Mr. Helsden's calm voice as he chatted with Miss Helsden about their recent activities, the sound so soothing and familiar that Pippa could hardly remember a time when she did not know it. Nor could she fathom a future without it.

"Miss Seymour," he said, a curious upswing at the end of her name.

Pippa started. Had he somehow read her mind? He so often seemed to know her thoughts that Pippa really did have to wonder just how connected they were, or if her fondness for the gentleman made every small and coincidental thing seem significant, written in the stars.

"Yes, Mr. Helsden?"

Though he had just addressed her, Mr. Helsden eyed something behind Pippa, brows knit together over his strong nose. He set his teacup down on the silver tray and leaned to one side to get a better view of whatever had captured his attention.

"Do you see that gentleman just there coming off the bridge?"

As gracefully as possible, Pippa peered over her shoulder. It took a moment and some squinting, but recognition finally dawned on her.

"Indeed! That must be Mr. Moorewell. I was employed by his family a few years ago on behalf of his youngest brother." She turned back to Mr. Helsden. "Do you know him?"

Mr. Helsden's face broke into a dazzling smile. "I certainly do. In fact, I would say our family is greatly indebted to him. He is an acquaintance from my first Season. We met several times last year as well. Mr. Moorewell was the one who gave me your name when I mentioned our struggles with Rebecca. He practically worshiped your skills and gave a glowing recommendation."

Pippa glanced over her shoulder again. She, too, was greatly indebted to Mr. Moorewell for the very same reason. Without him passing along her information to Mr. Helsden, she would have never met the most generous man she had ever known, or the kindest family to ever welcome her into their home.

"I should like to thank him for making the recommendation," Pippa said. "I am also very keen to know how young Master Adam has been these days."

"Excellent! I shall accompany you." Mr. Helsden leapt to his feet, something in the spring air and the camaraderie of the atmosphere energizing him. "Mama, may Miss Seymour and I greet our friend over there by the bridge?"

Lady Helsden angled her elegant neck back to peer up at her oldest child. Her eyes darted to Miss Rebecca, now artfully creating shapes out of a pile of grass she'd plucked.

"Yes, Jasper, you may go," Sir Arthur answered. With an understanding smile, he rested a hand upon his wife's knee. "We can manage Rebecca for a while. She has been quite well-behaved recently."

To Pippa's surprise, Mr. Helsden's mother turned to look at her, her clear blue eyes sparking, intense and observant where her son's were gentle and responsive.

"Certainly," Lady Helsden agreed after a long moment that turned Pippa's stomach to nervous ice. "Take your time and enjoy your friend's company."

Just as Pippa was about to suggest that she simply pass along a greeting through Mr. Helsden, the gentleman hurried over to her side of the blanket and held out both hands. She glanced from them up to his eager face. Goodness, she longed to take them.

Pippa gingerly placed her fingers over his, wary of acting

too obviously eager. Even if she did suspect Mr. Helsden had feelings for her, it would not do well to raise her employers' suspicions. As loving as they were, she still did not dare to imagine that they would easily accept any kind of relationship between their son and the governess. Lady Helsden's gaze remained far too impenetrable for Pippa to decipher her thoughts.

As soon as he wrapped his hands around hers, Mr. Helsden pulled up, easily lifting Pippa onto her feet in one fluid motion. She exhaled sharply, surprised and impressed by the casual display of strength. Keeping her bonnet angled down so Mr. Helsden would not see her blush, Pippa busied herself with fluffing out her summer green skirts and adjusting the bows adorning the pleats.

His hand appeared in her line of vision once more, palm upturned for her to accept. She finally had no choice, forcing herself to look up. He smiled expectantly, hopefully. Far too aware of the eyes of his family on her, Pippa kept her gaze focused on him. If she looked around and discovered their curiosity about this familiar gesture, Pippa would surely dissolve into a puddle of embarrassment.

Instead, she said a prayer for courage and once again took Mr. Helsden's hand. He pulled her toward him and turned, looping her arm around his and settling her hand on his coat sleeve. Without another word, he started the walk toward Mr. Moorewell, also heading in their direction with a young lady on his arm. Pippa stole a glance at her companion. Anyone else taking advantage of Hyde Park would surely mistake them for a courting couple. The thought felt both foreign and so very right to Pippa all at once.

Had her life gone as planned, her father still alive and her mother still happy and present, she and Mr. Helsden really could have been a couple. London was a large city and the *ton* spanned many, many families of influence.

There still must have been a chance that, in another life, she and Mr. Helsden would have crossed paths and perhaps found themselves doing this very same thing—only it would not have been strange at all.

"Why, Mr. Helsden, is that you?" Mr. Moorewell finally spotted them, lifting the brim of his hat a little to get a better view. "And, heavens, Miss Seymour!"

"Lovely to see you, my good man," Mr. Helsden called in return, offering a friendly wave.

Both gentlemen lengthened their strides, their ladies doing their best to keep up. A moment later, the two couples stepped off the walking path and onto the grass for proper greetings and conversation.

"Funny I should run into you out here, dear Mr. Helsden," Mr. Moorewell chuckled. "You always seem too busy to accept my invitations."

Mr. Helsden lowered his head with a sheepish smile. "My apologies. Mama has kept my schedule rather full until recently. I finally told her I could not continue at the pace she set and she graciously relented, bless her."

"Good!" Mr. Moorewell cheered, grinning so madly Pippa thought he might burst with joy. She glanced at the young lady at his side who wore a muted version of his smile, though no less excited. Perhaps she had something to do with Mr. Moorewell's exceptionally good mood. "Perhaps, then, you will be able to attend the engagement dinner Miss Presley's parents are hosting next week. I shall see if they will be able to accommodate you."

The other gentleman's eyes rounded, his head turning from Mr. Moorewell to Miss Presley and back again in rapid succession. Pippa stifled a laugh at his endearing surprise.

"You are engaged? Congratulations, my friend!" Genuine delight radiated from Mr. Helsden as he clapped Mr. Moorewell on the shoulder.

It filled Pippa with warmth, his everlasting happiness for others lifting her on a lighthearted cloud. She had worked hard over the years to overcome the jealousy and bitterness she had felt when she saw the happy families she'd always wanted, or thought about the future she could have had. Yet, no matter what challenges life threw his way, Mr. Helsden's natural love for others never diminished.

"Miss Presley, it is a pleasure to make your acquaintance," he added, bowing his head to the lady.

"The pleasure is all mine. Stephen mentions you all the time. He says you are the finest example of a gentleman he has ever known."

This time Pippa could not hide her smile. How could she, when Mr. Helsden looked so adorably flustered at a compliment? He shook his head forcefully, his hat nearly coming loose.

"Goodness, that is far too generous, though I do strive to do my best," he chuckled. "Heavens, I am so thrilled for you both! Of course I would be honored to attend your engagement dinner."

Miss Presley glanced from Mr. Helsden to Pippa, intrigued. "And will you be bringing…?"

Mr. Moorewell laughed and patted the lady's hand where it rested on his forearm. "No, no, dear Ethel. Miss Seymour here is actually a governess. And, since you two seem quite familiar, I take that to mean you have come to the Helsdens' rescue?" he asked, turning to address Pippa.

The cloud she had been floating on as she basked in the couple's joy evaporated. Of course she would have never presumed to accompany him to such a formal event with strangers. It was one thing to dine together amongst his family. Still, Mr. Moorewell's immediate response—though neither intentionally hurtful nor untrue—stung at Pippa's fragile heart. He had perfectly pinpointed the insecurity that prevented her from fully accepting her feelings for Mr. Helsden.

She was the governess, not someone he could bring as a guest to a friend's event, not someone he could parade around London with on his arm. Even this display was rather too bold in full view of the public, Pippa realized. She did not make any effort to remove herself from Mr. Helsden's side. It would hurt too much to show this newly engaged couple that she was painfully aware of the differences in their situations.

Mr. Helsden lightly jostled her arm and she snapped back to the moment. Everyone watched her, curious and slightly concerned. Uncomfortable heat rushed through Pippa from head to toe.

"Forgive me," she laughed awkwardly. "I have been quite tired of late from all the rescuing I have been doing."

The couple laughed and exchanged amused looks, their mutual affection evident. "Always so clever, Miss Seymour," Mr. Moorewell said when his laughter died away.

"Ah, then you must be the governess Stephen told me about, the one who helped dear little Adam through a difficult period," Miss Presley surmised.

"Indeed I am," Pippa said, that familiar twinge of pride temporarily smoothing her hurt. "Tell me, how has Master Adam been? I trust he has not given you any further problems?"

Mr. Moorewell shrugged. "Oh, nothing we cannot handle on our own now with the help of the new governess. But he is reaching that age where he thinks he knows best in all matters. At least now we do not have such horrible arguments as we used to."

Pippa's pride and happiness grew. She smiled, relieved to hear such an excellent report from a former student. Unfortunately, some did revert to their former behavior after she

THE NECESSARY LESSON

left if their families did not remain consistent with the things Pippa taught them. She'd had no doubt that Mr. Moorewell's family would succeed where others had failed, and she was happy to be proven right.

"That is so wonderful, Mr. Moorewell. I am so glad I was able to help, but your love and dedication made the most difference in the end."

"You are too humble for your own good, Miss Seymour. We would have been lost until the end of time had it not been for your patience and expertise. You truly turned our family around." The gentleman looked from Pippa to Mr. Helsden. "I am sure you will be saying the same very soon, my friend."

"I already do," Mr. Helsden admitted, smiling at Pippa with pure gratitude in his eyes. "We all do. She has only been with us a little over half a year and has already made a world of difference to Rebecca and the entire family. I hardly think any of us will want to let her go."

The engaged pair exchanged another glance, this one rather more suspicious. Pippa's heart seized, praying they would not pry. If anyone tried to confront her about possible affections for Mr. Helsden, surely she would say or do something foolish that would give her away long before she was ready to confess anything.

Mr. Moorewell spotted his mother behind Mr. Helsden and excused himself and his betrothed to join her, leaving Pippa's dignity intact.

"What a lovely fellow," Mr. Helsden said, shaking his head in friendly admiration. "And a very charming young lady as well. Shall we—"

They both heard it at the same time, pausing just as they started to turn back toward the family's picnic. Pippa and Mr. Helsden stared at each other in silence, straining to catch that sound again over the ambient noise of boots and hooves upon the gravel path and dozens of casual conversations surrounding them.

"Did you hear something?" Mr. Helsden whispered.

"I thought I did," Pippa admitted, turning one ear toward the direction the sound had come from.

"Well, perhaps it was nothing after all."

No sooner had Mr. Helsden completed his sentence than the sound repeated itself—a faint whimpering.

It tugged at Pippa's heart as well as her curiosity. "We should investigate," she suggested. The thought of some creature in need, its cries for help drowned out by the sounds of the bustling park, would not allow Pippa to rest.

Luckily, Mr. Helsden agreed wholeheartedly. With a determined nod, they headed toward the sound. They walked slowly, keeping to the grass to quiet their footsteps. It would not do to scare the poor thing off before they had a chance to assess the situation.

The closer they came toward the bridge spanning the Serpentine, the louder the pitiful sound grew. Pippa's heart picked up speed, her mind racing with all manner of possibilities. Would they find a baby duck separated from its family? Or perhaps a litter of abandoned kittens or puppies? The sound was so muffled it was impossible to identify. What should they do once they located the source of the crying? She supposed that would depend on what they found.

When they came just to the opening of the bridge, Mr. Helsden turned to Pippa with a finger to his lips. Pippa nodded, almost treading on her tiptoes as they rounded the bridge wall.

Pippa gasped, her hand instantly flying to her mouth to stifle the sound. The little one jumped and twisted around to stare at them with huge eyes, red from crying.

"What on Earth?" Mr. Helsden mumbled.

The boy, likely no more than three or four years old, tucked himself further into the muddy slope where the bridge wall met the bank and curved up over the water. Despite his initial hesitation, the child managed to mumble a tearful, "Help."

Acting as one, Pippa and Mr. Helsden lowered themselves to the boy's eye level. Still a little uncertain, the child scooted toward them in his crouched position, his feet squelching in the mud.

"Are you injured, my friend?" Mr. Helsden asked.

The boy shook his head, his woeful gaze piercing Pippa's heart. She longed to snatch him up into her arms and carry him away to safety, perhaps forever. But Pippa knew he must have someone out there who would miss him terribly, who was likely mad with fear at this very moment.

"I'm lost," he finally squeaked, his shoulders drawn up around his ears and thick brown hair a tousled mess. "Where is my mama?"

"You poor dear," Pippa whispered. "We do not know where your mama is, but we can help you find her. Do you think you can climb back up on your own?" she asked, eyeing the mud. If any one of them slipped on it, they could go toppling right into the river. She could not gauge from here how deep that jewel blue water might be.

He, too, glanced around the bank and shook his head again.

"Mr. Helsden, do you think you can reach him from here?"

The young man heaved a sigh and set aside his hat, turning his head to the left and right to determine the best course of action. "I am not sure, but I will try."

Dropping Pippa's arm, Mr. Helsden carefully stepped forward and planted his feet firmly on the solid edge of the bank. He bent at the knees and stretched out a long arm toward the lost child. "Take my hand, lad, and hold on tight."

Distressed, the boy only stared at Mr. Helsden's offered hand, his chubby face crumpling with alarm.

"It will be all right, I promise. I will not let you go," Mr. Helsden said with a reassuring smile. Pippa noted the sweat already dotting the back of his neck. If the boy panicked on this precarious ledge, they could both find themselves in need of rescue. Pippa had never thought to ask Mr. Helsden before if he knew how to swim.

"Come along now, darling," Pippa added, utilizing the soothing voice she had trained to perfection over the years. She crouched down beside Mr. Helsden, the position uncomfortable and certainly inappropriate for any lady. "Grab onto Mr. Helsden, and we will go find your mama together."

Timid trust slowly filled the boy's eyes as he looked from Pippa to Mr. Helsden several times. Finally, he reached out with one small hand and placed it on Mr. Helsden's palm.

"Ready?"

The child sniffled and nodded. Mr. Helsden gripped tight, his large hand wrapping right around the poor thing's wrist. With a grunt, digging his heels into the grass, Mr. Helsden pulled. His broad shoulders and strong back stretched under his tight coat. Had the circumstances been less perilous, Pippa would have guiltily enjoyed the way his muscles exerted themselves. Instead, she watched with apprehension, as the mud sloshed around the little boy's feet. She held up both hands, ready to catch them if they fell or started to slide away.

Mr. Helsden grimaced and with one last heave, he tore the child from the mud and up onto the bank. The momentum sent him flying back onto his bottom, the boy caught between his legs and clinging to his waist. Mr.

Helsden laughed and swiped at the sweat on his forehead with the back of his hand.

Pippa let out a deep, shaky sigh. Without thinking, she hurried around to the side and threw one arm around Mr. Helsden's shoulders, her other hand patting the boy's back.

"Thank goodness," she cheered, her own relieved giggle escaping. "Well done, Mr. Helsden. And what is your name, dear?"

Face still buried in his rescuer's stomach, the boy mumbled, "Maurice."

"And well done to you as well, Maurice," Pippa added.

As they gathered their minds and caught their breaths right there on the bank of the Serpentine, a few passersby paused to see if they needed assistance. Pippa asked Master Maurice to describe the dress his mama wore, but no one recalled seeing such a woman nearby. They moved on, leaving Pippa and Mr. Helsden to cradle the terrified child a while longer—until they heard urgent footsteps rushing across the grass behind them.

With Mr. Helsden's hat in hand, Pippa stood first, then grasped the man's arm as he hoisted himself and Master Maurice up. He situated the boy on his hip, little caring about the mud now adorning his coat and trousers. They turned to find Sir Arthur and Master Duncan running toward them.

"Is everyone well? We heard a commotion and saw you all in a heap on the ground," Sir Arthur huffed, concerned gaze sweeping over their little party. Behind him, the other Helsdens all stood together just off the picnic blanket, watching with bated breath.

"No one is injured—just a little frightened. But we will sort that out shortly, won't we, Master Maurice?" Mr. Helsden kept his attention on the child, giving him a playful little bounce.

Exhausted from his tribulations, Master Maurice's only response was to nestle his head against Mr. Helsden's neck and stick his thumb in his mouth. The sight twisted Pippa's heart into a frenzy of leaping shapes, so ready to burst through her chest at this unbearably sweet moment. She could not help staring, though she did not think anyone would fault her. She could claim she was dazed and flustered from the harrowing experience. It was nothing to do with Mr. Helsden looking so perfect with a child in his arms, a child he had rescued with both strength and kindness.

"Goodness, Jasper, I never would have guessed you to be the hero type," Master Duncan mumbled in awe.

Mr. Helsden lifted his other shoulder in a bashful shrug. "Anyone would have done the same."

Sir Arthur stepped forward and, surprising Pippa given the public area, cupped his oldest child's cheek in his hand. His smile brimmed with pride. "It does not seem that anyone else did. Excellent job, my son."

Pippa looked away, setting aside her own pride to give the father and son a moment of privacy. She turned her attention toward the crowded lawn, sweeping her eyes over every individual in search of a woman wearing a dark purple, almost black gown.

"Was he separated from his family?" Sir Arthur asked, gently stroking the back of Master Maurice's head.

"That is what he said, yes. But no one we have asked has seen a woman matching his mother's description."

Master Duncan planted both fists on his hips. "Well, she can't have gone far. She must still be in the park. What mother would forget about her child?"

The question, though it had nothing to do with Pippa, pinched at her already overwhelmed mind.

"There!" she cried, pointing in rather unladylike fashion

to a flash of movement on the opposite side of the Serpentine.

Everyone whipped around to look. Mr. Helsden jostled the boy in his arms. "Master Maurice, over there. Does that look like your mama?"

The boy blinked slowly and lifted his head. When his eyes landed on her, they widened and he sat bolt upright, kicking out his legs. "Mama!" he screeched.

"We will go return him," Mr. Helsden announced to his father and brother. "Thank you for coming to help."

Without wasting another second, Pippa and Mr. Helsden marched across the bridge toward the frantic woman pacing up and down the lawn. She grabbed onto every stranger she could find, head twisting around in all directions, her heart crying out for her lost child.

They were still several meters away when she happened to turn at just the right time. She caught sight of the trio, face breaking into heart-wrenching relief. Master Maurice wiggled desperately in Mr. Helsden's grasp as his mother snatched up her skirts and ran across the lawn toward them. The gentleman set the boy down on his own two feet. He ran the rest of the way on his own, leaping into his mother's open arms as she collapsed to her knees.

"Thank God! Thank God, my darling boy!" she cried into his hair as she crushed him to her chest. Tears streamed down her cheeks as she rocked them both back and forth and smothered his face in kisses. Master Maurice giggled, completely recovered from his frightful ordeal.

"And thank God for you two," the woman whispered when she finally managed to tear her attention away from her son.

"We are simply glad we were able to reunite him with his family," Mr. Helsden said, helping Master Maurice's mama to her feet. She clutched the boy to her, oblivious to the mess his muddy feet made of her stunning amethyst gown.

"I truly cannot thank you enough," she mumbled, her cheek resting atop the boy's head, eyes still brimming with tears. "I do not know what I would have done if I lost Maurice. I already lost his beloved papa just months before he was born. He looks so very much like him. If I lost Maurice, too, I am sure I would have died of heartbreak."

Pippa's own heart cracked at the woman's story—at how desperate a mother could be to cling to her child at all costs. Tears pricked at her eyes as she took in Master Maurice's mother, not much older than Pippa's twenty-three years. So young to have suffered such loss, and had narrowly escaped another devastating blow.

"Maurice, thank your rescuers," she continued, bouncing the boy in her arms.

He gazed up at Mr. Helsden and Pippa, his innocent eyes full of as much gratitude as a child his age could convey. He might not have fully understood what had happened, but he knew well enough that he had been saved from a sorrowful fate.

"Thank you, lad," he murmured around the thumb in his mouth, repeating the name Mr. Helsden had called him earlier. His eyes shifted between the pair, clearly meaning to address them both.

The gentleman chuckled and ruffled Master Maurice's hair. "Of course, little one."

"Now you be good and listen to your mama," Pippa added, taking his little hand in hers and giving it a gentle shake. "Stay by her side and you will always be safe. She loves you so very much." Her voice cracked over the last sentence, the emotion of the drama and the reunion overwhelming her.

"Come, my sweetheart," Mrs. Boone said after hurried

introductions, her watery smile turning into a joyful grin. "Let us get you home and cleaned up."

With a final fond farewell and a promise of a dinner invitation to repay them, Mrs. Boone and her little boy wandered off through Hyde Park, chatting happily without a care in the world.

"Well, I certainly had not expected anything like that to happen today," Mr. Helsden said with a weary sigh. He tugged at the cravat around his collar, no doubt sweltering from the physical exertion despite the cool touch of the spring breeze.

"That was quite an adventure indeed," Pippa agreed, dabbing under her chin with the back of her gloved hand. "But you did such a wonderful job. You truly are so natural with children."

Mr. Helsden turned his shy smile to the bright green grass beneath his feet. "It is so rewarding to help children in need. I know that now more than ever after seeing and influencing the transformation Rebecca has made. Despite all the challenges," he paused, brushing a clump of dirt from his trousers, "seeing a child happy and helping them grow is so much more worthwhile than I ever could have imagined."

"Ah, your hat, Mr. Helsden." Pippa held up the accessory and placed it in his outstretched hands, wishing she could return it to his soft curls herself.

"My hat," he chuckled with a fond smile. "Thank you, Miss Seymour. Once again, you know the whereabouts of my hat better than I do."

"It seems a small thing, but I know you would not like to lose it," Pippa admitted, turning away from Mr. Helsden's weighty gaze.

They started the walk back toward the Helsdens' picnic, taking their time and allowing their frantic energy to slowly melt away. They caught a few odd looks from other park patrons, eyeing the mud smeared across Mr. Helsden's body and Pippa's lopsided bonnet, but neither of them cared one whit.

"That is why I love being a governess," Pippa admitted after a few moments of silent contemplation. "Nothing can match or surpass that exact feeling you described, yet one cannot truly appreciate how meaningful it is until they experience it for themselves.

"When I was a girl, I always thought I would love motherhood and raising children through all the ups and downs of life. But it was not until I started as a governess that I truly understood what it means to mold a young mind, to raise them up to their full potential and comfort and encourage them when they encounter challenges. There is nothing else in the world quite like it."

Her companion hummed thoughtfully, his gaze unfocused as he looked out at the bridge. Pippa swallowed nervously, sure she had confessed far too much. Why had she brought up her old dreams of having children of her own when such a thing would never happen? Why did she even allow herself to indulge in the mere thought of it?

"I always wanted a big family like the one I grew up with. Perhaps even bigger," Mr. Helsden added quietly, a fond smile pulling up one side of his mouth. "A home full of children running about and playing and fighting. I know that does not sound ideal to others, but to me, it sounds like heaven."

For the first time in a long, long time, Pippa found herself truly wishing for the same. Usually, she was too preoccupied to mull over what she really wanted from life. That had suited her just fine—until Mr. Helsden showed up. His mere presence forced her to reconsider and confront those desires she had hidden away to protect herself.

The longer she spent in the Helsdens' home, the closer

she grew to Mr. Helsden, the harder it became for Pippa to ignore the deepest wishes of her heart. As much as she loved what she did, she wanted more than temporary placements in families that would eventually no longer need her services and send her on her way to someone else who did.

"I pray your dreams will come true, Mr. Helsden," Pippa whispered, half hoping he would not hear and half hoping he would.

He glanced down at her, his gaze so soft she wanted to melt. "I pray that yours will as well, whatever they are."

Those words, the longing in his tone, sent a thrill deep into Pippa's very bones. Could he be thinking what she was thinking? Could his soul long for the same thing…with her?

"Jasper, there you are!" Master Sidney called, running over as they crested the bridge. "Did you find the boy's mother?"

The heroes of the hour returned to the peace of the picnic, swarmed by curious family members. Pippa allowed Mr. Helsden to recount the details of their rescue efforts, drawing out the conversation.

Her mind wandered far into the future, one she had never allowed herself to entertain, even with her undeniably strengthening affections for Mr. Helsden. She saw him just like this, surrounded by loved ones, sharing stories and laughing and simply enjoying their company—but the loved ones she saw were ones they made together, some with black hair and some with red.

Surely, such a future could be possible with a man like Mr. Helsden. With him, there could only be pure love and happiness.

Pippa clung with all her might to that wild hope, praying that someday soon it would give her the courage to reach for that desperately desired dream.

CHAPTER 10

*A*fter such an exciting and eventful Season, Jasper had never been more glad to soak in the fresh air and calm atmosphere of Somerset. Unfortunately, not everyone in his family was as happy to return to Goddard House.

"Where is Amelia?" Rebecca asked as the family filed into the breakfast room on their first day back, taking their usual places around the long table. She stared quizzically at the empty seat beside her, usually occupied by her older sister.

"She is still feeling a little unwell and asked for a tray in her room," cousin Colette answered with a glum smile.

"Please, everyone, be sensitive to your sister's feelings until she returns to her normal self," Mama announced from her spot at the head of the table, trapping each child in her serious gaze in turn.

"And you two, no teasing about suitors or matches or anything of the sort," Papa added from the other end, narrowing his eyes at Duncan and Sidney. They lowered their heads and stared down at the ham, potatoes, and roasted vegetables on their plates.

Jasper's heart panged as he imagined poor Amelia curled

up in bed, most likely ignoring the breakfast that had been brought up for her.

She had not made a match despite several promising courtships. They all fell through for one reason or another, the main one being that she had not found herself head over heels in love. Naturally, with so many incredible examples to draw from within her own family, Amelia had accepted nothing less, even if it hurt to adjust her expectations for a poetically romantic first Season.

Despite many reassurances and promises of a better Season next year, Amelia had still taken the failure to heart. To expedite the healing process, Uncle Patrick and Aunt Eloise had sent Colette back to Somerset with them for as long as needed.

"Will she be all right?" Rebecca asked, an endearingly forlorn note in her voice.

"Of course she will be," Jasper offered, sending an encouraging smile to the youngest Helsden across the table. "Our Amelia is made of sturdy stuff—and she has all of us to rely on as well. Perhaps you could see if Miss Seymour will help you with a creative project to gift to Amelia. You know how she loves those gestures."

Comforted, Rebecca nodded and took up her fork. A moment later, a footman bearing a silver tray entered the breakfast room and presented it to Papa. As everyone else tucked into their morning meal, the baronet flipped through the post, sorting them into different piles of importance.

"Ah," Papa said, drawing Jasper's attention. He swallowed the bit of ham in his mouth and set his utensils down. "A letter for Miss Seymour has slipped into our post."

"I can deliver it to her. I will be going to the schoolroom with Rebecca after breakfast anyway."

"Very good." Papa nodded. He placed it on the corner of the table for Jasper.

Eager to start his day with Miss Seymour, Jasper nearly inhaled the rest of his breakfast, ignoring Mama's admonition that he could choke himself if he did not chew properly.

After their discovery of Master Maurice in Hyde Park, the rest of the Season had passed quickly. True to her word, Mama had stopped overloading Jasper's schedule with engagements, though she did insist that he attend an acceptable number of events to remain polite within the eyes of the *ton*. Jasper had been able to spend more time with Miss Seymour, yet they still did not have many opportunities for deeper discussions with Rebecca and his other family members always nearby.

With one last swig of hot tea, Jasper leapt up from his seat and excused himself after confirming that Rebecca would join him in the schoolroom as soon as she was finished. Letter in hand and heart humming, Jasper strode down the hall, a brief detour in mind.

As soon as he had snatched the letter, Jasper had been unable to resist peeking at the sender. It was Miss Seymour's mother, just as he suspected. Pausing in the drawing room, Jasper bent over a writing desk in the corner and scribbled the woman's name and address down. It could prove useful in the future.

"Miss Seymour," Jasper called as he entered the schoolroom. The governess looked up from a lesson book she was perusing and sent a smile that shot right to the center of Jasper's heart.

"Good morning, Mr. Helsden."

He crossed the room in a few long strides, stopping when he came toe to toe with her. It was too close to be considered appropriate, yet Miss Seymour did not protest or move away. In fact, if Jasper was not mistaken, her gaze lingered on his mouth for just a moment, tracing over it, before returning to his eyes. He did the same, admiring the pink curves of her perfect, perfect lips.

"I have something for you," Jasper mumbled, no hint of the awkwardness that usually crept into his voice. He held up the letter between them at chest level. "This arrived from your mother. It was mixed in with the rest of our mail."

Miss Seymour's eyes lit with anticipation as she took the folded paper from Jasper's hand, her fingers ghosting over his. "Thank you. I was worried she would forget that we were returning to the country and send it to London instead. Do you mind if I read it now before Miss Rebecca arrives?"

Jasper gestured with one hand upturned. "Not at all." He stepped away to give Miss Seymour and her letter some privacy. He did not wander far, glancing her way numerous times.

Whatever Mrs. Clark had written could not have been good. Miss Seymour's expression slowly fell from excitement to concern and eventually dismay. Jasper's chest lurched, fearing for the governess' mother.

Just as he took a step toward Miss Seymour, ready to comfort and commiserate, Rebecca burst into the room wearing a stern expression. Jasper's chest lurched again, this time with apprehension. The girl's mood had shifted drastically between the breakfast room and the schoolroom. Miss Seymour had indeed warned them that Rebecca would likely struggle to adjust to Goddard House and life in the country, just as she had when they arrived in London.

That was likely Jasper's fault. He should have waited for her so they could walk to the schoolroom together as they always did. Instead, he had put his excitement to see Miss Seymour first. Guilt churned in Jasper's stomach as he watched his sister cross the room with bated breath.

Miss Seymour quickly folded the letter, tucked it into the back of the lesson book, and smoothed her expression all within the span of five seconds. A professional through and through, no matter what occurred in her personal life.

"Good morning, Miss Rebecca," the governess chirped, sweeping one hand toward the table.

"Good morning," Rebecca grumbled as she threw herself into her usual chair.

Miss Seymour caught Jasper's eye, a warning in her gaze. He settled into his seat across from the ladies, tensed for whatever challenges his sister would throw their way.

To his surprise, their English history lesson went well despite Rebecca's surly expression and grumbled responses. At least she was participating and obeying, even if she was in a sour mood.

Until Miss Seymour closed one book and pulled out another—the dreaded French. Rebecca shifted in her chair and glared up at her governess.

"I want to jump rope outside," the girl stated, a demand rather than a suggestion.

Miss Seymour drummed her fingers against the leather cover of the French lesson book. "Perhaps later, Miss Rebecca, if you do well in your lessons. We must take care of our duties first."

"But why?" Rebecca whined. "The lessons will be there later."

"So will your skipping rope," Miss Seymour countered, cool and measured as always.

Irritation growing, Rebecca slid down in her chair and crossed her arms over her chest.

"Miss Rebecca, you know better than that," Miss Seymour chided gently. "Please sit up and correct your posture."

"I do not want to. I do not care about posture or French or all these wars from a million years ago. I do not want to think, I want to jump rope."

"Miss Rebecca—"

"Just leave me be!" the girl snapped, fury roaring across her face. "Just let me do what I want! I already had to endure boring London where everyone makes me do all sorts of things I hate. Why should I do more boring things I hate at home?"

"Come now, Rebecca," Jasper intervened. "I thought you enjoyed London after you grew used to it. We had fun visiting Gunter's and having picnics at Hyde Park. And we were able to have many dinners with our family we do not get to see very often, remember? You adore Aunt Harriet and cousin Margaret."

"Yes, but they are not here. And those are the only things I liked about London. Everything was boring and annoying. You wouldn't understand, Jasper!" Rebecca spat, her vehemence shocking him. "You are always happy to do everything everyone else tells you to do!"

"That is enough, Miss Rebecca," Miss Seymour snapped. She stood so fast from her chair that its feet scraped against the wood floor. "Apologize to your brother this instant."

Rebecca stood, too, squaring against the taller woman with all the might she possessed in her small frame. "Why should I? It is true, after all."

Pain and shame stung Jasper. Not knowing what else to do, he also rose from his chair, though he could not lift his gaze from the table. He knew Rebecca did not mean what she said when she was in this state. He had just not expected it to be directed at him. She had never tried to cut him like this before.

After several more minutes of heated arguing from Rebecca and repeated instruction from Miss Seymour, the child finally accepted a breathing exercise and willingly went to sit in the corner until she calmed down. With silence restored to the schoolroom, Miss Seymour and Jasper stared at each other in surprise.

"I am afraid I made a mistake," the governess whispered, standing beside Jasper and staring at the back of Rebecca's head from across the room.

"How do you mean?" Jasper scooted a little closer, his arm brushing against her ruched cotton sleeve.

"I should not have tried to return her to the regular lesson schedule the day after returning from a long journey," she sighed, fingers plucking at a pleat in her skirt, an unexpected pink that brought out the warm undertones of her skin. "Miss Rebecca's resistance to change is more severe than I thought, even after seeing how she reacted to our arrival in London. I thought she would adjust more easily when we returned to Goddard House, but I see now that any change will require a period of adjustment."

"I see," Jasper mumbled, frowning at the floor.

Miss Seymour shook her head and inched toward Jasper, her side pressed against his. "We will need to work harder to develop her coping mechanisms. Life is just too full of change for her to react so poorly every time. When she gets older and experiences more of the world's changes, it could very well destroy her if we do not help her learn to manage her fears and anxieties better. I think we should shift our focus there."

Jasper nodded, turning his face ever so slightly to watch Miss Seymour from the corner of his eye. He was glad she did not have to wear a bonnet or hat while indoors. It would have obstructed his view of her fierce determination and never-ending compassion.

"I agree, though I must confess I never thought life could change for the better to such an incredible degree until you arrived."

Tension filled the space between them, their pinky fingers just a breath apart. If Jasper lifted his a little, he could brush it against hers, perhaps intertwine them—a silent promise to weather any storm together, a reassurance that he needed her by his side.

"Miss Seymour?" a small, hesitant voice called.

The tension broke and dissolved.

"Yes, Miss Rebecca?" The governess stepped forward, leaving Jasper to stand alone with the tumultuous and increasingly uncontrollable feelings storming in his chest.

"I am ready to apologize," Rebecca mumbled, her expression penitent.

"Very good, dear." Miss Seymour crossed the room and held out a hand to her charge. The girl took it and offered the first apology to her governess.

Jasper only half listened, that familiar ache of conflict returning. Perhaps, because he had not been as involved with Rebecca's instruction while in London, he had forgotten that she must come first.

"I am sorry for saying hurtful things to you earlier, brother," Rebecca offered, her head bowed before Jasper.

"It is all right now, Rebecca," Jasper said as he took her into his arms for a hug. She snuggled in, burrowing her face in his chest. Jasper held her tight.

He glanced up over the top of her head to find Miss Seymour watching. Their eyes met, seeming to reach an unspoken understanding.

No matter what they felt, they could not let it distract them from the real reason Miss Seymour was here.

CHAPTER 11

Jasper's fingers trembled as he held the letter he had been waiting almost a month for. In the meantime, the tension between him and Miss Seymour only grew worse. It swelled to a delightful crescendo when he thought they might finally cross that bridge into something more. Then it was snatched back by the practicalities of life and the reality of their circumstances.

With this letter finally in his hands, Jasper felt that he could show Miss Seymour exactly what family meant to him, what she meant to him—and how important it was that she should have the opportunity to know what a loving family was.

He stared down at the letter for another moment, stunned that it had arrived at all.

Though he knew Mr. Clark monitored the frequency of his wife's correspondence with Miss Seymour, Jasper had not realized that might extend to others as well. He had even started to fear that perhaps Mr. Clark had intercepted his letter and forbade Mrs. Clark from responding.

But here it was at last, written in the woman's scrawling

handwriting, so different from Miss Seymour's elegant swirls. He scanned the page so quickly he hardly absorbed anything and had to force himself to go back to the beginning.

"Dear Mr. Helsden, I would be delighted to visit my darling Pippa at your home."

His breath caught in his throat, his eyes tripping over a word he had never seen before—Pippa. Of course, he knew Miss Seymour's given name was Philippa. He had not dared to venture into the realm of dropping all the formalities between them yet to even learn that she went by a nickname, a sweet, charming nickname that suited her so perfectly.

Pippa.

He tested it in his mouth, the letters rolling over his tongue with a strange mixture of reverence and exhilaration.

One day he would have the courage to say that name aloud. One day soon.

Forcing himself to return to the letter, Jasper read on and discovered that Mrs. Clark would need someone—clearly Jasper himself—to pay her travel expenses.

Alone in his room, Jasper let out a celebratory cheer, his fist pumping into the air. Joy buzzed through every inch of his body. Mrs. Clark had agreed to be reunited with her daughter! Surely, when the two women finally had some time to be alone together once more, they could reconcile and begin the journey of repairing their relationship.

With two letters tucked into his coat pocket, Jasper quit his quarters and rushed straight for the schoolroom, a beaming smile on his face. It faltered when he found the place empty. Had Miss Seymour told him they would be taking their lessons elsewhere today? Surely he would not have forgotten that.

"Excuse me, Anne, have you seen Miss Seymour and Rebecca?" he asked, stopping the first maid he came across.

"As a matter of fact, I just delivered tea to them and the other misses in the drawing room."

"Wonderful, thank you!" Elation rising once more, Jasper grasped the older woman's hand in both of his and gave it a hearty shake, grinning like a madman.

He did not wait to see her response, striding as fast as he could down to the other end of the hall. He arrived just in time to see Miss Seymour and Rebecca sinking into simultaneous curtsies. Amelia and Colette clapped at the display. When the latter noticed Jasper watching from the doorway, she waved him in.

"Jasper, Miss Seymour and Rebecca have been practicing their curtsies for us. So pretty and graceful, don't you think?" Colette asked, her eyes darting to the governess.

"Absolutely," Jasper whispered, looking only at Miss Seymour.

"Brother! Did you see? Miss Seymour says I am almost ready to curtsy at the palace," Rebecca cried with excitement and pride, forcing Jasper to tear his attention away from the governess.

"Yes, my dear, I did see," he lied, guilt pinching his heart. "It was beautiful. Can I convince you to show me again a little later?"

Rebecca pouted. "Can't I show you again now?"

Nerves mingled with the excitement currently making a mess of Jasper's insides. Now that he faced Miss Seymour, prepared with a special gesture, the possibility that she might not like this surprise finally dawned on him. He swallowed and forced that worry away. He had come too far to let that stop him.

"Not just yet, Rebecca. I require a word with Miss Seymour in private."

The air in the drawing room stilled, the young ladies curious while the youngest lady frowned in disappointment.

Miss Seymour watched Jasper, her gaze searching his. Jasper's heart fluttered under her thoughtful intensity. Did she sense something was about to happen?

"Is that so?" Amelia chirped, ruining Jasper's concentration once again.

He sent a desperate glance to his sister, praying she would come to her senses and let the curiosity pass without prying. This was not a conversation he wanted to have with an audience—especially if Miss Seymour did not have the response Jasper hoped for.

To his dismay, Amelia turned her head slowly between Jasper and Miss Seymour. "Well, surely it cannot be anything we—"

"Goodness, I am famished!" Colette cried, folding her hands over her middle with a sheepish smile. "I hope no one else heard my stomach grumble just now. Amelia, why don't we have some sandwiches brought out to the garden?"

Amelia pouted, looking very much like Rebecca. "But—"

"The day is so lovely, we should not waste it. Autumn will be here before we know it," Colette continued. She stood and smoothed out her skirts, looking at the other lady expectantly.

"But it has been quite hot recently," Amelia reminded. "In fact, I thought it nearly unbearable when I went to visit Hugh and Charlotte yesterday."

"Heat is so very tolerable when there is plenty of shade to be had," Colette insisted.

Crestfallen, Amelia finally relented and followed Colette from the drawing room, casting a dejected glance over her shoulder at Jasper. Colette eased the door closed, leaving just a crack for half of her face to appear. His back turned to Miss Seymour, Jasper mouthed a silent "thank you" to his wonderful, thoughtful, precious cousin.

"What's all the fuss?" Rebecca mused, looking between her brother and her governess with an air of suspicion.

"I believe Mr. Helsden said he wished to speak with me privately," Miss Seymour chuckled. "Would you go practice on the pianoforte for a few minutes?"

"But my pianoforte lesson is not supposed to be until tomorrow."

"So it is. But if you practice a little bit now, I will allow you to finish your lesson tomorrow early. Keep watch of your time and I will subtract it tomorrow," Miss Seymour offered.

Rebecca perked up and accepted the compromise. Jasper could not help smiling as he watched his sister bound away to the pianoforte and begin playing whatever she remembered, entirely certain that she would exaggerate the time as much as possible to shorten her lesson tomorrow.

Miss Seymour crossed the room toward Jasper, still lingering by the door. The hem of her dress—a very flattering apple green today—whispered over the rug.

Jasper could not wait another second. "I have had a letter from your mother," he burst, still mindful to keep his voice low.

The woman's eyes widened, fear flashing through them. "Has something happened?"

"Heavens, no," Jasper hurried, fishing both letters—his original request and the response from Mrs. Clark—from his coat pocket. He held them with the tips of his fingers, the pages rustling against each other, and looked down at the ground. Doubt crept up once more. "I...I hope you will not be angry, but I took the liberty of writing her to see if...."

Miss Seymour tilted her head so she could see his eyes again. "Do not keep me in suspense," she said lightly, most of her concern disappeared.

"I wanted to see if perhaps she would be interested in

coming here to visit you," he finished in a rushed whisper. Perhaps this had not been such a great idea after all, he chided himself. What if she preferred to keep their relationship confined to occasional letters? What if she did not wish to reconnect with her mother after what she had done—or rather, allowed her second husband to do?

"I am sorry for being so terribly forward—"

"What did she say?" Miss Seymour demanded. The eager rhythm of her voice soothed Jasper's nerves.

"She said yes," Jasper continued. "She wishes to come to Goddard House to spend time with you. If that is what you want, of course."

Miss Seymour stared at him, lips slightly parted in wonder. "But how? How did this all come about?"

Jasper offered a self-conscious shrug. "Do you remember the day I delivered one of her letters to you? I may have stolen her address from it."

She huffed out a chuckle, shaking her head. "My word, Mr. Heslden. You are full of surprises."

Heat threatened to flush Jasper's face. "I do not think anyone has ever thought me capable of surprise. So...you are not angry?"

Miss Seymour shook her head again, tears shining like crystals in her eyes. "No, I am not angry. No other family has ever offered to invite mine to visit, and I dared not ask for such liberties," she whispered. "I have not seen my mother in over five years, Mr. Helsden—not since I started as a governess. You have just given me the most incredible gift I could have ever dreamt of."

Jasper promised himself that that would not be true. He hoped to give Miss Seymour many other gifts in the future, ones even more wonderful than this. His feelings for her had long since become undeniable almost without his awareness.

They had grown so naturally over these past several

months that Jasper could no longer determine when his admiration and affection for Miss Seymour had turned into something more—something that made him hope that their dreams of marriage and children were not as far away as they thought.

Yes, Jasper loved the governess. Likely from the first moment he saw her. He wanted nothing more than to give her everything her heart desired—including a chance to renew her relationship with her mother.

"I am so very glad, Miss Seymour. If there is anything within my power to do for you, I am more than happy to do it."

"You are far too kind to me," she said, a touch of sadness in the words that made Jasper want to pull her into his arms at that very moment and never let go.

"You deserve kindness, Miss Seymour. You are an angel upon this Earth. It is an honor to be able to repay you for all that you have done for us in whatever small way I can."

"May I see those?" she asked, pointing to the letters in Jasper's grasp.

He passed them to her, allowing his thumb to trail over the back of her hand. "I can arrange the meeting and all the travel necessities with Mrs. Clark. You do not think Mr. Clark will prevent my next letter from reaching her, do you?"

Miss Seymour skimmed the contents of the letters, one in each hand, contentment settling over beautiful features. "No, Mother said he does not prevent her from communicating with others. Only me."

Her expression changed, eyes glued to Jasper's letter. "Look at when you wrote this," she whispered, turning the page so Jasper could see.

He leaned forward and squinted at the top right corner where he always penned the date. "Yes, it did take her some time to respond," he said cautiously, not entirely sure what seemed to have shocked Miss Seymour so. "Perhaps she needed some time to think of what she wanted to do, or to convince Mr. Clark to let her do it."

"No, it's not that," Miss Seymour chuckled. "You do not remember, do you?"

Jasper stood up straight and frowned at Miss Seymour. "Remember what?"

Amazement colored Miss Seymour's smile. "I have a letter from you, written on this exact date, when you asked me to come to Goddard House."

Unceremoniously plucking the letter from Miss Seymour's hand, Jasper brought it close to his face. Bells of recognition rang in the back of his mind. She was right. One year ago from that date, he had sent a desperate letter to Miss Seymour on an early September night begging for her help.

"What a strange coincidence," he mumbled, a shiver rippling down his spine.

"I think of it more as a little miracle," Miss Seymour replied.

When Jasper looked up from the letter, he found her gazing at him with all the certainty he felt in his own heart—certainty that they had been brought together for a reason. Only he did not agree that this was a little miracle.

Miss Seymour was the greatest miracle he could have ever hoped for, in ways he could not even begin to enumerate.

Now he had the opportunity to do something meaningful for the woman who had done so much for them. Jasper would ensure that Miss Seymour's visit with her mother exceeded her expectations.

And then…Jasper would finally admit all these things he'd kept hidden over this past long year.

Cozy under the covers, a single candle flickering on her bedside table, Pippa read and reread Mother's letter. Her heart soared as those words sparked a hope in her that she had long considered dead.

"I would be delighted to visit my darling Pippa at your home."

Mr. Helsden had done all this for her. He had extended a branch to Pippa's mother and had even gladly offered to pay her travel expenses.

It was all for Pippa. Her heart swelled at the thought and what it could mean—no, what it must mean. Surely he would only go to all this trouble if he had affections for her. Maybe he even loved her.

Pippa pressed Mother's letter to her chest, just over her heart.

"I hope he does love me," she whispered to herself. With this gesture, she could no longer deny that she certainly loved him. How could she not love a man who would do something so bold and so heartfelt for her? Not to mention the many other reasons that had built up over this past year. He had lifted her to heights of happiness she never thought possible. And it was all thanks to Mr. Helsden writing that fateful letter.

Mother was coming. Mother would hold Pippa in her arms again like she'd done before Father succumbed to disease and their lives shattered. Mother would see what a resilient woman her only child had become. She would see how Pippa had made something of her life and now made a difference in others'.

Perhaps, Pippa's heart whispered, perhaps Mother would return home and tell Mr. Clark that her daughter was no burden. Her daughter was someone to be proud of, someone they should be honored to have in their lives.

THE NECESSARY LESSON

As soon as that thought crossed her mind, Pippa's mood soured.

Mr. Clark. How on Earth would Mother convince her husband to let her leave? She hoped Mother had already discussed these plans with Mr. Clark and obtained his permission—not that she should need permission to visit her daughter. But if she needed it just to write, surely she would need it for this. Or maybe she had concocted some convincing excuse like the reappearance of a long lost relative.

In Pippa's childhood memories, Mother had always been so witty and bright and brave. That had all changed when Father was taken from them far too soon. A shell of her former self and terrified of the future, Mother had accepted the first proposal to come her way after her mourning period had ended. Pippa had never blamed her for making the most sensible choice during a time of terrible uncertainty, their estate passing to a distant cousin of Father's who had a large family of his own, leaving no room to spare for its original occupants.

Still, something strange tugged at the back of Pippa's mind as she tried to sort through the overwhelming emotions flooding her at the prospect of reuniting with Mother after all these years. She flipped onto her side and pulled the candle closer to the edge, angling the letter under the more advantageous lighting.

"I would be delighted to visit my darling Pippa at your home," she read again, forcing her eyes to absorb every letter, every stroke of the pen.

Pippa's brow furrowed as that feeling gnawed at her stomach. She moved the candle back and threw the blankets off, trekking across her dark room toward the desk, long hair spilling down to her waist. With growing apprehension, Pippa tore open the drawer where she kept all her letters and snatched a stack at the front—all the letters she saved from Mother.

Careful to keep them in order, she pulled out a few at the top and returned to her bed. She sat on the edge and bent toward the light of the candle, the one to Mr. Helsden in one hand and last month's in the other.

She examined them side by side, taking her time to analyze every individual letter. Ice seeped into her blood. The handwriting was not the same—not quite. This Y did not loop as generously as that one. That A was slanted in the wrong direction. The capital P that formed Pippa's name possessed the usual flourish, but something about it looked different somehow.

Panic threatened to overcome her as her eyes raced between all the examples she had spread over her pillows. Something was amiss. It had to be. After all, didn't this all seem too easy?

As her fear reached a boiling point, Pippa's heart yearned for Mr. Helsden. She needed his comfort, his calming presence. But it was far too late for her to do anything about all this. He was likely already asleep, and it would be highly inappropriate for Pippa to appear at his bedroom door at this late hour in her nightgown and robe.

Tomorrow, he would reassure her. The mere thought eased Pippa's mind just enough to convince her to stow the letters and return to bed.

Her life had been hard enough already, she reasoned as she burrowed herself under the blanket and blew out the candle. Darkness enveloped her. Her life had been hard enough, so why should it feel so far-fetched that something good could happen to her?

After all, she had met the most loving man she had ever known when she had thought herself beyond the reach of love.

She was simply looking for reasons why none of this would work. She had been doing just that over this past year, fighting with herself every step of the way to keep Mr. Helsden where she thought he belonged—far away from her heart. Now he had given her an opportunity to heal one of the greatest pains in her life, and she was trying to find fault with it.

Pippa turned onto her side and pulled over the other pillow, holding it in her arms like she hoped to one day hold Mr. Helsden as they fell asleep side by side. Her fears were irrational. And she no longer wanted to think about them, or even about Mother.

As the stiffness in her body eased, sleep slowly creeping up on her, Pippa thought about Mr. Helsden. She squeezed her pillow tight, burying her face in its soft fluff.

The man was a dream. Could someone so kind and thoughtful truly exist? Could he exist for Pippa?

She knew from her own experience with her step-family and many of the families she had worked with in the past that the tantalizing promise of happy endings often proved too good to be true.

Was Mr. Helsden too good to be true?

Pippa's very spirit rebelled against the thought. It felt wrong to her very core. Sleep finally claimed her, her last thoughts hazy yet undoubtedly certain.

Mr. Helsden was exactly the man he had always shown himself to be. That was the man she had fallen in love with.

CHAPTER 12

*P*ippa peered down at herself, admiring the gorgeous deep green gown Lady Helsden had given her for the special occasion. She inhaled and exhaled slowly, trying to calm the anxious fluttering in her stomach.

Just a week ago, Mr. Helsden had delivered the excellent news that Mother wished to visit Goddard House—to finally see Pippa again. She could hardly believe he had managed to make the arrangements so quickly. At least she still had a few minutes before Mother was scheduled to arrive. Until then, Pippa would do her best to preen herself, something she hardly ever had time for in her normal life as a governess. Mother had not seen her in years. She wanted to provide the best possible impression, to give Mother someone to be proud of.

A sharp knock at the door yanked her from her nervous reverie. Curious, she hurried to open it.

"Miss Harcourt, may I help you?" Pippa asked, her brows furrowing at the frazzled young lady.

"Jasper is waiting downstairs for you and for the arrival of your guest, but, well, we just received word from a servant at Attwood that your guest...your guests are there looking for you," she explained in one rushed breath.

"Oh dear," Pippa groaned, guilt and embarrassment warring with her nerves. "There must have been some confusion since the properties are so near each other. Mother must have thought I would be working at the big house."

"Perhaps," the young lady nodded, a swirl of deep auburn hair framing her face. She did not look entirely satisfied with that reaction, though Pippa could not guess why.

"I am ready now so I will meet Mr. Helsden downstairs," Pippa announced, then, a little quieter, "Do I look acceptable?"

Mr. Helsden's cousin grinned at Pippa, an expression for which she could not fault the girl. Miss Harcourt need not be held to the same standards of Society with her father working as the primary examiner of plays and her mother a seamstress who provided costumes for stage productions. Besides, Pippa took it as a good sign that she did indeed look acceptable.

"You look absolutely lovely, Miss Seymour," the young lady said, grasping Pippa's hand and giving it an earnest squeeze.

"Thank you," Pippa said, slipping out of her room and down the hall.

Downstairs, she found Mr. Helsden waiting below in the foyer. He paced up and down the space, hands clasped behind his back, until he heard Pippa's footsteps on the landing above. When he turned and caught sight of her at the top of the stairs, his mouth slowly fell open, eyes rounding as they roamed up and down her new gown.

Pippa prayed her heart would stop its mad stuttering by the time she reached the bottom of the stairs. Her prayer went unanswered. The thing jumped about her chest with renewed vigor when she stood before Mr. Helsden and saw up close the reverence with which he absorbed her. Slowly, instinctively, he reached one hand up and brushed a loose curl behind Pippa's ear.

"You are stunning," he whispered, standing close enough that his warm breath glided across her forehead.

"It is only one of Lady Helsden's old dresses," Pippa explained, though the compliment still sent her mind spinning. She did not simply look stunning to Mr. Helsden. She *was* stunning.

"But you bring new life to it," he countered, his voice low and soft.

"Mr. Helsden, the gig is ready for you," the butler announced.

Neither Pippa nor Mr. Helsden flinched or pulled away, not at all embarrassed to be caught in such an intimate moment. Pippa knew on the very day that he revealed his correspondence with Mother that they were both nearly ready—so close to finally closing the distance between them once and for all.

First, Pippa wanted to find some sort of closure with Mother, and perhaps even seek out her advice on what to do about a man. She had once dreamed of doing that very thing, relying on her mother's wisdom to help her navigate the winding paths of love—before life threw the last cruel blow at her.

In truth, Pippa did not feel like she needed advice when it came to Mr. Helsden. She knew what she wanted now. Her heart had known even longer. But it would be lovely to share such a moment of heartfelt bonding with her mother.

"Are you ready?" Mr. Helsden asked as he wrapped his hands around Pippa's and slid them up her forearms, resting at her elbows.

The touch was so foreign yet so very welcome, almost as

if Pippa had experienced it many times before and had somehow forgotten how much she adored it.

"I am," she said. She truly felt it. With Mr. Helsden by her side, they would clear up this misunderstanding and return to Goddard House with her mother.

The gig ride to Attwood Manor felt far longer than Pippa recalled. They walked to the big house most of the time, yet this ride stretched on even longer than that. She knew she was just moments away from seeing Mother again. The expectations, hopes, fears jostled inside her with every step of the horse's hooves.

"Mr. Helsden, Miss Seymour, right this way," the Attwood butler announced as soon as Mr. Helsden passed the reins to a waiting footman.

They hurried in behind the butler, though Pippa motioned for him to wait a moment before opening the door to the drawing room. The elderly servant dutifully looked away as Pippa turned to Mr. Helsden, silently seeking strength in his countenance. Mr. Helsden took her hands again, unconcerned about the presence of any staff who might see. His eyes gave her all the encouragement she needed.

Pippa turned to the door and nodded. The butler opened it and ushered them in with a regal announcement. Various familiar Harcourt voices greeted them.

Pippa's heart froze the moment she stepped into the room.

There stood Mother. And her stepfather.

Miss Harcourt's words echoed in Pippa's mind. She had indeed said something about guests. Pippa had been too flustered by everything to pick up on it, or else dismissed it as a mistake.

The couple turned and regarded Pippa and Mr. Helsden with vastly different expressions. Mother's slight frown turned into a wavering smile. Mr. Clark's upper lip twitched at one corner as if he wanted to snarl at his stepdaughter. Pippa saw no one else but them, preferring to ignore the curious gazes of Mr. Helsden's family.

"My sweet, sweet daughter," Mother gasped, extending her arms out as she crossed the room, her steps slow and uncertain, then gaining speed the closer she came.

Pippa's mind had gone so empty that when Mother pulled her in for a crushing embrace, she felt like a rag doll. She did not know how long it took for her to regain the use of her limbs and wrap her arms around the one she had missed so desperately for so long.

Her eyes remained locked on that horrid man, looming behind Mother like an insidious shadow. She knew hatred was not a virtue, yet she could not help hating Mr. Clark for tainting what should have been a joyous reunion.

"Mother," Pippa whispered into the older woman's graying hair, determined not to let him steal all her happiness—not again. "I missed you."

"I missed you, too, dearest Pippa." Mother's voice trembled with emotion, her fingers digging into the back of Pippa's bodice. "And you must be Mr. Helsden," Mother added, pulling away from Pippa just enough to address the gentleman.

"Indeed I am. It is a pleasure to meet you, Mrs. Clark," said Mr. Helsden from somewhere just behind Pippa. She could hear the displeasure in his voice. She could feel his comforting, reassuring presence at her back, supporting her. "And you must be Mr. Clark," he continued.

"Yes," the man replied in a lazy drawl that made Pippa's skin simmer with loathing.

She had been tricked. Somehow, someone had tricked her.

"Look at you," Mother sighed, holding Pippa at arm's length and eyeing her up and down. "So beautiful, my girl."

"Thank you, Mother. You look well. How was your journey?" Pippa asked. No matter how hard she tried, she could not infuse any life into her words. Not with the man who had stolen everything from her in the room, just a few feet away.

Mother mumbled something about the bumpy ride and perhaps staying at a different inn on the way back. Pippa could barely hear her, her ears rushing with shock and betrayal. This was not how this moment was supposed to happen. This was not how anything was supposed to happen.

"Why did you come to Attwood Manor and not Goddard House?" Pippa prodded when Mother ran out of things to say about their travels.

A light blush stretched across Mother's cheeks. "Well, Mr. Clark insisted this must be the right place even though the driver told us Goddard House was the smaller property just down the road. He made the man bring us here instead."

"Why? What does that matter to him?"

"Come say hello to your father, Pippa," Mother said, changing the subject. Those dreadful words sliced Pippa to her core.

"My father," Pippa said through gritted teeth, "is in heaven." She made no move to get any closer to Mr. Clark.

"Dear, look at how lovely our Pippa is. Do not be shy," Mother said over her shoulder, waving to her husband in a futile attempt to bridge the chasm between Mr. Clark and her daughter. He wrinkled his nose and remained in his spot.

Mother looked back and forth between them, her expression pinched and uncomfortable. She scurried to Mr. Clark and whispered something urgent in his ear.

Pippa took the opportunity to do the same to Mr. Helsden. "I want to leave. I cannot do this."

His expression softened, the pain he felt on her behalf just under the surface. He stepped closer and bent his head over her. "Stay just for a while. Talk to your mother. Perhaps there have been more misunderstandings than we anticipated. I will be just nearby the entire time, I promise."

Pippa gazed at him for a long moment, time slowing so she could process his words, his promise. She trusted him beyond the shadow of a doubt. Movement from the corner of Pippa's eye broke her concentration. Mother was walking back to her, Mr. Clark still immovable. That was perfectly fine by Pippa.

"He is so tired from the journey," Mother chuckled, shrugging with one shoulder. She always had an excuse for him at the tip of her tongue.

"Is that so? Perhaps he should not have made it then."

"Pippa, be polite. We have come all this way for you," Mother hissed, glancing nervously at the hosts she had accidentally intruded upon.

"Mr. Clark, I thought you might be interested in our card table over here," Lady Welsted chimed, entering Pippa's awareness for the first time.

She turned to watch the older woman, so dignified and self-assured in her later years, stride across the room toward her stepfather. Mr. Helsden's grandmother gestured toward a distant corner, far away from Pippa. Intrigued by the mention of cards, Mr. Clark followed, a wolfish glint in his dark eyes. The other Harcourts, including Lord Welsted and Mr. Helsden's Uncle Dalton and Aunt Winnie, resumed the flow of conversation, allowing Pippa an opportunity to speak with her mother without all eyes on them.

"What is he doing here?" she demanded under her breath. The careful composure she had worked so hard to train rapidly unraveled with every second she spent in the same room as Mr. Clark. "Mr. Helsden invited *you*, Mother. Not him. And you did not even think to mention that he would be joining you?"

Mother dropped her gaze to the floor, her expression miserable and forlorn. The look squeezed Pippa's battered heart.

"You would have changed your mind," she mumbled, sounding on the verge of tears.

Compassion never abandoned Pippa for long. She reached for Mother's bony hands and brushed her thumb across her knuckles. Still, she deserved answers.

"Tell me truthfully, Mother. Did he force you to let him accompany you?"

Mother did not answer right away. That made her eventual nod hurt all the more. "He intercepted Mr. Helsden's letter and crafted a response that I wrote out under his guidance. He would not have let me accept unless he came, too."

Pippa let out a sharp exhale and pulled Mother in for another hug. "Of course not," she muttered, unable to keep the bitter tone out of her voice, though she supposed she should be grateful that she had this opportunity at all. But there was more Mother kept hidden.

"I am so glad you could visit. I truly am," Pippa said, memorizing the feeling of her mother's arms around her once more. Who knew when she would experience this again?

"As am I, my dearest Pippa. I am sorry it took me so long."

For several minutes, Pippa and Mother maintained their little bubble as they reacquainted themselves with each other. True to his word, Mr. Helsden lingered nearby, his face always half-turned to the corner of the room where Mr. Clark played a card game with his uncle and grandfather. With him acting as guard, Pippa allowed herself to forget her stepfather's unwanted presence and simply enjoy her mother's.

Their reunion certainly had not matched any of her numerous imaginary scenarios, but Pippa was determined to salvage whatever she could. Eventually, Pippa felt herself easing back into the relationship she and Mother had once enjoyed, as if the years of letters had kept it alive in a muted state until they could finally be together again and revive what had once been lost.

"Mrs. Clark, I am ready to retire." That sharp voice cut right through the friendly atmosphere of Attwood's drawing room.

Mother winced and offered Pippa an apologetic smile. "Yes, we should be going now," she agreed. "Thank you for having us despite our mistake."

"Grandpapa, could we borrow another carriage to convey Mr. and Mrs. Clark to Goddard House?" Mr. Helsden asked as everyone else offered their farewells.

Mr. Clark passed right between Mr. Helsden and Lord Welsted on his way to the door, calling over his shoulder, "There is no need. We are staying at the inn in Caston."

Mr. Helsden and his grandfather exchanged a confused glance, both turning to Pippa's stepfather at the same time. "Though I must confess we were only expecting Mrs. Clark, we have ample room to accommodate you as well, sir," said the younger man, his tone as even and polite as ever. Only Pippa seemed to notice the fist clenched at his side.

"I would rather stay at the inn," Mr. Clark insisted. "Might as well, since this is a paid trip, is it not? That is what your letter said, eh, Mr. Helsden?"

Governess or not, Pippa could not stop her mouth dropping open at the man's bold rudeness. Her blood boiled under her skin. She was sure her ears would start steaming at any second.

"Mr. Clark," Pippa barked, directly addressing her stepfather for the first time, "Mr. Helsden has generously offered to pay for Mother's travel and lodging and arranged for her to stay at Goddard House for the week, which he has now extended to you. There is no need for you to take advantage of his kindness."

"Miss Seymour, they may stay at the inn if they wish. I am true to my word—always."

For once, Mr. Helsden's gentle hand on the small of Pippa's back did little to soothe her. She had never felt so completely betrayed, humiliated, and enraged all at once. How dare Mr. Clark make demands of Mr. Helsden when he had already deceived them once?

"Good man," Mr. Clark chuckled, his eyes dark as he stared down Mr. Helsden.

The gentleman did not flinch. Pippa marveled at his noble composure after such a slap in the face. When his fingertips brushed comforting circles through the fabric of her dress, Pippa knew how he managed to remain so calm in such an insulting situation. He did it for her, to protect her from an even uglier scene.

Pippa knew he would never be a violent man, but even a non-violent man could rage when someone caused his loved ones harm. Had she not been in the room, Pippa wondered if gentle Mr. Helsden might have delivered a tongue-lashing that would have gone down in history.

True to his word indeed, Mr. Helsden and Lord Welsted arranged for a barouche—per Mr. Clark's request—to deliver their guests to the local inn in the village. Mind an utter mess, Pippa spewed apology after apology to Mr. Helsden's family, who all repeatedly assured her that she was not to blame for any of this and that they would support her in any way they could.

Though she had just been sitting and enjoying a true conversation with her mother for the first time in years, Pippa had never felt the bonds of family more potently than in that moment. She did not belong to them—yet—but they still rallied around her. She trusted every single one of them to uphold their word if it came to it.

The gig ride back to Goddard House passed in almost total silence. Pippa had not a clue what to say to explain what had just happened. There really was no proper explanation. Mr. Clark was Mr. Clark, still. He always would be.

When Goddard House came into view, Pippa grew uncomfortable with the silence she usually cherished between herself and Mr. Helsden. She shifted on the seat. He did the same.

"Forgive me—"

"I am sor—"

They both started at the same time, slipping into another uncomfortable silence. Pippa gave him an imploring look. He nodded for her to go first.

"Mr. Helsden, please forgive me for that terrible display," she continued, the knot in her throat expanding until she could hardly take in enough air to form words. "I cannot believe…. I am so embarrassed and…hurt. And I hate that they have abused you like this."

He gave a dark chuckle, shaking his head and tugging the horse to a slow walk. When he looked at Pippa, his eyes only carried complete sympathy.

"Dear Miss Seymour, you have no reason to apologize. The poor behavior lies with them—with Mr. Clark, in particular. I suspect your mother could do little to stop him."

"Then you have nothing to be sorry for, either," Pippa insisted, gratitude swelling in her chest amidst the tumult of other bitter emotions.

"I do," Mr. Helsden continued in a whisper. "I am so very sorry that you had to endure all that, and I do not just mean today. I mean for the majority of your childhood and beyond. But, I can assure you, Miss Seymour, that we will endure it together from now on. You will never be alone in this ever again."

The tears finally came, slipping down Pippa's cheeks in a strong and steady flow. She no longer cared about looking a fool in front of Mr. Helsden. If he could so thoroughly accept where she had come from—and the scars that still remained—he would not mind a few tears. A few tears that turned into a seemingly endless stream when he gathered the reins in one hand and leaned over. With his free hand, he tilted Pippa's face up toward him and lowered his. His lips pressed to her temple, the first kiss of many, Pippa hoped.

Every deep, steady heartbeat confirmed what she had long since known: Mr. Helsden was always true to his word. And if he said that he and Pippa would survive this strange ordeal together, she knew he must be right.

That single kiss sealed this undeniable truth.

CHAPTER 13

"*There* she is!" Rebecca called, ushering Jasper toward the window with an excited grin.

Jasper joined his sister, one arm around her shoulder, and peered down at the front drive to find Miss Seymour returning to Goddard House from a walk with her Mother. Mr. and Mrs. Clark had been in the area for a few days now. Since Miss Seymour had the entire week off for the visit, Jasper had not seen much of her.

He understood, of course, yet his greedy heart could not help crying out every moment she was not by his side.

His anticipatory smile faded as she came closer, her expression clearer. Her brows were knit, her shoulders slightly rounded. Something troubled her. Jasper's mouth went dry. The connection his soul felt to hers rang a warning alarm.

"Let's go downstairs and welcome her home," Jasper suggested. Rebecca agreed with glee and skipped toward the sitting room door, oblivious to the multitude of emotions whirling in her brother's mind.

Home. The word solidified itself with every beat of

Jasper's heart. It felt so natural to associate that word with Miss Seymour. She was home, right here, with him.

So why did a cold dread fill his stomach as he and Rebecca made their way downstairs to the foyer?

"Jasper, I'm going to hide behind the big vase and pop out to startle Miss Seymour when she comes in," Rebecca whispered conspiratorially with a mischievous smile. She skipped over the last step with her growing legs and scurried behind the porcelain vase to the right of the stairs.

"I do not think that is a good idea, sister," Jasper hurried when he heard the voices of a footman outside greeting Miss Seymour. If she was in a sour mood, the last thing Jasper wanted was to scare her out of her wits.

"It will be a great lark!" Rebecca insisted.

Jasper was half a second away from pulling the girl from her hiding spot when the footman opened the door for Miss Seymour. She stared at the floor, downcast, as she entered. Her lovely, full mouth pulled in a frown like Jasper had never seen before.

"Miss Seymour, is something wrong?"

The governess jumped, her head snapping up. She had been so lost in thought that she had not even noticed Jasper standing right there in the foyer. The surprise subsided quickly, replaced by the same melancholy contemplation she had been wearing just a moment ago.

"My mother has asked me to return home with them."

Thunder clapped in Jasper's ears as his blood rushed to his head. Miss Seymour was leaving? His heart splintered at the mere possibility.

"Oh, I see…."

Embarrassment followed on the heels of his shock. He knew he should not have been so surprised, even after giving her that little kiss on her temple a few days ago. That foolish part of him that had been lost in the haze of falling in love had not thought for one second that this might happen.

What mother, when finally reunited with her daughter, would not wish for her to return to their family home? Surely Mrs. Clark, after living under her second husband's thumb for so long, would seize the opportunity to bring Miss Seymour back into her life. But…is that what Miss Seymour wanted?

"Does that mean you are leaving me, Miss Seymour?"

Rebecca's small, wounded voice sounded from behind the vase. Both adults turned in her direction as Rebecca slowly came out of hiding, half her body still tucked behind the vase.

Jasper's heart splintered again at the morose expression on his precious sister's face, her eyes round with dismay and bottom lip already trembling. They had known since the beginning that Miss Seymour would one day move on to another assignment. Despite the progress they had made over the past year, Jasper knew in that moment that Rebecca was not yet ready to let go. Perhaps, like Jasper, she would never be ready to let go of Miss Seymour.

"Miss Rebecca," the governess gasped, her own heartache and indecision clear on her face. "Well, I am not entirely sure…."

"If that is what Miss Seymour wants…." Jasper added, trying his best to tread carefully toward the potential of that reality without making any concrete statements.

After all, Miss Seymour could choose to stay.

No matter how tactful or noncommittal their answers, Rebecca had heard enough. Her lip trembled fiercely now. The tears burst through her dam a second later. Without a sound, she turned on her heel and flew up the stairs, her footsteps hammering in Jasper's ears in time with his throbbing heartbeat.

They both stared up the steps as she disappeared from view on the next landing. Jasper turned slowly toward Miss Seymour. They stared at each other for a torturous moment. He did not try to hide his own fear and misery.

The truth hung between them, impossibly heavy. Miss Seymour's face said it all. At the very least, Jasper could sense the inner workings of her mind drawing her toward accepting Mrs. Clark's offer.

Could he blame her? If he somehow became estranged from his family with only letters passed between them for years, would he not race back to them the very moment they called?

Miss Seymour lowered her head once more. Jasper hated that. He hated to see her so torn when she was normally so self-assured.

All the while, Jasper could not think of a single thing to say or do. He was frozen, trapped on the precipice of their future—if there was any future for them at all.

CHAPTER 14

*P*ippa could no longer bear the sorrow in Mr. Helsden's eyes, knowing she was the cause. If nothing else—even that sweet kiss—had proved his feelings thus far, the pain she saw there was all the confirmation she needed. She only wished it did not have to happen like this.

As much as she longed to comfort him, Pippa did not know what she could say. She herself did not know which path she would choose. One of them would no doubt bind them together for the rest of their lives. The other would break his heart.

There was another hurting soul Pippa needed to address first.

"I should go to her," she mumbled, not sure her voice had made any sound.

Mr. Helsden only nodded, a multitude of emotions passing across his lovely, handsome face that had populated so many of Pippa's dreams for months. It was that very face and the spirit behind it that made this decision so difficult for her.

For now, before she gave her mother's proposal any more

thought, she needed to put her charge first. She moved toward the stairs behind Mr. Helsden, her hand longing to reach out for his as she swept past, drawing parallel for just a moment. Somehow, she resisted, the thought of poor Miss Rebecca caught so off guard spurring her on.

Pippa sped through Goddard House, the place that had been the most loving, welcoming home she had known in almost all her life, and arrived at the bedroom shared by Miss Rebecca and Miss Helsden in the blink of an eye.

Time moved so strangely, without a care for Pippa's needs. It was too slow on the walk from the village inn. Now, it was far too fast, giving Pippa no opportunity to gather herself or straighten her thoughts before trying to comfort the troublesome, sensitive, unique, charming child she had come to cherish.

Sniffles greeted her through the thick wood door, slashing at Pippa's heart. With a shaky breath, she summoned the courage to knock.

"Miss Rebecca? May I come in?"

More sniffles. Though she preferred to give children their space in most situations, knowing they would come to her when they were ready to process their thoughts and feelings together, Pippa recognized this was not one of those times. This was serious, life-changing—for both of them.

She inhaled another shallow breath and opened Miss Rebecca's door. The girl had collapsed in the middle of her bed, curled into a ball with her trembling back facing the door. Miss Rebecca did not acknowledge the governess' presence.

Pippa stepped into the room. Miss Rebecca's sobs pierced her like a hot knife to her very core. She sat on the edge of the girl's bed and settled a tentative hand on her shoulder. Miss Rebecca jerked to shake off Pippa's hand. Pippa retreated, but remained on the bed.

"Miss Rebecca, please allow me to explain," she started, praying with all her might that her own emotion would not crack through. She needed to be strong for Miss Rebecca now more than ever.

"What is there to explain?" the girl hiccuped as another sob racked her body. "You said you would be busy this week spending time with your family. You did not say you would be leaving with them at the end of it."

Pippa drew upon all her years of training and experience, all the fortitude she had been forced to develop through her circumstances, to say what she must say next.

"Darling, nothing is settled just yet," she started slowly. Pippa paused, realizing that she was trying to convince Miss Rebecca as much as herself. "It is…a complicated situation, one that I do not take lightly. I love my mother, you see, just as you love yours. I have missed her very much. There are many things I must take into consideration.

"But you know, Miss Rebecca, that even if the time comes for me to leave Goddard House, I will never truly leave you. You are a strong, resilient young lady. Parting is always sad, but that does not mean our friendship will end—"

"Stop! Just stop!" Miss Rebecca screamed, snapping upright and whipping around to glower at Pippa with fury and agony flaming in her eyes. Pippa reeled back, nearly slipping off the bed. "You are going to abandon me, abandon all of us, just like everyone else! And here I thought you might marry Jasper some day and stay with me forever."

Her last few words trailed off into another gargled cry. They seared Pippa like a brand.

She squeezed her eyes shut as she answered, "I…we…your brother and I never discussed that, Miss Rebecca." The truth of her own statement slammed into Pippa's chest, knocking the wind out of her. They had certainly danced around it, each waiting for...what, Pippa could hardly remember.

It did not matter now. It was too late. They had waited too long.

"But," Pippa continued, her composure fracturing, "you know we can still write to each other as often as we like, and perhaps even visit. Wouldn't that be nice?"

"It will not be the same!" Miss Rebecca hissed, her small hands clenched into fists so tight her knuckles had gone white.

Pippa could not stop herself from looking away, her emotions surging far too close to the surface. If she did not get a grip on herself, she would break down in front of Miss Rebecca. The child did not need to see that.

"I am sorry, Miss Rebecca...."

Pippa's mind betrayed her, flashing memories of Mr. Helsden behind her eyes. She knew Miss Rebecca was right. If she left now, nothing would ever be the same between them. After spending this past year with these loving people, did she really want to become a stranger to them again in favor of a stepfather who had thrown her away and a mother who had allowed it to happen?

It made no sense, yet Pippa could not deny the pull she felt toward Mother. She was her only true family left in this world. Over the years, she had fantasized about this very situation, about Mother making amends and begging Pippa to return. There had never been a man like Mr. Helsden to muddy the waters of her decision. Of course, Pippa's imagination always conveniently left out any mention of Mr. Clark.

If she went back with Mother, she would be going back with him, too—the one who had set her on this winding path of surprising fulfillment that had eventually led her to Mr.

Helsden's doorstep. And possibly one of the greatest heartbreaks of her life.

"Leave," Miss Rebecca demanded, that single word embedded with such loathing that Pippa had never expected from a child her age. It sent a painful chill through her. "Leave!"

"Forgive me, Miss Rebecca," Pippa whispered, shame and confusion tearing through her as she crossed to the door. "I am not going anywhere just yet. Perhaps we can talk again later."

Miss Rebecca did not deign that offer with a response, instead throwing herself back amongst her blankets and pillows. Pippa quit the room, wondering where she might find another family member to come look after her.

Rapid footsteps down the hall caught Pippa's attention, her hand still on the doorknob. She would not have to find anyone after all. Miss Harcourt and Mr. Helsden marched toward her, one looking right at her and the other staring at the floor. Pippa met them in the middle, her gaze on Miss Harcourt.

"I will go in with her," the lady announced quietly, nodding to Pippa with sympathy in her eyes. She hurried toward Miss Rebecca's door and entered without knocking.

Mr. Helsden and Pippa stood alone in the empty hallway, several feet apart. The distance, both physical and emotional, felt so forced and unwanted.

She had grown used to being near him, nearer than a governess should have allowed. She had wanted that, her desire increasing with each passing day until her heart tricked her into thinking it would always be this way, that it had become an integral part of them. Even something she once thought was integral could crumble right before her eyes.

"Mr. Helsden, I am so sorry for causing such a mess of

things," she started, forcing the words out around the painful lump in her throat.

When he did not answer right away, Pippa's eyes drifted up, terrified of what she would see.

The gentleman—the man who had so unexpectedly won her heart—watched Pippa with a misery that matched her own. Yet there was that compassion, ever present. There was something intrinsic that could never be diminished, no matter what the world threw at him. It was the very foundation of his being.

"It is not your fault, Miss Seymour." The slight upswing at the end of her name gave Pippa pause. Emotions warred across his face once again. He looked like he had so much more he wanted to say.

"Did you enjoy your time with your mother?" he asked instead.

"Yes, I did. After that first meeting, we were able to return to how things were between us before Father died, like nothing had changed," Pippa answered honestly.

Keeping things hidden had done them no good so far—though perhaps she might still feel just as torn even if she and Mr. Helsden had ever found the time to make their affections known. It might even feel worse. Someday, Pippa would come to see this as a blessing in disguise, that they never gave voice to their hearts and made what was to come even more painful.

Mr. Helsden gave Pippa a strained smile that did not reach his beautiful eyes. "Good, I am glad to hear it. And I am happy to have done something special for you because— Are you really going to leave?"

The question spilled out in a rush of breath and wrapped itself around Pippa's collapsing heart.

She contemplated in silence for a long moment, allowing her muddled, frantic thoughts to converge into one key sentiment. It came to her lips, though Pippa did not have the strength to look him in the eye as she made clear the deepest truth she had carried all her life.

"I have only ever wanted one happy ending—a loving, caring family. And I have had that dozens of times over through my work when I leave a family feeling more whole than when I arrived. I have wanted for nothing more, until…. Years ago, I left a broken family behind. Now I have a chance to repair it."

Though Pippa did not lift her gaze all the way, she could still see Mr. Helsden's slow, thoughtful nod. "I admire that greatly, Miss Seymour. Not many could do what you do, yet you manage it with such grace and patience. You have been an invaluable part of our family, but…I understand if it is your time to go. What a wonderful opportunity you have been given. None of us would wish to deprive you of it."

Pippa gripped her skirts and dipped her head further. She had once thought herself a strong person, able to withstand all of life's challenges. Perhaps she had finally met one she could not look in the face.

"I need more time to consider it," she muttered.

It was true, no matter how desperately that part of her cried for a new start with her mother, to make up for these five years they had lost. She could not deny that her work with Miss Rebecca was not quite finished. Pippa knew if she left now there was a chance the girl would recover and maintain a portion of the improvements she had made. But that chance was slimmer than Pippa liked to admit.

And there was Mr. Helsden. Sweet, kind, generous, steadfast Mr. Helsden. The man who had given Pippa hope that she could have a permanent family—a love that would never abandon her.

"I know you will make the right decision for yourself and your happiness," Mr. Helsden said, a strange finality in his words, as if he already knew what Pippa would choose. Maybe he did.

There was something undeniable between them, something that connected them as if they were one spirit in two bodies.

Mr. Helsden had nothing further to say, dashing Pippa's hopes that he might finally put everything he felt for her into words—that he might ask her to stay.

Instead, he turned his back to Pippa and slipped into Miss Rebecca's room, leaving the governess alone once more.

CHAPTER 15

The parlor at the inn was devoid of guests save for Pippa and Mother. The lunch placed before her was devoid of flavor. Nothing felt right with this storm cloud casting a shadow over Pippa's every waking moment.

"Dearest, you have hardly eaten your potatoes. Hurry, before they grow cold. You still like potatoes, do you not?" Mother urged as she speared a small seasoned carrot onto her fork.

"Do I?" Pippa mumbled. "Yes, I suppose I do." She did as Mother told her. The thing might as well have turned to dust in her mouth.

"Pippa," Mother started with a heavy sigh. She set her utensils down and looked up from her plate.

"Yes, Mother?"

"I know you must be torn over all this," she continued, those eyes Pippa loved so much brimming with sincerity.

Pippa pressed her lips into a tight line, not quite a smile or a frown. Torn was an understatement. She felt as though she had been broken open, her entire past and all her possible futures laid bare for her to pick apart and try to stitch back together into something merely acceptable.

Mother frowned and reached across the small table, cupping Pippa's cheek in her hand and lifting her face. Their eyes were the same—the same shade of blue with the same beaten, defeated quality.

"I know your work is important to you now, daughter, but…I wish so desperately for you to return with us," Mother continued, her voice cracking.

"You know, you would not necessarily have to give up being a governess either. Perhaps you could rest for a while. You have been working so hard. Surely you have savings you could lean on for a while."

"I do not have much in the way of savings, Mother," Pippa confessed, her worry deepening. "I have some, but not enough to manage my own expenses without relying on Mr. Clark's money. Some governesses never even receive an allowance. I am lucky in that I possess specialized skills that families pay me for, but even still, it is not as much as you think."

Mother's frantic hope only slightly diminished. "In that case, perhaps you could find a local family to hire you on as a permanent governess. No more of this moving all over the country every few months. Wouldn't that be nice, dear Pippa? We could always be near each other."

Pippa nodded numbly. It all sounded lovely. At some point in time, Pippa would have thought it sounded fantastic. But she had gone and made the mistake of falling in love.

Love always complicated things, especially when caught between two divergent loves—love for her mother and love for Mr. Helsden.

Had it not been for Mr. Helsden, the decision would have been easy. Wouldn't it?

That same nagging feeling Pippa had experienced a week

ago when Mr. Helsden had given her her Mother's letter pricked at her again.

She had tried to interact with and talk about Mr. Clark as little as possible during this visit, but knowing what he had done to deceive his way back into Pippa's life…. There was more Mother had not yet told her.

"Mother, has Mr. Clark's financial situation improved at all? The last time you wrote, before Mr. Helsden contacted you, you told me that he was still indebted to someone and would need to sell even more land to pay it back. What became of that?" Pippa inquired, keeping her voice even, without any accusation. Mr. Clark might have no shame when it came to his money—or lack thereof—but Mother certainly did.

"Well, Pippa…."

"Please, Mother, be truthful with me."

The older woman glanced from her daughter to her half-eaten lunch, shame deepening the lines around her eyes and mouth. "Well, yes, things are a bit difficult right now, and we could use your help. But please believe me when I say, Pippa, that I want nothing more than to be in your life again. My precious, precious daughter."

Mother choked on the last word. When she lifted her eyes to Pippa once more, they shone with tears. Pippa's chest caved in on itself. No matter what part Mr. Clark played in all this, no matter the mistakes Mother made in the past, Pippa could feel her sincerity reaching out to her, seeking to make amends.

"I have always, always regretted not fighting harder to keep us together," Mother continued. A few tears cascaded down her sunken cheeks. "And, if it is not too late, I would like to apologize for the misery I have put you through. When life set a challenge before me, I crumbled under the pressure. But you, my dear, you rose above it and became stronger. You found a purpose. I...I only found loss, the loss of both you and your father. And I am more proud of you than I can ever hope to express. Could you ever forgive me, Pippa?"

Tears welled in Pippa's eyes now, too. She laid her hand over Mother's and pressed her face deeper into the touch, inhaling her scent and absorbing the feeling of this comfort she had needed so many times throughout these past several years.

"Of course I forgive you, Mother," Pippa sighed, allowing her emotion to spill out and pool under her mother's palm. "I will admit I was angry and bitter at first...for a long time. But I came to understand why. I know Mr. Clark is not an easy man. If he sets his mind, nothing can dissuade him. Especially if he never had any intention to provide for us both. None of that is your fault."

"So what do you think, darling? Will you come home with us?" Mother asked with a grateful, anticipatory smile.

Pippa did not answer right away. A significant part of her longed to accept, despite everything in her past. Surely, now that she was a grown woman and confident in herself and her abilities, she could stand to deal with being in the vicinity of Mr. Clark. If they needed some help to stay afloat, Pippa had ways to provide it, just as Mother had suggested. It would not be much, but it was something.

Goodness, how she dreamed of having a real relationship with her Mother again, preferably one that consisted of more than a single letter each month. As Miss Rebecca had so painfully pointed out yesterday, writing simply was not the same as sharing lunch together every day, taking walks around the area, talking about everything and nothing without worrying about running out of space on a page or getting lost in the post.

"I love you, Mother," Pippa finally said, forcing a smile.

That was what Pippa had wanted all along—family. And family came first. She could even learn to tolerate her stepfamily.

What she left behind did not matter. It must not matter.

"I love you, too, my wonderful daughter." Mother's expression flooded with expectation, a grin stretching across her face. She knew Pippa's answer.

CHAPTER 16

*J*ust like yesterday, when everything they had built over the past year had started to unravel, Jasper watched the front drive from the drawing room window.

The tiny dot that was Miss Seymour appeared at the end of the gravel path, returning from lunch at the inn with her mother. Even from this distance, he knew. His heart faltered. It had known all along.

Slowly, the woman he loved came closer to Goddard House—the home they had shared for months, the home in which they had fallen in love, the home in which Jasper had dreamed of growing old together.

He had learned so much about Miss Seymour during that time, both consciously through the things she shared with him, and unconsciously through the habits he observed. She walked with her shoulders lowered, head down, gloved hands twisting around each other.

There was no doubt in Jasper's mind that she had made her choice. It was not the one he'd selfishly prayed for.

Jasper placed one hand on the wall beside the window

and rested his forehead against the cool glass, gritting his teeth against the terrible truth—and the part he had played in it. Even now, with a pain he had never known crushing him from the inside out, he still could not remove his eyes from her.

As Miss Seymour greeted the waiting footman, her bonnet angled to keep her face from view, Jasper longed to kick himself. This was his doing. If he had never written to Mrs. Clark, thinking he was being gallant—

No. Jasper pushed himself back from the window and shook his head. No, he would not regret providing this opportunity for Miss Seymour to have a second chance with her family. She had made it so clear, time and time again, how dearly she loved her mother and how sorely she missed her. Now they could live happily together again thanks to Jasper.

He could, however, blame himself for never making his own feelings clear, for always worrying about waiting for the appropriate timing. He had waited too long. The right time he had been looking for had sailed right past him.

Now that Mrs. Clark wanted to reunite permanently with her daughter, perhaps that would not have mattered in the end.

When he heard the front doors open, Jasper rushed from the room and flew downstairs, taking the steps two at a time. Miss Seymour stared at him in shock, frozen as she untied her bonnet ribbon. He landed before her and, completely ignoring his plan to approach her casually without betraying his heartache, snatched her hand and dragged her toward the downstairs sitting room.

What point was there in hiding his pain? The more he realized that the woman he loved was going to leave, the more rooted that pain became until Jasper felt sure it would soon become a permanent feature, as innate as the breathing of his lungs.

Once inside the sitting room, door still ajar, Jasper spun around to face Miss Seymour. He took a moment to appreciate her beauty, her elegance, her heart that deserved to finally have the happiness she always wanted. He only wished, if this was to be the last time he ever saw her, that it could have been with joy in her eyes instead of sorrow.

"You know," she started, her whisper deafening.

"I think so," Jasper nodded, his hands flexing. He had to keep them busy lest he lunge forward and grasp for her, unable to let go.

Miss Seymour dropped her gaze to the ornate rug. "I plan to return home with Mother and Mr. Clark," she said. "But not immediately. I wish to remain for another two weeks so I can wrap up my duties with Miss Rebecca and help her start the transition to a new governess. I am sure you will need some time to post notices in the papers as well."

"Yes, yes," Jasper nodded again, ice freezing his limbs. His hands loosened and rested limp at his sides. "Yes, that does sound like a good plan."

He looked away. That necessary lie killed the last flicker of hope fighting against the darkest corner of his heart.

So this would not be his last glimpse of Miss Seymour. He must endure another two weeks in her presence, recalling all the wonderful times they had spent together in this very house and banishing any fantasies of the future he had painted with increasing vibrancy over this past year. If these last few days had been torture, how could he survive the next two weeks?

"Miss Seymour…."

Her name slipped past his lips so effortlessly that he could not determine when he had decided to actually speak. Her Christian name—Pippa, lovely Pippa—balanced on the back of his tongue, tempting him to speak it aloud just this once like he had dreamed of doing since receiving Mrs. Clark's response.

How many times had Jasper imagined calling her that after all this was over when he declared himself to her? Saying it now would be a mistake. He swallowed the desire and locked it away in that box that would contain all the rest of his hopes and dreams involving the governess.

"Yes, Mr. Helsden?"

Jasper started. Without thinking, he looked up at Miss Seymour again. Her gaze was both curious and remorseful. Had she ever imagined saying his Christian name? Jasper had. His mind had recreated all the lilts and melodies of her voice into a new shape—Jasper. He would never hear that either.

"I hope you know, Miss Seymour, that I will miss you terribly," he continued, not bothering to hide the emotion tugging at his words. "We all will. We will never forget your presence in our lives. I also hope that we might keep in touch. We would be very happy to know that you are doing well wherever your future takes you. And of course you will receive an excellent reference."

Miss Seymour gave a smile that contained too many emotions for Jasper to interpret. It would have been futile to try.

"I thank you from the bottom of my heart, Mr. Helsden," she whispered, each word another punch to his gut. "You and your family have shown me such kindness. I will never forget you either."

Not knowing what else to say, Jasper offered a sharp nod of farewell and marched toward the door. He felt an almost physical sensation of his heart tearing from his body with each step he took away from Miss Seymour. It would not leave her so easily, even if the rest of Jasper tried to.

One final selfish thought roared to the front of his mind when he reached the door, his palm against the smooth wood. He had one last thing to say. After this, he would begin the long, unbearably slow process of trying to let go.

Jasper turned his head, not quite looking over his shoulder. Miss Seymour was nothing more than a dark shape in his peripheral vision.

"Are you really, truly sure about this?"

Time stood still as he waited for Miss Seymour's whispered "Yes."

As soon as the word escaped her, the word Jasper had been expecting, he pushed the door open and left her behind.

There was nothing further he could do or say. Miss Seymour had made her decision, and an admirable one at that. Not many would have forgiven a mother and stepfather who had acted as Mr. and Mrs. Clark had done.

That was just Miss Seymour. If anyone had the heart to welcome them back into their life, it was her.

Jasper stormed through Goddard House to his bedroom, ignoring inquiries from servants and a concerned call from Amelia. All sound was muffled under the splintering of his heart.

Despite the pain that made him fall to his bed with a ragged gasp, Jasper could hardly blame Miss Seymour for any of it. It would have been far easier to do just that, to transform her into a villain in his mind.

Jasper would not. He could not. This heartbreak was all his own. He must bear the responsibility for it.

CHAPTER 17

*T*ime could be a blessing or a curse. Today, it was a curse. Or perhaps love was the curse. Pippa could not think straight enough to assign proper blame.

They both marched on into the next day, ignorant of the grief Pippa suffered as she faced the closing of this chapter of her life. Regardless of how she felt, she still had responsibilities.

Said responsibility currently sulked in the chair beside her and had been ignoring her all morning. Miss Rebecca radiated rage and loathing, her keen eyes burning holes into the mathematics lesson book. All the problems Pippa had written out weeks ago remained unsolved. Her charge had refused to say a single word to her, refused to pick up a pencil, refused to acknowledge her existence in any way. How Lady Helsden had managed to force Miss Rebecca into the schoolroom that morning, Pippa did not know.

"Miss Rebecca, I know you are upset, and rightfully so, but please try at least one problem," Pippa begged for the umpteenth time. "Just one sum and I will release you from lessons for the rest of the day."

THE NECESSARY LESSON

The amazingly stubborn girl did not even flinch when a knock echoed through the schoolroom door. Pippa swallowed, her throat dry. Could it be Mr. Helsden? She hadn't explicitly told him that she would not require his assistance during her final two weeks. It had seemed quite obvious yesterday that neither of them would want that when she told him the news.

"Come in," she called.

"Miss Seymour," the maid said with a curtsey. "You have a visitor in the drawing room."

Pippa nodded. "Thank you, Anne. Would you fetch Mr. Helsden and have him look after Miss Rebecca until I return?"

The maid accepted her mission and hurried away down the hall. As much as Pippa did not want to be there when Mr. Helsden arrived, she also did not want to leave Miss Rebecca alone. Even if the girl refused to speak to her or anyone else, Pippa knew she needed someone by her side.

Her cowardice won out when she heard Mr. Helsden's familiar footsteps down the hall. Pippa fled in the opposite direction, knowing he would be with his sister in just a few seconds. She kept her eyes to the ground, terrified that he would somehow materialize before her and force her to look at the pain she had caused.

"Mother," Pippa said as a footman opened the drawing room door. Once again, she froze at the sight of her stepfather, her eyes narrowing. "Mr. Clark…. May I help you? If you wish to discuss travel arrangements, could I visit you at the inn for dinner? I have my duties—"

"Blast your duties," Mr. Clark snarled, a hint of laughter in his rumbling voice.

Pippa hated herself for shrinking at the uncaring blackness in his eyes. Mother shrank, too, looking everywhere but

Pippa. Her fingers worried at the skirts of her plain dress, the same one she had worn for their lunch yesterday.

"Pardon?" She managed to force out that single word, praying for strength to endure whatever nonsense the man had planned.

"Mrs. Clark told me you want two more weeks here. I do not care to wait two weeks. I have made arrangements for us to leave tomorrow, so you had better start packing."

As if he had not just pulled the rug out from under Pippa once again, Mr. Clark examined his fingernails and picked at one, flicking off whatever dirt or grime he had scraped away. Apparently, Pippa's feelings were worth even less than the gunk that grew under his nails.

Heart breaking anew, Pippa looked from Mr. Clark to her mother, desperate for any help. Mother continued to stare at the floor, half hidden by her husband.

Pippa shook her head in disbelief. This could not be happening. She thought she would have more time to say her goodbyes and—if she was lucky—mend things between herself and Mr. Helsden so when she did leave, they could leave as friends.

That had been Pippa's problem from the start, from the moment she met Mr. Helsden. Time. She had thought she would have more time—time to uncover his feelings, to uncover her own, to decide if she could allow herself a future with him, to summon the courage to lay her heart naked before him.

Once again, Pippa's time had been stolen.

Could she salvage it just this once, just long enough to leave on her own terms?

"I cannot say I understand your haste, but you need not wait for me. If you wish to leave tomorrow, then do so. I will follow after I have finished my time with the Helsden family."

Mr. Clark rolled his eyes and fixed Pippa with a bored stare. "I said I want to go tomorrow—all of us. No dilly-dallying and waiting around for you to change your mind."

"I will not, I swear—"

"Then you and your dear mother can return to once monthly letters, hm?" The man crossed his arms over his wide chest, a foul smile dancing on his lips. "Hope you haven't given these folks your notice. They might not want you back once they see how easily you would leave them in the lurch. But, who knows, maybe they will be generous and leave you with a decent reference."

"If I do not come with you tomorrow, then I cannot come at all?" Pippa's voice came out as a pitiful squeak, horrified tears swarming her eyes.

They blurred her stepfather into an imposing, cruel monster. Her mother was merely a fleck somewhere in the distance. Despite what Mother had said at lunch yesterday, there was no fight left in the woman. She said she regretted not fighting for Pippa in the past, yet she could not fight for her now either.

But Pippa was a woman grown now. She must either fight for herself or....

"Yes, we can leave tomorrow."

Pippa accepted defeat.

What difference would two weeks make, really, when her future with her mother hung in the balance?

"Good," Mr. Clark announced, sweeping past Pippa back out into the hallway. Mother trailed after him, silent, without a glance at her daughter.

Knees buckling, mind reeling, Pippa slowly managed to force herself back to the schoolroom. Mr. Helsden had left the door open. When Pippa appeared in the doorway, only he looked up. Miss Rebecca kept her head turned away.

"I am very sorry to deliver such sudden news, but I am

leaving tomorrow. Since I do not have much time, I must make haste and gather my belongings," she said in a lifeless monotone, as if she had rehearsed the speech in her mind so many times it became second nature. Nothing about this was natural, but Pippa had no energy to project a liveliness or normalcy she did not feel.

She did not wait to see their reactions. Pippa was already halfway out the door when the last words left her parched lips. Eyes glued to the staircase at the end of the hallway, Pippa took a few feeble steps.

A burning hand grasped her wrist, spinning her back around. Pippa's heart shot to her throat, eyes wide. She would know the feel of that hand anywhere, from the shape to the precise pressure of the grip to the warmth.

"Pi— Miss Seymour, what on Earth is happening?" Mr. Helsden demanded. Even his demands were tender, though the fire in his eyes was fierce, aching.

Had he just been about to say her name? Pippa ignored that. It did not matter. Of course she wanted to hear her name on his lips. Pippa knew by now that life was not inclined to ever give her precisely what she wanted. There would always be some catch.

"Mother and Mr. Clark were just here to see me," she explained. "Mr. Clark wishes to leave for Hampshire tomorrow and I am to come with them. I tried to convince him to let me stay for the rest of the two weeks as I promised, but he said if I did that I would not be returning to Hampshire at all."

"Miss Seymour," he whispered, looking just as shocked as Pippa felt. "You do not need to go through with this," he urged, both hands claiming hers and lifting them to chest height, the space between them closing with his fluid movement. "We can find a way to convince him otherwise, I am sure of it."

"No. I am sorry, Mr. Helsden." Pippa shook her head with a wry smile. "This is how Mr. Clark has always been. He gets his way, and the rest of us must play along. This is how it must be. I cannot…." she inhaled, fresh tears stinging her eyes. "I cannot miss this opportunity to be with my mother again."

Using all the strength she could muster, Pippa pulled her hands away from Mr. Helsden. He opened his mouth to say something. Pippa ignored him. She rushed down the hall and up the stairs, lifting her skirts to keep from tripping.

The momentum whirled Pippa around her room like a storm, not allowing her to stop for one second to think or reconsider. She snatched up her luggage and packed away everything she owned into those three cases.

Only one thought rang in the back of her mind the entire time, punctuating every tedious motion of taking one dress from the armoire, folding it, and tucking it in her suitcase.

Why was this happening to her again? Why must she be torn from something and someone she loved so dearly?

At least this time she had somewhere familiar to land. She had Mother. Last time, she had had no one to turn to, no one to wipe her scared tears.

Pippa slammed the first case shut and flipped the clasps. If she knew she had another opportunity to be with Mother, why did she already feel so devastatingly lonely?

CHAPTER 18

The drawing room window had become a fast friend of Jasper's. No, friend was not the right term. One should not feel so distraught when meeting a friend. But it did allow him to privately wallow as footmen loaded a carriage with Miss Seymour's belongings.

He should have confessed earlier. Weeks ago. Months ago. If he had, maybe she would have chosen to stay. Or maybe she still would have decided that her love for her mother must come first. Jasper would not have stopped her then either.

Their brief, terribly awkward, and terribly painful goodbyes echoed in his mind as he watched Miss Seymour say something to his parents who had gone out to see her off. It would haunt him, he knew. He had barely managed a full sentence on the very last time he would ever speak with the woman who owned his heart, mind, and soul.

If he had said any more than that, Jasper was sure he would have fallen to his knees before her, begging her to stay and making her position needlessly difficult. He could never,

THE NECESSARY LESSON

ever forgive himself if she chose to stay out of guilt rather than the truest desire of her heart.

Down below, everyone's heads snapped around to the door. Jasper could not hear what they said or who they addressed. He did not need to. A second later, Rebecca burst into view, running at full speed toward Miss Seymour.

He choked out a despondent chuckle. Rebecca had been so furious at the prospect of Miss Seymour leaving. He had been almost afraid of it, certain that no other twelve-year-old to ever exist had expressed such wild rage.

Despite all that, Jasper had no doubt that when the time finally came, Rebecca would not let her governess go without a proper goodbye. She threw her arms around Miss Seymour in what looked like a crushing hug even from here, nearly knocking the lady back.

Jasper so wished that could have been him. Only he would not have the grace to let her go as Rebecca now did, swiping at her eyes with the back of her hand. Mama and Papa came forward and each wrapped an arm around their daughter's shoulders.

With one final curtsy, Miss Seymour stepped up into the carriage, her skirts disappearing just as the footman closed the door.

That was it. That was Jasper's last view of her. And on the very same day as last year, when he had received her response that she would come to Goddard House as Rebecca's governess.

The timing of these past few weeks left a bitter taste in Jasper's mouth. What had once seemed miraculous now felt like an insulting slap across the face.

The driver climbed atop the box and tapped the reins. The horses lumbered around the circular drive, then broke into a light trot down the straight path, carrying Miss Seymour out of their lives.

They would likely have to start over again with a new governess. Rebecca's behavior would surely regress if her temper these past three days was any gauge.

Jasper's heart would have to start over, too. That seemed an even more impossible challenge than Rebecca.

Now that he had known love with a woman as perfect as Miss Seymour, how could anything else compare? Jasper felt his future slipping out of his grasp as Miss Seymour's carriage grew smaller and smaller.

"Here he is," Colette called, the proximity of her voice startling Jasper. He turned from the window. There was nothing for him to see out there any longer.

His cousin waited just inside the door, regret and empathy writ large in her eyes as she offered a glum smile to Jasper. She would miss Miss Seymour, too. They all would. At least Jasper was not alone in that.

A moment later, Mama and Papa entered the drawing room, looking just as melancholy as Colette. "Take Rebecca to her room, please. Amelia is already waiting there," Mama whispered to her niece. Colette nodded, sent Jasper another sympathetic glance, and hurried away.

Mama and Papa slowly approached Jasper, as if he were some wounded animal liable to bolt. He hated that. He hated that they had watched him fall in love, had cheered him on and supported him as much as possible, and watched him lose it.

"I noticed your farewells with Miss Seymour were a bit… lukewarm, son," Mama started. She never was one to mince words or dance around the truth. Jasper envied that trait. If only he could have inherited that.

"Yes," Jasper mumbled, not sure why she brought it up.

Her bright eyes flashed with heartache for her child. "That, to me, only further confirms what we already knew. You are indeed very in love with Miss Seymour."

Jasper stared down at the tips of his shoes. "How so?"

"Because, my boy, when you love someone so much, you can hardly force yourself to endure the agony of saying goodbye," Papa added. He slipped his arm around his wife's waist and held her close. Jasper tried not to lament for the hundredth time just that morning that he would likely never experience the same enduring love his parents shared.

"What happened, Jasper? Really?" Mama prodded. They had come close enough now that she could take her son's hand in hers and swing it back and forth gently.

Jasper let out a pained laugh. "Where to begin? I suppose we should start with me being a complete and utter fool."

To his surprise, Jasper found that telling the tale of how he fell for the governess, how he had planned this surprise as a stepping stone to declaring himself, and how fate had stolen the opportunity from his hands with the arrival of Mr. and Mrs. Clark did not hurt as badly as he thought it would. It certainly stung, yet it also solidified for him just how significant of a role he had played in all this.

His inaction, his hesitation had cost him the one thing he wanted more than anything in this world. Now he would have to endure that reality and pray that wherever she was, Miss Seymour was happier.

"Oh, my poor dear," Mama whispered, pulling away from Papa to wrap her arms around her oldest child in a rare display of physical affection. Mama showed her love in many ways, from genuine compliments to generous gifts, but hugs were not one of them. Though it was meant to comfort, it only drove home once again just how badly Jasper had made a mess of things.

"Do not fret over me, Mama," Jasper mumbled, resting his cheek against her hair. "After all, I should consider myself blessed to have known love, even if it was not meant to be. I am sure I will feel that truth…someday."

Mama pulled away from him, breaking their comfortable embrace. She glared up at Jasper, her usual stubbornness returning in full force. "Is that all?"

"Is what all?" Jasper groaned. He did not have any strength left to argue his case to his secretly romantic mother.

"She is the love of your life and you are simply going to let her leave? And you will spend the rest of your days in misery, is that it?"

Jasper bit down hard on his bottom lip and turned away. He already felt bad enough without seeing the disappointment in his parents' eyes.

"If this is what she wants, then yes. How can I be so selfish as to ask her to stay with me when she has missed her mother for so long?"

Mama and Papa regarded each other, silently debating what to say next. Jasper did not give them the opportunity.

"Isn't that what I always say?" he continued. "Family is everything. Surely you of all people can understand that. Now she is reunited with hers, and we should be happy for her."

Papa took a step closer, his perceptive gaze shooting right to Jasper's aching heart. "But you know, Jasper, that you are her family now."

His words froze Jasper to his spot. How could such a thing be possible? They were not married. He had not even proposed. They had never so much as exchanged those three crucial words. How could they be a family?

As if reading his son's mind, the baronet continued. "When you love each other, that makes you family. Even if you never said so aloud. Love, more than blood or lineage or legalities, is what makes a family."

"But she has her mother now, Papa. It would be too cruel of me to make her choose between us."

Papa took another step and rested his hand, so careful and gentle for its size, on Jasper's shoulder. "Son, I understand your reasoning, and it is very noble. But sometimes when it comes to love, you must bare your heart to the one who holds it and worry about all the rest later."

Jasper's brows slowly lifted, his mouth falling open. "Are you telling me to…act impulsively?"

He could hardly believe the words as they left his mouth. If anyone knew what to do in this situation, however, it would be his patient, thoughtful, cautious papa. Long before Jasper was born, Papa had waited and waited to share his feelings with Mama. He, too, had almost missed his chance.

"Yes I am," the older man chuckled, fine lines crinkling at the edges of his eyes.

"Your father is right," Mama added, pride shining in her eyes as she gazed at the man she had loved almost all her life, though she had not realized it for a very long time. At least they had both arrived on the same page at some point and had made their dreams come true.

Could Jasper really do the same?

"Now please, darling, for my sanity's sake, go make Miss Seymour an official part of our family," Mama added, her usual sharp edge softened by adoration for her son and hope for his future.

Jasper frowned. "For your sanity's sake? Not for my heart's sake?"

"Well, yes, that as well," Mama laughed. "But goodness, I cannot deny that Miss Seymour is just the kind of daughter-in-law every mother prays for."

Jasper laughed as well, already feeling ten times lighter. His road was still paved with uncertainty. At least he had his parents' strength and wisdom to draw on when he fought for the woman who had made his life more whole than he had ever thought possible.

"Hurry now," Mama said, sweeping her hands toward Jasper to shoo him. "We already had a horse brought round the front in case you needed it for a romantic declaration."

This time Jasper's laugh filled the drawing room. He grabbed both parents and squeezed them tight. "Goodness, my genius mama, you truly do think of everything."

"Get going, son, before your mother steals that horse and proposes to Miss Seymour herself," Papa whispered into Jasper's ear.

Planting a swift kiss on each of their cheeks, Jasper rushed from the room on dizzying wings of hope. He had not the faintest clue what to say when he caught Miss Seymour's carriage. He could only pray that the right words would come to him at the right time—for once.

"Jasper, wait!"

He skidded to halt at the top of the stairs and whirled around. "Colette, I am sorry but I really must make all haste. And Rebecca—"

"I know, I know," the young lady hurried, jogging the rest of the way to Jasper. "Amelia is still with her. And I know you must hurry. But I simply wanted to say good luck." She smiled, Jasper's sudden optimism mirrored in his cousin's face.

"I have faith in you. And in Miss Seymour. I have spent the last year watching the two of you fall in love, after all. You are meant to be together, and I fully expect to see the two of you walking through those doors hand in hand in a few minutes."

Heart brimming with all the courage he gained from his loved ones, Jasper surprised them both by grasping Colette's face in his hands and planting an enthusiastic kiss on her forehead.

"Thank you so very much, my favorite cousin," he chuckled breathlessly.

CHAPTER 19

*G*oddard House shrank behind Jasper as he catapulted down the gravel drive. His horse surged forward with unimaginable power, every muscle responding to Jasper's reins and heels. After just a few minutes of hard riding, the back of Miss Seymour's carriage came into view, nearly at the end of the lane that would branch in one direction toward Attwood Manor and in the other toward the village where her parents waited.

Spurred by the mere sight of it, Jasper urged his horse to push a little faster until he was finally close enough to see her silhouette shifting through the narrow back window.

"Stop! Stop!" he shouted, surprised that his mild voice could ever be that loud. It worked. Alarmed, the driver pulled his horses to a stop. Jasper did the same.

"What is the meaning of this?" the man demanded.

Jasper ignored him and leaped from his horse, running the rest of the distance to the carriage. "Please mind him for a few minutes," he demanded as he handed his horse's reins to the driver. "Up the road a ways, if you would," he added quickly. The puzzled man did as he was bid and led the creature away from the carriage, affording them some privacy.

Heart hammering and lungs clawing for air, Jasper pounded his fist on the carriage door.

"Miss Seymour! Please, I must speak with you!"

"Heavens," the governess gasped as she threw open the door. She gaped at Jasper, by far the least ladylike expression he had ever seen on her. It only made Jasper love her all the more.

"Pippa," he exhaled, relishing the way her sweet name felt as it passed through his lips. He extended a hand to her.

When she took it, Jasper's heart soared to the clear blue heavens.

"Mr. Helsden, what is the meaning of this?" she asked when she emerged from the carriage, surprised and curious. Then her eyes widened. "Did you just call me…?

"Pippa," Jasper repeated. "Please stay. Here, at Goddard House. With me."

"Jasper," she whispered.

His heart, already lost among the clouds, exploded in a burst of light and warmth. His name wrapped so tenderly in her beautiful voice. There was nothing on this earth that could compare—except….

"I love you, Pippa. I love you to the depths of my heart and beyond. I am sure that I will fall deeper in love with you every single day, whether you are by my side or at the opposite end of the world."

He reached forward and took Pippa's other hand. Lifting them both, he touched his lips to her knuckles and wished that gloves had never been invented.

"And I know," he continued, drawing a long breath, "I know that you have your mother to consider. But I hope you will also consider that we could be a family, too. You and me.

And the rest of my family, for they love you nearly as much as I do."

Pippa giggled through her tears, her perfect mouth trembling.

"But you and me, Pippa. I know I said family is everything, and I stand by that—especially the family we will create together. That is what I want, so, so desperately. I have spent far too much time hiding from that for fear of being selfish. Over this past year, you have taught me a crucial, necessary lesson—that one must not be afraid to seize love lest it slip away forever. Now, before I lose my chance again, I wish to selfishly ask you again to stay here with me.

"You will always be cared for no matter what happens. You will always have a place in my home, in my arms. And I have no doubt that we will still find a way to continue changing lives. I know how important your work is, and I admire it so very much. I am not sure how yet, but I am sure there must be some way—"

"Jasper."

He fell silent, realizing for the first time that Pippa was smiling at him in that bemused way he so adored.

"You are rambling again," she chuckled.

Heat shot up Jasper's spine right to the tips of his ears. His fingers fidgeted with hers. "Forgive me. I seem to do that when I am nervous."

She slipped one hand out from under his and brought it to his face, pressing her palm to his cheek, then sliding her fingers into his hair, and finally coming to rest along the back of his neck.

"Do not apologize," Pippa whispered. "I love that. I love you, Jasper."

"You do?" he mumbled, dumbfounded. Even her fingers playing with the tendrils of hair at the nape of his neck still could not quite make him believe it.

"Did you not think so? I was afraid it was painfully obvious."

"Well, I suspected. I hoped. But I did not want to assume, of course. Did you suspect that I love you?"

Pippa nodded, her heartfelt smile turning melancholy.

"Then why did you want to leave?" The words barely rose above a whisper. He knew Pippa would hear. They were so connected in ways he had never thought possible with another person. If his heart asked the question, she would hear it.

"It is interesting that you should mention that," she mumbled, pulling her gaze away from Jasper. "I have been wondering that myself since I stepped foot inside this carriage. Second guessing myself. I even considered turning around more than once."

"You did?"

Pippa nodded again. "The further I got, the worse I felt. In truth, I have been miserable since the moment Mother asked me to return home—to Hampshire—with her. If I really was so happy to be with her again, why did I feel so wretched when it came time to leave?

"I realized two things on this short ride," she said with a light laugh. "First, I realized that I love you too much to ever truly be happy anywhere but by your side."

She paused and leaned forward, her forehead resting against Jasper's lips.

"Second?" he asked, his mind performing somersaults at the feel of her so near.

"Second, I realized that, as much as I love my mother and want her to be in my life...it is time that I put myself first. I am not unsympathetic to her situation, and perhaps what happened to me was inevitable, but it is time I moved past that and found happiness for myself. That is the lesson you taught me."

Touched, Jasper slid his arms around Pippa and held her close against his chest. He hoped she could feel the rhythm of his heart beating, chanting her name with every pulse.

Pippa. Pippa was his now and forevermore. Jasper knew it to the core of his bones.

"I think you are right about that, my love," he whispered into her stunning red hair. He hoped their children would look just like her, with a hint of him. But mostly her.

"I think so, too. But as much as I wish to return home with you this very moment and start our new life together...."

"Of course. We must tell Mr. and Mrs. Clark," Jasper agreed. "But first, will you allow me to fulfill another dream of mine?"

Pippa tilted her head up to gaze at Jasper with anticipation, desire. Her tongue flicked across her lips, waiting for him. "If it is the same dream as mine, then yes, please do."

And a good thing, too. Jasper was not sure he could have waited a second longer.

One arm around her waist, the other hand cradling the back of her head, Jasper tipped Pippa back and joined his mouth to hers, something he should have done months ago.

Yet, even as they shared this long-awaited first kiss, their hands grasping at each other and their hearts drumming in perfect synchronization, Jasper could not really regret anything that had happened—even the pain of the past several days.

It had all led them here. The heavens smiled upon them, answering all their prayers and more yet to come.

Her taste, her scent, her body pressed to his set Jasper aflame. This exceeded all his expectations of what love and kisses could feel like to an unfathomable degree. And he would never, ever tire of it.

They did, however, have to eventually pull apart for air.

They did not let go, remaining content in each other's arms for a long moment of silent staring. It felt nothing short of miraculous.

"Are you ready?" Jasper asked, remembering the last time he had asked Pippa that question—on the day her mother and stepfather had arrived and sent them hurtling toward a great despair that had transformed into their greatest joy.

"Yes," Pippa answered. He could see her nerves just under the surface. Deeper, he could see her remarkable strength.

"I will be by your side the entire time," he reminded, just as he had last time.

"I love you, Jasper."

"I love you, Pippa."

"Let us put the past behind us and hurry home."

CHAPTER 20

When Pippa and Jasper descended from the carriage, the same one that had been about to take her away forever, he paused and pointed up. Pippa followed his finger to the large window at the front of the house that belonged to the drawing room. There, several faces crowded the panes, wherever they could find a space.

"I think they are excited to welcome you home," Jasper whispered into her ear, his lips so soft against that sensitive skin, without a care that almost his entire family was currently spying on them.

Pippa giggled. She did not care either. They would be her family soon, too. In many ways, they already were. She would never be ashamed to show just how much she loved Jasper.

"Then let us give them something to really be excited about." Lifting up a little on the tips of her toes, Pippa placed a gentle kiss on her love's cheek.

He grinned at her, eyes brimming with adoration. Pippa had seen it there so many times in the past, though she had sometimes been oblivious and sometimes in denial. Never again.

"Let us see their reaction," he suggested, tilting his head back to peer up at the window.

"They disappeared," Pippa gasped. "That was quite quick."

Expression full of pure bliss, Jasper slipped his hand into Pippa's—a perfect fit. "Come, let us not keep them waiting."

After a quick glance over his shoulder, Jasper led them up the front steps of Goddard House and to the next floor. The drawing room door was already ajar. When he pushed it open with his free hand, cheers and claps erupted all around them.

Pippa laughed, a full, real laugh, without bothering to politely hide it behind her hand. Her joy simply could not be contained. She let it spill forth over and over again as Jasper proudly pulled her against his side and they accepted congratulations and many warm hugs from the wonderful Helsden family and cousin Colette.

"I knew you could do it," the young lady said with a teary grin. She grasped one of their hands in each of hers. "I knew from the first moment I saw you together that you were meant to find each other and keep each other."

"And I have you to thank for much of this, dear Colette," Jasper said, his voice thick with gratitude. "You often seemed to know what I needed better than I did—and you kept Amelia from badgering me into insanity."

Colette chuckled and shook her head. "I am afraid you have just made that task much harder for me. With wedding excitement in the air, she will be insatiable."

"Look at you two," Lady Helsden sniffled, a hand pressed over her mouth. "You are simply perfect." Sir Arthur stood with his arm around her shoulder in silent wonder and relief.

Pippa could not help blushing at her future mother-in-law's emotional display. She had never seen the calm and collected lady so overcome.

It certainly eased her anxieties about integrating herself into the family—properly this time. Jasper had revealed to her in the carriage that Lady Helsden might very well have proposed on his behalf if he failed to muster up the courage. She wanted Pippa in their family so badly.

When the merriment died down, Jasper leaned toward Pippa's ear again. "I am so in love with your laugh. Please allow me to hear it every day."

"Only if you allow me to hear yours every day," she whispered back.

"Oh, Jasper, Miss Seymour, you must tell me all about how it happened," Amelia begged, clasping her hands over her heart as if they were romance novel characters come to life. "The grand declaration, the proposal, everything. I must have every detail."

"Ah, about that," Jasper chuckled.

"The details are forthcoming," Pippa added quickly when she saw disappointment cross her new sister's face. "There is still one more person we would like to speak to first. And please, everyone, I would be honored if you would call me Pippa from now on."

"And…." Jasper continued, looking over his shoulder again. Pippa's eyes effortlessly followed his face. Even knowing they would have a lifetime to enjoy each other's presence, she still could not get enough of him. "Pippa," he whispered, breaking her loving reverie.

Pippa glanced behind them as well, suddenly realizing that no one else in the drawing had mentioned the surprising presence of another…because she was not there. Jasper nodded toward the door.

As much as she never wanted to leave her sweetheart's

side again, Pippa knew she must. There was one other important announcement—or rather, request—to make.

Just as she suspected, Mother lingered in the hall, hidden by the partially closed door. She gazed down at the floor, her mouth scrunched to one side and brows upturned with worry.

"Mother, come into the drawing room with us," Pippa coaxed, holding out a hand to the poor woman. The years of living under Mr. Clark's tyranny had done her nerves no favors.

Mother glanced from Pippa's hand to her face, full of fear and uncertainty.

"Everything will be just fine, I promise," Pippa continued. "No matter what happens, we will find a solution."

Finally, after another long moment, Mother took Pippa's hand. "You do not have to do this, you know," Mother muttered, not quite looking her daughter in the eye. "I hardly deserve it. And what if…what if they do not like me after everything that has passed? And what if you prefer your new family to me?"

"Oh, my darling mother," Pippa sighed, wrapping her arms around Mother in a tight hug that she hoped would convey all her feelings. Certain words still needed to be said, however. "They understand your situation. As do I. And I want more time to heal our wounds and start anew. For that, you must stay by my side. Whatever happens, you will always be my mother. My love for them will never diminish my love for you. So, let us go do what we must, shall we? Together."

Her head nuzzled against Pippa's neck, Mother nodded. When she pulled away, Pippa's heart leapt to see a flicker of hope and that flame of her old brightness fighting against the shadow she had been living with for so long.

Hand in hand, Pippa and her mother rejoined the rest of

the family in the drawing room. All heads turned to them, curious. Jasper's did as well, his handsome face full of love and acceptance for both women.

He extended a hand toward them, a peace offering and promise of the future they could all build together. Pippa took it, her groom on one side and Mother on the other. Jasper looked out at his family, brave and determined.

"I am sure you all remember Mrs. Clark, Pippa's mother," Jasper started.

"After Pippa and I agreed that she would remain here and become my wife one day very soon," he paused, sending a radiantly happy glance her way, "we went to the village to discuss the change in plans with Mr. and Mrs. Clark. After a…heated talk and no small amount of convincing, Mr. Clark has agreed that it would be better for his wallet if his wife were to remain with us—with Pippa."

"I-If you will allow it, of course," Mother added, stumbling over her hasty words.

Pippa could feel her trembling. Her heart ached with sympathy for the woman. She had so rarely had any opportunity to exercise her voice since Father's death. "I do not wish to impose upon your hospitality, as I have already done. So I would be happy to seek employment in the village, or even in this house if you require it. I have lost too many years with my beloved daughter, and I would like to stay as near her as possible now that I have been set free…in a sense."

Lady Helsden stared at Mother, considering. Yet Pippa did not see any anger or distaste in her expression, only thoughtful compassion. At times like this, she looked very much like her oldest son, even if they were different in every other regard.

Mother flinched when Lady Helsden strode forward and stood before them. She tried to hide herself behind Pippa, eyes desperately searching the floor, as the other woman took her free hand and held it up in both of hers.

"Mrs. Clark—or, if I may—Hester, it would be our pleasure to welcome you into our household alongside your brilliant daughter," Lady Helsden announced, loud and proud for everyone in the room. "We shall leave the past in the past and look forward to happy, comfortable days."

"I quite agree. We are a household that is always happy to welcome new members," added Sir Arthur, stepping up beside his wife with that generous smile he had passed to his son, that Pippa prayed would pass to another generation.

Everything in Pippa burst with euphoria, the unexpected joys of the day surpassing anything she could have ever imagined. Of course, she and Jasper had been sure that Lady Helsden and Sir Arthur would not deny their request, but a little twinge of fear in the back of Pippa's mind had kept her from being completely positive.

"Do you truly mean that?" Mother whimpered, her face distorting with the effort to hold back her tears.

Lady Helsden smiled and squeezed Mother's hand. "Of course we do, my friend."

"How absolutely wonderful!" Pippa cried, releasing Jasper to snatch Mother into another breathtaking hug. She held on tight, rocking them side to side. What she had done to deserve this incredible happiness, Pippa did not know. She accepted it with an endless cascade of thankful prayers deep in her heart.

"Come, Hester, why don't you have a seat? We can chat over wedding plans for these two over some tea," Lady Helsden suggested, offering her elbow to Mother.

With a grateful smile that still looked a little hesitant, Mother accepted and allowed the other woman to lead her deeper into the drawing room.

"There is someone else who will be thrilled to hear your news, don't you think?" Sir Arthur reminded gently.

Not that Pippa or Jasper could have possibly forgotten. There was simply so much to do and say and sort out. They wanted this particular moment to be slow and free from distraction.

After throwing out their temporary farewells, the couple rushed to the schoolroom. Pippa was glad that Miss Rebecca —no, her sister, Rebecca—had not been present in the drawing room. She wanted to earn her blessing privately.

"What are you doing in here all by yourself, silly?" Jasper asked as he eased open the door, keeping Pippa hidden just behind it.

"Why are you here?" Rebecca grumbled. Though hidden from view, Pippa could perfectly imagine the girl's petulant expression.

"I would not have guessed you would choose to be in the schoolroom when you had no lessons," Jasper continued, sidestepping her question.

Fabric rustled as Rebecca shifted in her seat. "Well, I couldn't think of anything else to do. I am used to coming here every day. Besides, everyone else was in the drawing room and I wanted to be alone."

A smile burst across Pippa's face, so wide her cheeks hurt. Rebecca did not hate her after all. She could hear it in the melancholy undertone in the girl's words. Though her former charge had come out at the last second to give Pippa a goodbye hug, she had feared that the girl would understandably vilify Pippa once she was out of Goddard House for good. Luckily, Rebecca would not have that opportunity.

"Do you still wish to be alone?" Pippa asked, too impatient to let Jasper step aside. She lifted his arm and slipped under it through the narrow doorway. The air in her lungs stilled. This moment felt far more nerve wracking and significant than their announcement to the drawing room.

Rebecca's mouth dropped open so quickly Pippa could not help laughing out loud again. The girl's head snapped back and forth between her former governess and her brother, a dozen questions popping up behind her round eyes.

"Miss Seymour…."

"You may call me Pippa now."

She took a few slow steps into the schoolroom, hoping not to distress the sensitive child—even if she did want nothing more than to run across the room, throw her arms around her, and apologize for everything that had happened these past few days. That could wait a little longer, until Rebecca was ready.

"Pippa…. Is that your name?"

"Indeed it is. A beautiful name for a beautiful lady, don't you think?" Jasper said. He came up beside Pippa and looped his arm around her waist. "Pippa will not be leaving. She will be staying right here with us—forever."

"Forever," Rebecca whispered in awe. "Does that mean you two are getting married?"

Pippa chuckled, playfully narrowing her eyes at the girl. "Now, what makes you think that?"

Rebecca frowned at Pippa as if she could not believe anyone would be so dense. "Well, since you spend so much time together, I already figured you have been courting this whole time."

Jasper let out a booming laugh, the intensity and volume both shocking and delighting Pippa. With his body pressed against hers, she could feel his joy reverberating through her, echoing her own.

"Well, I suppose we have, if you think about it."

"That was why I was so upset when I heard you were

leaving," Rebecca continued. Her expression turned melancholy in an instant, shoulders rounded and head bowed. "I was upset for myself because I was going to miss you very much. You were my favorite governess I have ever had. No one was ever as kind or patient as you. But I was also sad for Jasper. I knew he was fond of you, and I knew you leaving would hurt him a lot—even more than it did me."

The air in the schoolroom stilled as the couple contemplated Rebecca's words, so wise and so very tenderhearted. Tears pooled in Pippa's eyes, her chest aching with love for the girl who had once been just another student. For all her tantrums, Rebecca truly possessed one of the most generous hearts Pippa had ever known.

"I am so sorry for causing you such pain, dear Rebecca," Pippa mumbled, swallowing the knot in her throat. "I hope, in time, you will forgive me—"

"I will forgive you right now," Rebecca announced, sitting up straight with blazing eyes. "I will forgive you right now if you marry my brother this instant."

Pippa and Jasper exchanged looks of both amusement and longing. She knew without a doubt that if it were possible, they would do exactly that.

"Unfortunately, sister, we must wait at least three weeks before we can marry," Jasper explained with a shrug. "Weddings take time to plan, and the banns must be read."

"What are banns? And why do you need to plan anything? Can't you go to the church and tell the vicar you wish to marry?"

"I will explain the banns later, I promise," Pippa offered, her smile growing. They had Rebecca's blessing now, and quite an enthusiastic blessing at that.

"And we are forgetting one more thing," Jasper added as he pulled away from Pippa, turning to look at her.

"There's more?" Rebecca groaned. "Getting married seems like an awful lot of fuss."

"It is, but it will be worth it in the end. And before we can be married, we must first be engaged."

Pippa's stomach erupted into a frenzy of flutters, her mind spinning so quickly she almost swayed on her feet. They had agreed to wait for the official proposal until Rebecca could be with them. She was such an integral part of their relationship that it had felt wrong to consider taking this step without her.

Now that the moment had clearly arrived, anticipation dancing through Jasper's eyes, love touching his soft smile, Pippa could hardly think straight or keep herself tethered to the Earth.

The man of her dreams took both her hands in his and kissed her knuckles. His gaze locked onto her, strong and steady and certain.

"I love you so very, very much, my darling Pippa. I have for so long, and I will until the end of time."

"I love you so very, very much, my wonderful Jasper. More than I could ever hope to express in a single lifetime."

"Will you marry me?"

Those beautiful words rang like church bells in Pippa's ears. Her heart beat so powerfully she thought it might leap from her chest and into Jasper's, snuggling up next to his where it belonged.

"Say yes," Rebecca whispered loudly from somewhere behind them. Pippa had almost forgotten she was in the room. Everything had melted away into a blissful haze, just her and Jasper frozen in this moment of long-awaited bliss.

"I think Rebecca is right," Jasper also whispered, softer, right against Pippa's ear. His breath trailed down her jawline and neck, raising gooseflesh across her exposed skin.

She inhaled deeply, grinning like mad. "Of course I will marry you, Jasper!"

Without wasting a second, Jasper snatched Pippa into his arms, crushing her to him and forcing every last hint of air from her lungs and sense from her mind.

When his lips molded themselves to hers, moving with promises of passion and love, all earthly concerns and considerations vanished. This must be heaven, Pippa thought to herself as she deepened the kiss, her fingers twisting into Jasper's dark hair.

Nothing could be better than this—being in the arms of the man she wanted more than anything in the world, knowing without any doubt that he loved her just as profoundly as she loved him. And they would have the rest of their lives to bask in that glory, surrounded by their precious family.

The moment could have lasted forever, as far as Pippa was concerned. Rebecca, however, had other plans. Racing across the room, she slammed into the newly engaged couple with full force, knocking the wind out of them and nearly sending all of them toppling to the ground.

"Yay! This means you will be my sister, Pippa!" she cheered, her arms wrapped tight around their waists. She tilted her head back, grinning up at them with glee in her eyes.

"Yes I will, my dear girl. And you shall be mine as well." With a silent promise to return to Jasper's arms as quickly as possible, Pippa disentangled herself from her betrothed and dropped to her knees before Rebecca. She pulled the girl to her chest and rested her cheek atop her head, so incredibly content.

This day had not turned out how she expected. The same could be said for the entire year. Just one year ago, Pippa had no idea the journey she would find herself on to arrive at this moment—discovering a new family, reuniting with old family, and falling heart first into a love she had never thought possible.

But it was possible. And it was hers, forever and always. Jasper had proved that time and time again.

Perhaps one day far into the future she would stop feeling like she was in a dream. As Jasper—the man who would soon be her husband—kissed her again, Pippa knew that would not happen. Every day with Jasper would be a dream, no matter the challenges they faced in the future. As long as he was by her side, she would be living that impossible dream her heart had protected for her all this time, just waiting for her to learn how to accept it.

"So will the wedding be three weeks from today?" Rebecca asked, grounding Pippa back to reality, though the hazy delirium of the dreamlike quality did not disappear completely.

Jasper chuckled and rested a large hand on the back of Rebecca's head. "Not quite. We must wait for a Sunday."

"Then the Sunday three weeks from now," Rebecca insisted, bouncing on her toes in anticipation.

"If that sounds agreeable to my bride." Jasper turned to Pippa. The hope and excitement in his eyes mirrored her own.

"Yes, that would—"

A new thought struck Pippa like lightning.

"My love? Is something the matter?"

"No, quite the opposite," Pippa whispered, amazement washing over her. "It will be perfect. But think of the date, Jasper."

Her future husband frowned in thought. "Yes, October.... Just a moment, isn't that—"

"Yes," Pippa said breathlessly. "The very day I arrived at Goddard House, exactly one year later."

Jasper grinned, laughed, and pulled Pippa into his embrace. Lifting her off her feet, he spun her around in several dizzying circles, much to the amusement of Rebecca.

When he set her back down, the world still swirling around her, he grasped her face in his hands and gazed deep into her eyes, into her very soul.

"That shall be our wedding day," he announced.

"How strange, the way these things work out," Pippa sighed as she slipped deeper into his arms—her new home.

"Or perhaps perfectly miraculous."

EPILOGUE

London bustled with life, with spring, with love. Or perhaps that was only Jasper's newlywed joy coloring the world around him. Either way, he did not mind. His wife clung to his arm, walking by his side wearing a beautiful smile of peace and comfort, his heart made material outside his body.

"Here, Jasper?" Pippa asked, pausing before a townhouse in a more modest area of the city.

"Indeed. You know, I still cannot believe you convinced Colette to join us for a walk," Jasper said as he ascended the steps to his Uncle Patrick's and Aunt Eloise's home. "She is so determined not to have a Season that she refuses any activities even remotely resembling one."

Pippa gave a proud shrug, nothing too scandalous that would draw the ire of *ton*. Not that Jasper cared. His wife could shrug as much as she wanted, smile as widely as she wanted, laugh as loudly as she wanted. He would cherish it all.

"There you are!"

The married couple whipped around at the sound of

Colette's panicked voice. She raced down the street toward them, lilac skirts lifted off the pavement and bonnet teetering dangerously to one side. They hurried down the steps and met her halfway, ignoring both curious and irritated looks from passersby.

"Cousin, whatever is the matter?" Jasper demanded, letting go of Pippa for the first time that morning to grasp Colette's upper arms and give her a light shake.

"Come…come look," she gasped out between sharp inhales. "Hurry."

Concern flashed between Jasper and Pippa. They jumped into action, following closely on Colette's heels as she led them toward an alley at the end of the street. That explained the fine layer of dust clinging to the hem of her skirts. Aunt Eloise, the talented seamstress who had brought this beautiful garment to life, would no doubt have something to say about that.

Fear pulsed in Jasper's ears as they rounded the corner, unsure what to expect, what could frazzle their calm and collected Colette.

All fear and uncertainty evaporated immediately when his eyes landed on the cause—a little girl, coated in dirt and trembling with terror, cowering behind a pile of wooden boxes.

"Heavens," Pippa exhaled, clutching Jasper's coat sleeve with one hand, the other over her heart.

"Colette, what—"

"I was feeling a little anxious earlier after arguing with my parents before they left to spend the day in Papa's office," she rushed, still struggling to catch her breath. "So I was looking out the upstairs window counting the carriages going by while I waited for you to take my mind off it. I saw this little girl run down the street and came to investigate. I found her cowering here."

"Poor dear," Pippa whispered, eyes brimming with worry. With all the caution gained from her years as a governess, Pippa carefully approached the child and knelt before her, not caring about soiling her emerald skirts.

"Did you try looking for her family?" Jasper asked.

Colette shook her head, exasperated and overwhelmed. "I was going to do just that, but the girl says she has none. She must be an orphan."

Brows furrowed, Jasper turned back to the mysterious child. Upon closer examination, he realized with a pang in his stomach that that very well could be the case. Her shoulder length brown hair was terribly matted, her plain gray dress covered in all manner of stains. Worst of all were the hollows under her large black eyes. The pang tightened into a sharp twist.

"Hello, little one," Pippa said in her most soothing voice, one bare hand outstretched. Jasper had not even noticed that she had removed her gloves.

"I thought you and Pippa would know what to do," Colette continued. "She says she ran away, though she would not say much more than that. I am not sure she is capable of it."

Jasper nodded, his expression turning dark for a moment until he realized the girl was glancing between him and Pippa. He tucked those painful theories away. For now, they needed to find some way to help this poor child.

The idea hit Jasper square in the chest. It was unusual at best and mad at worst. If anyone would understand and appreciate it, it would be his wife.

"Colette, why don't you return home for now? I am afraid our walk will have to wait until another day. We will manage the situation from here."

"Will she be all right?" Colette asked, wringing her hands around each other.

Jasper nodded, never removing his eyes from the girl and his wife. "Yes. We will make sure of it."

Alone in the alley, Jasper knelt beside Pippa with a gentle smile directed toward the little mystery. "What is your name, dear?" he asked.

She shrank deeper behind the boxes, as if she could disappear through the wall behind her if she tried hard enough.

"Martha...or...Fanny."

The newlyweds exchanged curious glances. "You have two names?" Pippa prodded.

The girl's bottom lip trembled as she retreated further into herself. Clearly, she had not experienced much kindness in her short life.

"Sometimes," she finally mumbled.

"There is nothing to fear," Jasper added, instinctively wrapping his arm around Pippa's shoulder. "We only want to help."

She watched them with her round, downtrodden eyes for a long moment, debating the sincerity of their words. After what felt like a century, she nodded.

"Very good," Pippa said quietly. She held out her hand once more. Still shaking, the girl placed her small, dirt-stained hand just on the edge of Pippa's fingertips. "Do you have a name you prefer?"

The question seemed to intrigue the child. Her eyes darted up, her mouth scrunched to one side. "Hmm...I like...May."

"May," Jasper repeated, infusing that simple word with all the warmth in his heart. "That is a lovely name. It suits you."

May blinked rapidly and looked away, though she did not let go of Pippa's hand.

Jasper took the opportunity to bring his mouth close to his wife's ear to whisper his strange idea. In fact, it was a rather monumental request. Deep in his bones, he knew

Pippa would be of the same mind. After all, they often said they were one soul in two bodies.

After a moment of thought, possibilities racing through her mind, Pippa finally smiled and nodded. There was still much to sort out, but that could wait.

"We have a question for you, May," Jasper started. He, too, offered his hand.

"Darling, would you like to come home with us?" Pippa asked, a slight tremble in her voice, both hopeful and anxious.

One brow, partially caked with mud, lifted as she eyed the couple before her. To their surprise, she slowly scooted out from behind the boxes and wrapped her fingers around two of Jasper's. Encouraged, Pippa brought the girl's other hand into her palm, engulfing it protectively.

May—the girl they would make their daughter, their first child—nodded. The corner of her mouth twitched up in the faintest smile.

It was enough. It pierced both Jasper and Pippa to their cores, burrowing deep into their hearts. They looked at each other, grinning from ear to ear. They would make a difference in this child's life by providing her with a loving, happy, comfortable home.

Just like that, they started their family—unexpectedly, miraculously, perfectly.

That had always been their story, and it would continue with May.

***

THANK you for reading Jasper's and Pippa's story! You can join the family again in Colette's story here. If you want to stay updated on my new releases, you can sign up to my newsletter and receive my stand-alone novella, *A Lifetime Of Love,* or you can hang out with me in my private Facebook group.

If you would like to read my complete Regency Romance series, The Harcourts, to learn more about Jasper's parents you can read them here. You can also read my other series Resolved In Love here.

ABOUT THE AUTHOR

Penny Fairbanks has been a voracious reader since she could hold a book and immediately fell in love with Jane Austen and her world. Now Penny has branched out into writing her own romantic tales.

Penny lives in the Midwest with her charming husband and their aptly named cat, Prince. When she's not writing or reading she enjoys drinking a lot of coffee and rewatching The Office.

Want to read more of Penny's works? Sign up for her newsletter and receive A *Lifetime of Love*, a stand-alone novella, only available to newsletter subscribers! You'll also be the first to know about upcoming releases!